The Viscount's Marriage of Inconvenience

BARBARA RUSSELL

OLIVERHEBERBOOKS

Cover art by Dar Albert at Wicked Smart Designs

Published by Oliver-Heber Books

0 9 8 7 6 5 4 3 2 1

one

ALTHOUGH VIOLANTE HAD never ridden a sledge, she believed she wouldn't have any problems rushing at high speed down the steep slope of Windy Ridge. It couldn't be that difficult, could it? So many people enjoyed themselves on a sledge. She wanted to be one of them, especially since her papa had finally bought a sledge after years of begging him for one. It wasn't her fault if the snow had fallen rather inconsistently that autumn; she hadn't had the opportunity to practise and Papa had strict rules—too-strict rules—about who, when, and where she was allowed to use the sledge.

Too dangerous, too cold, too inexperienced.

But never mind. Now the frosty slope belonged to her. Papa didn't need to know.

She straightened the sledge, closing one eye to check the trajectory wouldn't send her against a pine tree. Her thick gloves didn't make the job of dragging the sledge easy, and her scarf got in the way, but she set the sledge in a steady position. Giggling, she sat on the narrow seat, excitement sizzling, and...nothing happened. The sledge remained there, well-planted in a few inches of snow. She shifted back and forth, her coat brushing the fresh snow, but the contraption didn't budge, as if agreeing with Papa about how dangerous sledges were.

"Come on." She pushed with her hands and feet, but the stupid thing was stuck. Perhaps too much snow.

Bother. She stood up to get the sledge unstuck when the treacherous device shot forwards and slid at breakneck speed down the steep slope. Sprays of snow flew at its passage, glittering in the sunlight.

She sprinted after the sledge, but the snow she'd so admired a moment ago now hindered her. Her boots sank into the soft layers, slowing her down. Icy snow froze her stockings and soaked her skirt. A gasp left her when she spotted a lonely man carrying a heavy-looking sack at the bottom of the slope. Whoever the man was, he was right on the wild sledge's path.

She cupped her hands around her mouth. "You. Watch out!" Her voice echoed on the quiet hill.

The man stopped in his tracks. His hood fell back as he turned towards the sledge.

"Move," she yelled.

He dropped his load and ran, but the snow encumbered his progress while the sledge sped up. Violante pushed her legs forth, but no matter how much energy she put into the run, the sledge's speed was no match for her. Or for the unfortunate man.

The sledge kept changing trajectory as if it had a mind of its own, seemingly shadowing the man's movements. She clamped a hand over her mouth as he fell down to his waist into a snow well. The sledge hit a bump in the snow and flew high into the air, its shadow running over the slope. The man scrambled out of the well but stumbled and fell over. Unless he moved, the sledge would crash against him.

"Move, move." She wheezed and pushed forth, desperate to do something, although reaching the man in time to save him was impossible.

She winced as the sledge hit the man with a loud bang of shattered wood. The man cried out, covering his head with his arms. Wood splinters darted in every direction, ending the sledge's escapade and likely her future freedom. Heavens. She hadn't only injured a poor man but destroyed her father's sledge as well. Not to mention Papa had forbidden her from going to Windy Ridge alone in winter, with or without a sledge.

Her breath turned into mist around her mouth as she ploughed through the snow towards the bottom of the slope. "Are you hurt?"

The man groaned, hunching over.

"I'm so sorry." She dropped next to him and shoved aside the sad remains of the sledge from the man's back. "The thing went wild on me."

The man rubbed his shoulder. Snowflakes rained from his tattered jacket where a hole opened on the elbow. His threadbare gloves missed a finger or two. Not even his youth could assuage the gauntness of his cheeks and his excessive pallor. He raked a hand through his midnight hair. It was so dark it stood out against the snow.

"I'm so sorry," she said again.

"I'm all right, miss." He didn't look up at her.

"But you can't be. The sledge hit your back."

He shrugged but grimaced. He had to be around her age, maybe a little bit older. Eighteen or nineteen. It was difficult to tell so thin he was.

She took his arm and tried to haul him up. "My house is over there at the bottom of the valley. It's Sharpe Manor. My father was an army physician. He'll take a look at you."

He shook his head. "I'm fine."

The tension in his features belied his pain. When she tugged at his arm again, he staggered to his feet and brushed the snow from his clothes.

She steadied him although he towered over her a good foot. "You aren't well. And it's my fault. Please come with me."

He gazed at her. His deep black eyes were a stark contrast to his skinny face. They held a fierce strength and something else that sent a chill down her back. Contempt? Disgust? She had hurt him, after all.

"I can't come with you. My master will beat me if I don't return with the chestnuts I purchased for him in the town." He pointed at the sack he'd dropped.

Oh, no. She wouldn't allow his master to beat him. He'd been hit by her sledge. He wouldn't be beaten as well. All because of her recklessness. Papa had a point when he told her to be less impulsive. Lesson learnt.

"My father and I will escort you home and explain to your master what happened. You can trust my father. He's a man of his word."

He narrowed his gaze.

"All will be fine. I promise. If you don't trust me, you'll trust Papa." She went to lift the sack, but goodness, it weighed a tonne. "Please let me help you." She yanked at the rope tying the sack, but she slipped back and ended up in the snow, hitting her rear on a rock or something. *Ouch!*

He exhaled and stretched out his hand. "Are you sure your father will be happy to help me?"

"More than sure. He's the kindest man ever and has strong opinions on how masters should treat their servants. He's a war hero and a fair master. Ask any of the people who work for him." Although her papa might not be so lenient towards her once he learnt about the whole sad affair. He would punish her for disobeying him.

She accepted the man's hand, feeling the bones in his rough fingers.

He hauled her up, and she ended up an inch from him, nearly bumping against him. She put a hand on his chest for balance. His heartbeat pounded fast. Perhaps anger or fear. He kept frowning. The cause for his quick heartbeat couldn't be relief. He might resent her not only for having hurt him, but because she came from a wealthy family. Resentment towards wealthy families had been a widespread sentiment as of late.

He stepped back so quickly she staggered on her feet.

"I'll carry the sack," he said in a gruff tone.

"You shouldn't. Your back is injured."

He slung the sack over his shoulder and gritted his teeth. His knees buckled, and he fell again, muttering a curse. The sack sank into the snow with a huff.

"We'll come later to retrieve the sack." She pulled him up, and this time he let her help him. "My name is Violante Sharpe, by the way."

"Violante?" He said her name as if trying how it sounded on his lips.

She took some of his weight. "It's an Italian name, a variation of Viola and Violet. My mother is...was Italian." The sting that came when she mentioned her mother should be familiar by now. But it never failed to hurt.

"Sorry for your loss, miss." His tone softened a tad.

It was a loss, but also it wasn't. Her mother wasn't officially dead as far as Violante knew. She'd left Sharpe Manor one night in secret like a thief, leaving only a measly note saying, '*I have to go. I can't stay here.*' No explanation, no future contact, not even 'I love you.'

Violante pressed her lips against the bitterness in her mouth that thinking about her mother always left behind. Why did she waste her time thinking about her mother? Her papa was more than enough, the only one she trusted.

"I speak Italian as well," she said for no reason. "It's a beautiful language."

He barely nodded.

"What's your name?" she asked, steadying him when he staggered again.

"Keith Ryan, miss. I work at Sir Howard Glenister's manor. My master and his family are here for a holiday."

"Nice to meet you, Keith. I wish we'd met under better circumstances."

A corner of his mouth was pulled tightly. "So do I, miss." His breathing came out rugged.

Goodness, she hoped he didn't have a broken rib. He didn't look like someone who could endure a serious injury. Sir Howard didn't treat his servants well, judging by how thin and weak Keith was. To be a member of the House of Commons who professed to care about people, regardless of their social class, Sir Howard did a very poor job of taking care of his servants.

"I'm sorry for the incident," she said as they slogged through the snow towards the manor. "I meant to ride the sledge, but it slipped."

He shot her a glare of reproach. "Windy Ridge is too steep, and the snow freezes quickly, causing the sledge to slip faster. You should try the other side. It's gentler and warmer."

"I don't think I'm going to try any sides any time soon. Besides, I annihilated the sledge. Papa won't be happy."

He stopped, a hand on his ribs. "Will he punish you?" A sharp note crept into his voice.

"Alas, he will."

He resumed walking. "Maybe I should go to my master then. I don't want to cause you trouble with your father. Will he beat you?"

She gave him a horrified look. "My papa? Goodness, no. He would never, ever physically punish me. Oh, he grumbles and mutters a lot, but he's never hurt or scared me. His punishments are more about restricting activities I love or my freedom, but he would never lay a hand on me or his servants, for that matter. You'll see for yourself."

Another scowl. Perhaps he didn't believe her.

"You can lean on me," she said as he tottered again. "I won't let you fall."

"It's hardly appropriate, and we're alone." His tone could cut glass.

"I only mean to help."

He didn't say anything, and she didn't insist. Besides, he had a point. Her body pressed to his, and they were practically hugging. Anyone looking at them would think they were a couple. Thank goodness Hampstead wasn't London. Her reputation wouldn't be ruined simply because she helped an injured man, and well, no one was around aside from them.

He groaned in pain as they trudged through the snow. They sped up a little once they reached the clear path that led to her house.

He breathed heavily, rubbing his ribs. "I think I broke a rib."

There. All because of her. "Dash it, I'm sorry. But fear not. Papa will fix you. I learnt a little from him. A broken rib will take a couple of weeks—"

"A couple of weeks?" His voice rose. "Sir Howard will kick me out if I can't work for a fortnight."

She cursed her decision to go to Windy Ridge again. "I'm sure my papa will find a way to help you."

A deep, deep furrow marred his brow. "You have too much faith in what your *papa* can do."

Right. She wouldn't push the subject further. He would see it for himself. The more they walked, the more he grimaced. He shuffled his feet onwards, and a tremor went through him. The incident couldn't be the sole reason for his weakness.

She rolled her bottom lip between her teeth. "I don't mean to pry, but you..." Bad idea. How was she supposed to tell a boy he looked frail without offending him? "Never mind."

"What?" He leant against her, and she had to focus on remaining straight and not trip on her feet.

"Nothing really. We're nearly there."

He shivered in his worn jacket. "I know how I look," he said through yet another grimace. "When my master isn't pleased with my work, he doesn't feed me. He'll be even less pleased after today."

"Maybe if he fed you properly and treated you well, your work would be to his satisfaction. Just because he's rich and powerful, it doesn't mean he's better than you. It's the nineteenth century, for Pete's sake. Social classes—" The words rushed out of her mouth before she could stop them. "Sorry. It wasn't my place."

Her words were potentially dangerous. One might think she sympathised with the anarchists who were bombing London and killing people. She sympathised with their ideas but not with their methods.

He flushed either in shame or anger, but if he was offended or instead shared her view, he kept his opinion to himself.

They walked the rest of the way in silence. Along the path, his breathing grew more laboured and his legs weaker. She hoped the sledge hadn't caused any internal damage. Papa had told her of soldiers who had died because of the internal bleeding from wounds not visible from the outside.

The more she thought about all the possible injuries Keith might suffer, the more her pulse spiked. By the time she arrived home, she was frantic to see her father. Keith cried out when she helped him up the short flight of stairs to the back entrance.

"I can't..." He panted. "I must stop."

"Sit here." She nearly lost her balance, helping him onto the bench in the hallway.

He rocked back and forth, his hand on his ribs. His mouth was twisted in a grimace.

"Don't die. Please."

He gave her another glare. "I'll do my best." The words stammered out of him.

She rushed along the corridor without caring about the trail of mud she left behind. Even the housekeeper would be angry with her. The parlour was empty. The sitting room was deserted. Where was her papa?

She reached the main entry hall and spotted him. "Papa!"

She ran towards him in a combination of relief and urgency. He had a hand on the knob of the front door but paused upon seeing her.

"What's the matter?" he asked, inspecting her face. "Are you feeling unwell?" Instant concern tightened his voice.

"Not me...not me..." She took his hand and tugged at it. "You must come."

"Who's injured?" He shed his mackintosh coat, tossing it on the floor.

She inhaled deeply, running back towards Keith. "It's my fault. I took your sledge—"

"My sledge?"

"I went to Windy Ridge to try it."

"Violante." He stopped and searched her face with his clinical look.

She held up a hand. "I'm fine, but a boy named Keith is injured. He's here."

"How did he get injured?"

"Can we discuss the details later? He needs your help. I think he's dying." Her voice cracked.

They ran towards the rear entrance. Keith staggered to his feet and shuffled back closer to the door with wary steps, surely ready to bolt away if her papa raised his voice.

"Keith," she said. "No need to worry."

He reminded her of those wild animals she met in the forest and who didn't trust her.

"Sir." His dark eyes widened either with fear or pain. Or both.

"Please, Papa, help him," she said.

Her father's physician attitude snapped into place. She could tell by the way he straightened and his gaze focused on Keith. "Keith, I'm Mr. Sharpe. May I examine you?"

Keith gave a brusque nod, keeping his gaze on the floor.

Papa took Keith's face gently and stared into his eyes. "You feel dizzy."

"I do," Keith whispered.

"Can you walk?"

Keith shook his head. A faint blush crept over his cheeks.

"I'll carry you to my examination room."

"That's not necessary, sir," Keith said so low she barely heard it.

"I must insist. I don't want you to faint in the hallway. You might hit your head hard." He pointed a finger at her. "We'll talk later, young lady."

"I know." She gave Keith an encouraging nod he didn't return.

With a swift move, her papa gathered Keith in his arms, seemingly without effort. Keith shot her a final glare from above her father's shoulder.

Yet, she could bet he would thank her later.

two

KEITH CLOSED HIS fists on the soft, pristine bed where he was sitting in front of Mr. Sharpe. His head spun, and his stomach churned with nausea, but he'd rather throw up than faint in the room of this stranger. He'd heard enough frightening stories about what happened to servants at the mercy of rich people. Sir Howard wasn't an example of virtue to start with. Keith would be stupid to fully trust the stranger.

Mr. Sharpe loomed over him, examining Keith's back with probing fingers. The man was a blond giant with the same peculiar violet eyes as his daughter. Father and daughter also shared the same wavy spun gold hair. But where Violante's features were soft and delicate, her father's lines were strong and harsh. Even his gaze had a hardened quality Keith had seen in soldiers. Not in the gaze of any aristocrats he'd met.

"Did the sledge hit your head?" Mr. Sharpe asked.

"Only my back." Keith bit down a gasp as Mr. Sharpe rubbed a salve over his back.

"You have a broken rib." He touched Keith's spine. "And a large ecchymosis."

"Sir?"

"A bruise and a swollen area. Your muscles are rather stiff." Mr. Sharpe started to wrap a bandage around Keith's torso. "The bandage will help with the pain, but there isn't much I can do for the broken rib. I can give you a mild opiate."

Keith tried not to cry while Mr. Sharpe tightened the bandage. Pain shot up his spine, and nausea burned the back of his mouth. A buzzing noise rang in his ears as his head turned lighter.

The next thing he knew was that he lay on the bed, and Mr. Sharpe's face filled his field of vision.

"You fainted," he said, checking his pulse.

A funny taste filled Keith's mouth. "I feel tired."

"I bet you do. Your weakness has nothing to do with the incident, although the sledge could have broken your neck." Mr. Sharpe wiped his hands with a cloth. "Plenty of rest and food. No lifting heavy weights. No work whatsoever. You should be better in a week or two."

Keith rubbed his aching forehead. "I can't afford to rest for two weeks, sir. Sir Howard will give me the sack." Or worse.

At the mention of Keith's master, a cold glint lit Mr. Sharpe's gaze. "You're too thin to do any chores. Your muscles are underdeveloped because of malnutrition. Your skin has an unhealthy colour that makes me suspect your liver isn't in good shape either. And your rib won't heal unless you take care of yourself. If you don't rest, the broken rib might puncture your lung."

Keith's face burned in shame. Now he understood where Violante's bluntness came from. "I can't," he muttered. "I need to work."

Mr. Sharpe dragged a chair close to the bed and dropped himself into it. He didn't look less menacing or commanding because he was sitting. "Why does Sir Howard treat you so beastly? You don't have the energy to do any chores."

Keith should be careful. If he spoke ill of his master, he wouldn't simply lose his job. The peelers might arrest him for some ridiculous crime, like subversion or anarchism.

He licked his dry lips. "Sir Howard is a busy man."

"So every politician says, but I hardly see the results of their so-called hard work. Certainly, they have the bloody time to attend brothels and opium dens."

Keith sat up and dragged his shirt over his head, ignoring the dizziness. While he agreed with Mr. Sharpe, he had to work to live.

"I should go. Thank you for your help, sir."

"Lad." Mr. Sharpe's voice held a commanding quality Keith couldn't ignore. He put a hand on Keith's chest and gently pushed him back. "Sod Sir Howard. You aren't leaving my house until you're properly healed."

"Sir Howard would kill me." There. He'd said it. If bluntness was what the Sharpe family wanted, he'd give it to them.

Mr. Sharpe clicked his tongue. "We'll see. He'll have to go through me. I risked my life on the battlefield to save the lives of the soldiers who fought for this country, because Sir Howard and his politician friends decided it was a good idea to deploy an army in some distant land that had done nothing to us." He tilted his head up, showing a thin but long scar cutting deep into his neck. "I almost died in a foreign land more times than I care to count, and for what? To return home and be scorned by the very politicians who ordered me to fight for them in the first place. I'm not alone in my predicament. Many soldiers, who lost limbs and peace of mind, are treated like unwanted, embarrassing guests. I'm not friends with whoever abuses their power to mistreat those below them. The best way to judge a man's value is to see how he treats people beneath him."

Keith agreed with everything Mr. Sharpe had said, but his situation wouldn't change. "I have nowhere to go. No family. No friends." Confessing to his loneliness hurt more than he'd care to admit.

"You have me now." Mr. Sharpe patted Keith's shoulder. "I'll send a message to Sir Howard and personally talk to him. I'll demand he let you stay here. If you wish so. You'll have a place here in my house and certainly receive decent meals at least thrice a day and a nice, warm bed. Your stomach will not be empty ever again. What do you choose, lad?"

It wasn't really a choice, was it? Sir Howard would punish him for being late, and it was a matter of time before he'd kick Keith out, or Keith would die from exhaustion. Mr. Sharpe's offer caused a knot to tie in Keith's throat. Gratitude and shame overwhelmed him.

He swallowed past the knot choking him. "Why do you want to help me?"

"Because it's the right thing to do. Because I hate seeing a lad like you being mistreated. Because I was *you* a long time ago. I come from nothing. I starved and worked hard while powerful people abused me. I want to change my beloved country, helping one person at a time." Mr. Sharpe squeezed Keith's hand. "You aren't alone."

Those last words broke him. A sob ripped out of him, leaving a path of pain and fire across his chest and back. The more he tried to contain his tears, the more they fell. He shouldn't fall to pieces in front of a stranger. He covered his face in shame, trying to muffle a painful sob in his tattered shirt. Mr. Sharpe lifted him and held him gently without saying anything. For the first time, Keith experienced a father's hug. He gave up trying not to cry as Mr. Sharpe held him, careful not to hurt him.

"Perhaps my daughter's recklessness wasn't a bad thing, but don't tell her I said that." Amusement laced Mr. Sharpe's words. "I gather you wish to stay."

Keith wiped the tears with the back of his hand. "I do, sir, and I promise I'll earn my keep."

"It's all right. We'll discuss that later. You have to recover first."

Keith had been wrong about Violante. She'd told him the truth.

Yes, perhaps the incident at Windy Ridge had been a good thing.

VIOLANTE HAD NEVER BEEN prouder of her papa. She'd never doubted he would help Keith, but seeing his plan come to fruition filled her with happiness.

As she, Papa, and a very silent Keith waited in the sitting room for Sir Howard to arrive, she couldn't stand still. She paced from the warm hearth to the window overlooking the front drive to check if Sir Howard's carriage was in sight. Papa smoked his pipe in the armchair, reading the newspaper. Keith stared at his hot cup of tea as if waiting for a monster to come out of it. His shoulders were hunched, and his head hung on his chest. Why wasn't he happy? The housekeeper had given him a fresh shirt, a jacket, and a pair of trousers. The cook had prepared a rich broth only for him. Yet he kept staring at everyone with a wary expression.

"You don't have to be afraid," she said, jolting him.

Some of his tea spilt, ending up on the floor. He paled further. "Apologies, sir." He went to wipe the tea with a napkin, but she stopped him before his ribs and back hurt.

"I'll do it." She put her hand on his arm.

He withdrew his arm immediately. "I'm nervous," he said among short breaths.

"You can trust Papa." She'd said that a dozen times. She cleaned up the floor with a napkin. "He won't let anything happen to you."

"I know," he whispered.

She inched closer. "If anything, I'm more worried about Sir Howard. Papa is an excellent fighter." She mimicked throwing a punch. "He can knock out an opponent in three seconds straight. He can shoot a target at two hundred yards with his rifle. And he can—"

"I think Keith got the point, darling," Papa said.

"I didn't tell him about your knowledge of gunpowder." She waved her arms around. "He made fireworks for my last birthday.

Beautiful peonies and crossettes. It was the most beautiful birthday party I've ever had."

Keith flashed a fleeting, timid smile. It lasted a moment but brightened his thin face.

"She's exaggerating," Papa said from the armchair. "I had help with the fireworks, and I haven't sparred in a while. I'm afraid I'm rusty."

She shook her head. "He's being modest."

Papa lowered his newspaper, puffing on his pipe. "Your praise won't distract me from the fact you stole my sledge—"

She lifted a finger. "Borrowed without permission, Papa."

"—destroyed it, and injured this young man." He pointed his pipe at her. "Not to mention that Windy Ridge is too steep for someone as inexperienced as you are, as I told you many times. You explicitly disobeyed me. You could have been seriously hurt. You could have hurt Keith more seriously. If the sledge had hit his neck at that speed, we'd be having a very different conversation now."

It was her turn to hang her head. There was a serious note in her papa's voice she couldn't dismiss. He was right. She shouldn't have taken the sledge. She shouldn't have gone to Windy Ridge.

"I'm sorry, Papa. I really am. Because of me, Keith is injured. That's inexcusable."

"I'm glad you recognise your mistakes." Papa exhaled a puff of smoke. "No dancing for four months."

What? Her jaw hung open. "Four months? Papa, that's unfair. Christmas is coming. I want to dance. A new style of gallop is in fashion. I have to practise it before the ball at the town hall. Everyone will be there."

He arched his eyebrow. His hard features spelt the end of her Christmas dream. "No reading novels for a month as well. You'll only read books concerning your studies. One more word," he added when she opened her mouth to protest, "and it'll be two months. You'll have time to ponder the gravity of your actions. If you keep complaining, you won't even go to the Christmas party."

Tarnation. She folded her arms over her chest, fuming as much as Papa's pipe. No dancing for four months and no novels for a month. She'd go mad with boredom.

"Sir..." Keith said in a low voice. "I'm all right. I mean, I'm alive. Nothing terrible happened."

His attempt at helping her eased her frustration. "Papa is right. As usual. You aren't all right."

The look of pride her papa gave her was worth the admission of guilt. Almost. The noise of a carriage stopping in the driveway broke the moment.

She ran to the window. A sleek black carriage with Sir Howard's crest shone in the sunlight. "He's here."

Keith stiffened, his fingers clenching around the cup. Papa acquired that determined look that sent a chill down her back. There was the noise of the front door shutting. The footman said something she didn't understand. Footsteps sounded from the hallway. The closer they came, the tenser the atmosphere.

The footman opened the door and bowed. "Sir Howard."

Papa put down his pipe. "Thank you, Mark."

Sir Howard strode inside in a flutter of his black cloak that made him look like a giant crow. He removed his gloves with a yank, sweeping his gaze around as if surveying a heap of rubbish. The fact he hadn't left his coat and hat to a servant meant he was in a hurry.

"Mr. Sharpe. What is the meaning of this *urgent* meeting? I'm a very busy man even when away from London."

Keith shoved to his feet, a tremor going through him. He paled so much she was worried he might faint. Her papa stood up as well, but his wide stance had a menacing quality Violante had rarely seen. No, she hadn't exaggerated when she'd mentioned his prowess. She loved him dearly, but she was aware her father could be lethal when he wanted to.

"Sir." She bobbed a shallow curtsy.

The politician's gaze lingered on Keith. "Have you stolen from these people? I swear if you did something wrong, I'm going to whip you myself."

Violante gasped. Whip? What kind of monster was this man? Papa worked his jaw.

Sir Howard stepped closer to a shivering Keith. "What did you do now, cur?"

"Keith did nothing," Papa answered before Keith could say anything. "There was an incident this morning, and Keith got injured. We took care of him."

Sir Howard didn't soften. His sharp chin, covered by a trimmed goatee, added to his Gothic novel villain's persona. "I apologise for any inconvenience my clumsy servant might have caused you. I'm afraid Keith is slow both in the body and head. One of my servants found the sack of chestnuts he was supposed to fetch at the bottom of Windy Ridge. I should have known you were up to no good."

"Keith dropped the sack because of me," Violante said, ignoring Papa's warning stare to stay silent. Likely, he would forbid her to read for another month. "My sledge hit him. His back is injured, and he broke a rib."

"Thank you for your concern, miss." Sir Howard grabbed Keith's arm and gave it a yank. "We'll take our leave now."

Keith let out a muffled cry of pain. She shot forwards to free Keith, but her father was faster.

"Don't touch him." Papa closed the distance between himself and Sir Howard with two long strides. "Your behaviour is unacceptable." He gave Sir Howard a shove that was light enough not to be rude but strong enough to force him to release Keith.

The shocked expression on Sir Howard's face would be comical if not for the possible consequences of his wrath.

"How dare you?" he hissed.

Her father didn't flinch. "Keith is under my protection, and I mean to employ him at my service."

Keith grabbed the back of the armchair for support. Pain twitched his mouth. His serious glint matched Papa's.

"Whatever for?" Sir Howard was flustered. "As I told you, he's a poor servant and a lazy worker. Not worth your time."

"Then you won't mind losing him." Papa wrapped an arm around Keith's shoulders. "The lad stays here."

"Does he agree?" Sir Howard angled towards Keith.

Everyone stared at him. He swallowed a couple of times, moving closer to Papa. "I want to stay with Mr. Sharpe."

"You ungrateful brat." Sir Howard raised a hand, but Papa blocked him before he could hit Keith.

"Get out of my house." The air vibrated with the power of Papa's warning.

"You stole my servant."

A tendon in Papa's neck beat a quick tempo. "You don't remember me, do you?"

Sir Howard collected himself quickly as a good politician. "Should I?"

"I served overseas with the Royal Army Medical Corps in the Royal Warwickshire Dragoons. At that time, you worked for the Council of War and made the decision to send my men and me to war. You visited the garrison to wish us good luck before our departure, telling us how proud the empire was of us. You shook my hand and told me not to disappoint my country. I'm sure you're aware of how few of us returned. Our operation was marked as the most disastrous one in terms of lives lost in a century." He fell silent, but Violante had the feeling he restrained himself from adding something else.

Sir Howard remained still for a long moment. Then he fiddled with his cravat, seemingly unaffected by Papa's words. "Do what you want. You'll regret your decision, Mr. Sharpe, mark my words. This boy will cause you nothing but trouble."

He marched out of the room in a wave of dark fabric, leaving his ominous words lingering in the sitting room.

three
Three months later

THE LIVELY MUSIC—a quadrille or a gallop, Keith couldn't tell—echoed off the high-vaulted ceiling of the town's communal hall. Christmas wreaths, tinsels, and branches of mistletoe hung from every corner. He'd never seen a room more lively and decorated. The bright colours were almost distracting.

He sipped his glass of mulled wine, watching the couples twirling around on the dance floor as those who weren't dancing clapped their hands in rhythm with the music. He was happy to just watch and enjoy the show.

It was amazing what rest and good meals could do to the body. He'd been with Mr. Sharpe for only three months, but he'd never felt stronger. His broken rib had healed in a couple of weeks, and his muscles had grown. His clothes strained over his bulging muscles. Muscles! A novelty for him.

"I lit the stove in our room before coming here," Paul, one of the stableboys, said. He was another novelty. Keith's first friend. "So you won't complain about the cold."

"Thank you."

Paul rolled his eyes. "You know, you must stop thanking me every two seconds. It's annoying," he quipped.

Keith elbowed him. "If it annoys you, then I'll do it more often. Thank you."

Paul laughed. "We'll see in tomorrow's boxing practice if you'll thank me when I knock you out."

"You have to hit me first."

"I'll hit you, all right." Paul straightened his jacket, staring at a girl on the other side of the ballroom. "As much as I love chatting with you, I want to dance with a pretty lady."

"Good luck." Keith raised his glass as his friend winked at him, heading to the girl.

Keith walked around, careful not to spill his wine. Happy families danced and laughed together, and the sight didn't bring the usual pang of loneliness into his chest.

He didn't remember his father, but for the first time since he was born, he didn't care. Mr. Sharpe showed him what it meant to have a father every day. Speaking of his benefactor.

Keith paused away from the loud music and the laughing crowd next to the set of double doors opening to the porch. Between the people dancing and the roaring log fire, the hall was so hot that a bit of fresh air was needed.

Mr. Sharpe stood right outside of the hall, talking with a man in a dark cloak, and Keith stepped closer to them. A thick scar crossed the stranger's face, passing over the bridge of his nose. Whatever they discussed, it had to be a serious subject, judging by how tense their faces were. Mr. Sharpe beat a fist on his chest. The scarred man nodded, waving an arm.

Keith didn't mean to eavesdrop on their conversation, but he remained still when the word 'explosion' reached his ears. The Fenians—the anarchists who wanted to affirm their principles with bombs—were the terror of the moment in London. Explosives were their bread and butter, and the police had warned the population to be careful and avoid crowded places and trains.

He chuckled bitterly. Perhaps there was something wrong with him. He heard the word explosion and immediately thought of the Fenians. He blamed his quick dark thoughts on the fact that his mother had been killed by a Fenians' bomb when he was little. Something he didn't remember either.

Mr. Sharpe was probably organising another fireworks show for Violante. As if sensing the attention, Mr. Sharpe met Keith's gaze, and for the first time since moving to Sharpe Manor, a cold chill had set into Keith's bones. Ridiculous. There was no man more honourable and kind than Mr. Sharpe. He was intense, yes, even dangerous, but not a Fenian.

Keith sucked in a breath when Mr. Sharpe walked to him. "Evening, sir."

The harsh expression on Mr. Sharpe's face vanished. "Keith, are you all right?"

He bowed his head. "Perfectly fine." He caught a glimpse of the other man closing the doors and leaving quietly.

Mr. Sharpe gave Keith an assessing glance. "You have recovered more quickly than I thought. You're strong, lad."

"I have to thank you for that, sir, which reminds me..." He cleared his throat. "I'm ready to start doing more serious, heavy work. Anything. I can work in the fields and stables or help rebuild the old barn. Wherever you decide."

He was eager to earn his keep. After weeks of doing nothing but eat, rest, wander Sharpe Manor as if it were a hotel, and help in the kitchen and with the housework, he wanted to return the favour and make himself useful before Mr. Sharpe decided he wasn't good enough.

Mr. Sharpe smiled. "I'm not going to kick you out. I'm your physician as well as your employer. I know when my patient is ready to do heavy work."

"I can do more than light chores or peel potatoes. I wouldn't mind working in the barley field."

Laughing, Mr. Sharpe raised his glass. "After Christmas, I'll find something for you."

Keith hadn't realised how desperately he wanted to do some real work until Mr. Sharpe said yes. "Thank you. You won't be disappointed. I'm a hard worker and—"

"I know." Mr. Sharpe squeezed Keith's shoulder. "I'm not Sir Howard. You don't have to prove yourself to me."

"Thank you. I'm fully aware of the differences between you and Sir Howard."

"Sir Howard is a parasite," Mr. Sharpe hissed the last word. "He sucks the life out of our society. People like him should—" He exhaled. A muscle in his jaw ticked. "Why don't you search for Violante? She's still angry with me because I won't let her dance. She might need some company."

Keith pretended not to notice Mr. Sharpe's angry words. In the current, tense climate, words like those would grant Mr. Sharpe a close investigation from the police, maybe even an arrest.

"I will find her, sir. Thank you." He weaved through the crowd, a nagging feeling at the back of his head. But then again, Sir Howard deserved Mr. Sharpe's scorn, and the two of them had a past.

He found Violante in an empty corner. Arms folded over her chest, she glowered at the dancers, swaying her hips in rhythm with the music. Her pretty blue gown enhanced her violet eyes, and her golden curls framed her heart-shaped face. Despite her troubled expression, she was lovely, beautiful, perfect.

His chest, cheeks, and whole body warmed instantly, faster than the mulled wine could ever do. He dallied, searching for something clever to say. She'd offered to teach him how to read and write, and he looked forward to starting his lessons, although being alone with her made him nervous and excited. She always carried a book with her, and after the one-month ban imposed by her father, she'd devoured novels at a speed he didn't believe was human. Wherever she went, her nose was stuck in a book. If she didn't read, she talked about books.

He wanted to understand what made books so fascinating for her. But if he was going to be honest, the reason he'd agreed to be taught by her wasn't only his curiosity about books. He had no right to feel anything for her. She was the daughter of the man who had saved him from a life of hardship and suffering, maybe even death. He was no one, owned nothing, and most likely his situation wouldn't change in the future. He couldn't offer her any of the comforts she was used to enjoying in her manor. Besides, she'd marry someone who was rich and could write his own name.

Keith's body didn't listen to his cold logic. A stirring started in his chest every time she smiled, and when she frowned as she did now, he wanted to smooth those worry lines with his lips. He shook his head. Dangerous thoughts. That path would lead to his demise. Nothing more.

She waved when she saw him, and he couldn't dally any longer.

"Are you enjoying yourself, Miss Sharpe?" he asked.

She pouted. "Violante. How many times must I tell you? And no, I'm not enjoying myself." She eyed his mug. "Mulled wine? May I take a sip?"

"I'll fetch a mug for you." He went to leave, but she took his wrist, sending shivers up his arm.

"Please don't bother. I'll never finish a whole mug. I'd like only a sip unless you mind, of course."

Curse him to hell and back. "Not at all." He offered her his mug.

Something really had to be wrong with him, because for some reason, watching her drink from his mug started all sorts of stirrings, and not only in his chest.

"Thank you. I needed it." She handed him the mug. Her tongue darted out to catch a ruby drop on the corner of her mouth, and he thought he was going to die with the sensations rushing through him.

She huffed. "No dancing for Christmas. So many gentlemen want to dance, something rare, let me tell you, and I had to refuse all who asked. Can you think of a more cruel punishment?"

Being whipped? "Actually, I can."

She unfolded her arms. "I'm sorry. I must look so silly to you. It was a figure of speech."

"There's no need to apologise."

"You're too kind." She touched his hand, and he nearly dropped his mug.

No, he wasn't kind. His thoughts weren't kind at all at that moment. He wanted to taste the wine on her lips and tongue, hold her, and feel her body against his as he danced with her. If he could dance, that is. He gazed around. Mr. Sharpe was nowhere to be seen.

"Maybe you can teach me to dance," he said. "You wouldn't exactly be dancing but teaching me."

Her violet eyes brightened. "Yes...no. I don't want to cause you trouble. I almost broke your neck. That's enough."

"We won't get in trouble if we dance away from the dance floor, like in the other room for example." He pointed in the direction where the anteroom was. "And if your father complains, I'll take the blame."

A crease appeared between her delicate eyebrows. "That wouldn't be fair."

"He won't catch us. I'm sure of it. And we'll be quick."

She rose on her tiptoes to glance over his shoulder. "Papa won't be happy."

"We'll be careful." He put the mug on the windowsill and stretched out his hand. "May I have the honour?"

After a moment of hesitation, she laughed and slid her delicate fingers over his rough palm. "Yes."

"I must warn you. I really can't dance. You'll have to teach me."

"It's all right." She laced her fingers through his, and he hitched a breath.

Right now, she could ask him to lift the entire hall with a finger and he'd do it. She led him to the end of the hall behind the Grecian columns that formed a dimly lit arcade. The music came muffled but was loud enough to follow it. Maybe it was a waltz.

He wrapped an arm around her waist and pulled her closer, ignoring the hot turmoil in his chest. He had no idea what he was doing, but it didn't seem to matter. She laughed as he made her twirl in the shadows of the arcade. Her skirt flapped around, enveloping them in a cloud of blue muslin. He copied the movements of the couples in the ballroom, but if he did a poor job, she didn't complain about it.

When the music ended amidst the clapping couples, she sagged against him, laughing. Her cheek rested on his chest, and the fresh scent of her hair teased his senses. He wanted to stroke the shiny golden curls and tangle his fingers through them to see if they were as silky as they looked. He wanted to bury his face in the crook of her neck and get lost in her softness.

She reclined her head to meet his gaze. He could spend the whole night trying to decide what colour her eyes were. There was violet, blue, and a hint of green, but they changed with the light.

"I'm happy you're staying with us," she said.

His pulse spiked in a moment. She was happy.

She inched back, and he missed her warmth. "You're the best friend I've ever had."

His heartbeat plunged. Instant destruction. A cold shower wouldn't be more shocking. Friends. There was no more devastating word in the English language. He was a friend to her. But then again, what did he expect? He scratched the back of his neck, not sure about what to say. It was better that she considered him only a friend. If he repeated that a few times, he might believe it.

"I'd better see where Paul is," he said, stepping back from her. "I promised to help him keep an eye on the horses."

She took his hand, stopping him. "Thank you for the dance. I enjoyed it."

He slid his hand out of hers. "So did I, Miss Sharpe."

four
Four months later

VIOLANTE WASN'T SURE what was happening to her. As she walked across the garden, she wondered if the changes within her were only due to her growing into a woman or something else.

She'd never cared about boys. Heaven knew if they were a messy lot. Too loud and boisterous for her tastes, especially when they were busy in Papa's gymnasium. Since Papa had turned an old barn into a training hall, everyone who worked on his estate was welcome to lift weights or learn how to throw punches and spar. The boys seemed to have a penchant for punching each other. Not her cup of tea. She found sparring amusing for two minutes and then she wanted to do something else, like take a walk, read a book, or both.

But from the moment Keith had arrived, she found she didn't mind being around him. Quite the opposite. She'd told him he was her best friend that day at the ball, and he was, but she wondered if there was more to the tingling of her body when she was with him than friendship.

Months had passed since the sledge incident. Christmas had arrived and gone. After the ball at the town hall, he'd turned not exactly cold but a little distant. Even when they were alone, he behaved too much like a servant would behave with his mistress, and she didn't like it. She must have done something that had offended him.

The snow had melted, new leaves had sprouted on the trees, snowdrops dotted the field...and Keith had put on a lot of muscles.

Muscles she admired right now. Not that she meant to. Or maybe she did. She had searched for him for their daily reading session—she was teaching him how to read and write, and he was a great student—and she'd found him in the backyard, shirtless, throwing hay bales around with the other stableboys. Not really throwing around. There was a method to the madness, but she was distracted by the sweat glistening on his skin, the sharp ridges of his muscles, and the way the sunlight gave blue hues to his sable hair. Although she was being unfair towards him because, while his muscles were a work of art, she admired his kindness, sharp wit, and gentleman-like manners above all.

Paul said something that apparently was funny because Keith threw his head back and burst out laughing. Oh, his Adam's apple. She'd never noticed that particular male feature before, but for some reason, it fascinated her now. His voice had changed in the span of a few months. He rumbled deep and low, and even when he read to her the most boring passage in a book, she remained fully alert and enthralled. He could read the housekeeper's shopping list with that baritone, and she would sigh at each word.

But her newfound fascination with boys couldn't be simply because she was growing up or some other wild reason connected to the moon's phases. Because Paul was shirtless too, and she guessed he was a handsome chap as well, but looking at him didn't stir parts of her that shouldn't be stirred. Then again, as the cook's son, Paul had grown up in Sharpe Manor and then worked as a stableboy. He was family.

Keith was another matter. It was amazing how his body had transformed in less than a year. He didn't resemble the scrawny, pale young man she'd met in the snow. He was broad, tall, brawny, and had a skin that acquired a lovely brown shade because he spent so much time outdoors. Had she mentioned his hardened lines? Or the stubble that permanently darkened his jaw? When she'd met him, she hadn't been sure about his age. Now there was no mistaking the fact he was a man.

Perhaps Papa was right, and she read too many novels. Maybe the odd stirring would go away once spring passed. She couldn't imagine battling with it for a long time. It was exhausting. Yet here she was, spying on him. Well, she wasn't spying. Merely taking a peek and observing young men's behaviour for a purely scientific reason.

He met her gaze, and the air charged with the energy of lightning. He stopped laughing, his strong jaw tightening. There. He turned cold when she was around. Although...she might be wrong, her lack of knowledge in romantic affairs was spectacular, but she could swear a flicker of interest heated his gaze. It was a predator's stare, and she shouldn't like it.

"Mates, a lady is here," he said over the rowdy voices.

He pulled his shirt on. The movement caused his abdominal muscles to flex. Not a trace of the sledge accident was left on his body. Not a visible one, at least.

The other boys followed suit, muttering a greeting in her direction and wiping sweaty brows.

"It's only Violante," Paul said, buttoning his shirt.

"Hey!" She propped a fist on her hip. "What do you mean by that?"

"That you don't care about us being shirtless, and we don't care about being seen by you." He took a sip from a bottle of water.

Oh, but she did care about one boy in particular.

"It doesn't matter," Keith said. "It's propriety."

Paul nearly choked on the water with a burst of laughter. "Since when do you care about propriety?"

Keith jumped off the hay cart with a graceful leap that brought him a few feet away from her. His hair reached his shoulders, devilishly tousled by his outdoor activities. "I've always cared about propriety, except when you're around."

"Bugger off." Paul lunged.

Keith laughed, pretending to punch Paul. They wrestled, shoving and pushing each other among laughter and the others inciting them. Violante shot her gaze skywards. The fight could go on for hours.

"Keith?" she said. "We should start."

"Go." Paul pushed him again. "A gentleman never makes a lady wait."

"Shut it." Keith gave Paul a final shove before striding towards her.

She expected Paul to make fun of Keith for taking reading lessons, but he never did. A testament to the respect between the boys.

Keith towered over her by more than a foot, and goodness, she liked it. Yes, spring would pass, and she'd be normal again.

"New book today, right?" He wiped his face with a cloth tied to his belt.

"Yes." She found it difficult to meet his dark gaze. "I didn't mean to rush you. Maybe we can start later if you're busy."

"No, we were just fooling around, but I'm sweaty. I should clean up."

"Don't!" she nearly shouted.

He came to a stop, his eyebrows reaching his hairline.

"I mean, it doesn't matter," she said. "It's such a fine day that we can study outside. No need for ceremonies. I put a picnic blanket under the sycamore. I brought a basket as well. Oat biscuits and ham and cheese sandwiches."

He beamed so widely that a pair of dimples appeared on his cheeks. "It sounds perfect."

She smiled, too, but in triumph. The man ate like a couple of starving horses. The cook kept feeding him, having taken him under her wing, and Keith took full advantage of that. So did she. *All is fair in love and war.* But she wasn't in love. No sir.

He adjusted his shirt until the fabric stretched nicely over his broad chest. "What are we going to read today?"

"*Wuthering Heights.*"

"The Brontë sisters again."

"Yes. I thought about trying the newspaper, but goodness. Only bad news." She shook her head, wishing she hadn't read the gruesome details of the latest terrorist attack. "London is being riddled with bombs by the anarchists. Two days ago, the Fenians bombed the Palace of Whitehall, also hitting Scotland Yard itself. The police fear an underground station would be the next target."

"Bloody hell. Pardon me." He rubbed his forehead. "The Fenians are becoming more active. Your father was in London two days ago."

"Yes. It's scary. Thank goodness nothing happened to him."

"Thank goodness." A strained note snuck into his voice.

"The Fenians are desperate. Papa says they have nothing to lose because the government pushes them to a corner and refuses to acknowledge their rights for an independent Irish republic and for equal treatment of every social class."

"Their cause might be noble. Their methods are not."

She nodded. "I don't want to read about the Fenians."

"I agree," he said after a long pause.

"You're going to love *Wuthering Heights.*"

It took a moment for him to smile. "I'm sure I will."

The breeze carried his hearty scent to her. It was a combination of sweat, leather, and the citrus soap he used. She sat next to him on the blanket, wondering for how long her papa would let her enjoy being in Keith's company unchaperoned. They didn't stand on ceremonies at Sharpe Manor, but Papa had talked about her having a Season in London. Bad sign. He wanted to find her a husband, which wasn't necessarily a horrible thing. She loved dancing and meeting new friends, and Papa would never force her to marry someone she didn't like, but London had to be overwhelming in addition to dangerous.

Her gaze drifted towards Keith of its own accord. The problem with having a Season was that it implied a chaperone, rules, restrictions, and well, staying in London away from her forest, green hills, and too close to the Fenians. And too far from Keith.

He plonked down onto the blanket and crossed his thick legs at the ankles with a sigh.

"Book or sandwich first?" She opened the basket, already knowing the answer.

"Sandwich, please. I'm famished." He eyed the basket with pure hunger. It wasn't a bad stare. Intense and focused.

She chuckled. "As usual."

She handed him a sandwich, and their fingers brushed. It wasn't the first time. Months ago, before he turned serious and detached, they'd hold hands during long walks on the hills. When they played cricket, they grabbed each other's arms and sometimes they hugged—it depended if they played in the same team or not. Touches happened constantly. Or they'd happened. He'd grown more careful with their closeness as of late. And today...today her skin tingled at the contact with the rough pads of his fingers. The sensation spread from her hand and crawled along her arm to sit comfortably in her heart.

He withdrew his hand quickly, avoiding her gaze. That was another thing that often happened, him putting distance between them. He obviously didn't feel the same way she did, and there was safety in that. Her heart wouldn't break if he was honest with her. Besides, she wasn't sure what her feelings entailed. Perhaps nothing. Perhaps everything.

By the time she finished her sandwich, he'd devoured three of them with a few big morsels and washed them down with tea. He worked so hard his hunger was understandable. He performed all sorts of jobs in the stables, fields, and even in the kitchen. He cleaned the gymnasium as well, making sure the floor was polished and fresh towels were stacked in the cabinets. Papa had to tell him —no, *order* him to rest.

"Now, *Wuthering Heights*." He wiped his mouth and hands with a napkin before opening the book. "I'm ready for a new adventure."

"Take your time. No need to rush. It's only practice."

He frowned at the first page. She let him study the words. No need to push him.

He cleared his throat. "*1801—I have just returned from a visit to my landlord—the solitary neighbour that I shall be troubled with...*"

He didn't read smoothly but stumbled, especially when a word started with a 't.' He took long pauses as well, but she didn't mind. The haunting story told in his deep voice held an achingly desperate note she loved.

"I'm butchering it," he said once he finished the first chapter.

"No, you're improving."

"Not fast enough." He scoffed. "I learnt to box in a matter of weeks, but it's taking me months to read. It can't be normal."

"You're too harsh on yourself. No one learns to read perfectly in a few months."

He closed the book with a reverence she approved of. "I've never thanked you."

"For what?"

"For hitting me with your sledge." He flashed one of his rare, full smiles. Not the arrogant smiles he showed around to the other lads or the adoring ones he reserved for her father only. It was his secret smile, the vulnerable one. The one that told her he'd suffered and that he was scared to be hurt again. He kept that smile for her only.

She returned the smile. "You shouldn't thank me."

"If you hadn't hit me, I'd still be at Sir Howard's service." He touched the book. "Unable to read or write my name. Hungry. Cold. Weak. Dying."

Yes, the thought was disturbing. She handed him another sandwich. "My father gave you the opportunity to stay here, not me."

He took the sandwich. "He's the best man I've ever met. He's more honourable than my own father."

She tensed a little. Keith had never talked about his parents, and she hadn't bombarded him with questions since he never asked about her mother. She assumed he didn't ask questions because he didn't want to be questioned. But then, not even Papa talked about her mother. Never.

"What happened to your parents?" she asked.

He wolfed down the sandwich and didn't say anything until he sipped his tea. "My father drank himself to an early grave. I wasn't born yet. He died when my mother carried me. She died in the Clerkenwell bombing by the Fenians." His tone remained flat, but the way he hunched belied his sorrow.

She drew in a breath in shock. "I didn't know. I'm so sorry."

He fiddled with a buttercup, touching the pretty petals with a finger. "She worked for Sir Howard in his London house. She was walking by the New Prison when the bomb exploded. The police said she was in the wrong place at the wrong time. Bad luck. It didn't feel like bad luck but like a tragedy. I was four. I learnt everything I know about that day from other servants." He clenched his fist until the tendons in the back of his hand stood out. "I don't even remember the sound of her voice or her face. I don't have anything of her, neither a picture nor a pendant. I grew up with Sir Howard's servants, taken care by whoever of them had time for me. Sometimes, none of them had and I was left alone," he whispered the last words.

She put her hand over his, her chest tightening for his pain. For once, he didn't move his hand but let her stroke his knuckles.

"I'm so sorry," she said. "I can't imagine my life without Papa. He's never made me lack for anything, material or emotional."

He turned towards her, slipping his hand out of hers. Unfortunately. "You told me your mother left. May I ask why she left?"

She lifted a shoulder. "I don't know. In the year before she left, she and Papa argued a lot although I don't know about what. She grew anxious, distant, and easily startled. When I asked her what troubled her, she always said nothing. Then one night, she vanished. She didn't say anything to anyone." She had to take a deep breath to ease the sense of betrayal in her heart. "She wrote a note and left it on my nightstand. *I have to go. I can't stay here.* That's all. No explanation. No last hug. No begging for forgiveness. She left most of her belongings behind as well. Her beloved star-shaped pendant is in my father's safe. I don't know why she didn't take it."

Keith frowned but didn't look as outraged as she expected he would be. "What did your father say?"

"He was furious," she said. "He never said that Mama had a lover, but that's what I thought happened. She must have left with whomever she'd fallen in love with. Papa refused to talk about her. He said we had to accept the fact she was gone. Even now, he can't bear to talk about her. She never returned or sent a word. Papa searched for her, but he never found any clues about her. I have beautiful memories of her, of us sharing every secret, going to the market together, singing, and then she became someone else. I imagine she has a new husband, and maybe, a new daughter, and doesn't care about us." Her voice cracked, just like her heart.

He inched his hand closer and let it hover over hers for a split second before closing his strong fingers around hers. He didn't say anything. The warmth and strength of his hand around hers were the best comforts she needed.

She pushed the good memories out of her mind because they were too sad. "But I'm lucky to have Papa."

"As I'm lucky to have you." Papa's voice came from behind them.

Keith removed his hand faster than she could blink and shot up to his feet. "Sir."

"As you were." Papa clapped Keith's shoulder. "You did an excellent job with the horses. Thank you."

Keith flushed. "You're welcome, sir."

Papa crouched and kissed her cheek. The smell of worn leather and tobacco brought her back to when she was a child and sat on his lap while he signed bills and wrote letters at his desk. She'd fallen asleep on him on those occasions, lulled by his calm breathing.

"I love you, darling." He stroked her hair.

"I love you too, Papa."

"What are you reading?" He tilted his head to read the cover. "*Wuthering Heights*." He clicked his tongue. "Sorry, lad. I was wondering when you had to endure the Brontë torture."

"Papa." She swatted his shoulder. "*Wuthering Heights* is a wonderful book."

"Depressing and hopeless." He turned serious. "Too similar to real life." He straightened. "I need a word with Violante, Keith."

"Of course, sir." Keith bowed and waved at her before taking the book. "I'll see you later."

Goodness. Papa wanted to forbid her to spend time with Keith? That was it. The end of her happy time with him.

Papa sat next to her. "He's a good lad."

"He is. What did you want to tell me, Papa? Is it about Keith?"

His eyebrows drew together. "No, why?"

Oops. She forced a laugh. "Nothing. Nothing."

"Did he behave inappropriately towards you? Did he do anything? I swear, I'll have—"

"Papa." She touched his arm. "Calm down. Nothing happened. Keith is nothing but a gentleman. I promise."

He didn't soften. "Good. I'm fond of him, but if he disrespects you, I won't hesitate to throw him out."

"No need for that. Keith is very respectful and devoted to you." So much so that he was afraid to touch her. "What is it?"

"Sir Howard is throwing a party to celebrate his daughter's birthday."

"That explains all the carts I saw driving in and out of his estate in the past days when I walked up Windy Ridge. Are we invited?" She wouldn't mind. Music, good food, and lots of people.

"No. And even if we were, I wouldn't set foot in that devil's house for all the gold in the queen's vault." He didn't sound amused but determined. "In fact, I want you to stay away from his estate for the next few days. No more horse riding or walking towards Windy Ridge."

"But Papa, this way I can't even see the lady guests' gowns or the fancy carriages."

"Please, just this once, do as you are told." He patted her cheek. "Promise me you'll stay away from Sir Howard's house. He invited a bunch of politicians and members of the *ton*, and with everything that is happening in London, I'm worried." His tone carried such gravity she could only nod.

He was overreacting. Who would bomb an estate in Hertfordshire? Her corner of the world was nothing but peaceful.

five

WHATEVER OUR SOULS *are made out of, his and mine are the same.*

That sentence would stay with Keith forever. He couldn't stop reading *Wuthering Heights*. He was slow, had to stop to read a few passages again, and some words were difficult to pronounce even in his thoughts. But the ache and longing in the story ripped him apart because he understood them too well. Dusk crept along the garden as he walked back to the manor, reading in a low voice.

He knew why Mr. Sharpe had wanted to talk with Violante. She was going to be a debutante and find a husband in the next Season. She'd move to London and forget him, as it was the natural order of life. Yet it hurt. Deeply. Intimately. He should be used to being alone, but from the moment he'd moved to Sharpe Manor, he'd understood what a family was, and now he was addicted to the feeling of being part of one.

He walked towards the manor while reading, his eyes glued to the pages. He pushed the front door open and took a few steps before bumping into someone. The book slipped out of his hands.

"Careful, lad." Mr. Sharpe snatched the book before it fell to the floor. "Violante won't be happy if you scratch her copy of *Wuthering Heights*."

"Not happy? She'll kill me." He took the book. "I didn't see you, sir. Sorry."

Mr. Sharpe smiled. "I'm glad to see you're learning. Nothing is more important than an education. You're doing well. What would you like to do with a proper education?"

"Learning to read makes me think. If I could I..." He shook his head. "Sorry. You aren't likely interested."

"Quite the opposite. If you could?"

"Well, I'd like to build a place like the one you did for the lads. A gymnasium where people can learn to box and stay busy. Staying busy would improve the lives of many boys and keep them off the streets."

Mr. Sharpe raised his eyebrows. "You're on your way to becoming a great boxing teacher. When the time comes, I'll help you open your own gymnasium."

If Keith hadn't already respected and loved the man, he would now. "Really, sir?"

"I hate losing you, but if this is your dream, I'll help you. Why do you want to keep people busy?"

He hesitated, skimming the book, but Mr. Sharpe didn't prompt him to answer. "I grew up in Sir Howard's house in London. I saw many boys wasting their time and lives on the streets of the rookery, turning to crime. It sounds silly, but I believe that if they have something to do during the day, something they might turn into a career, they won't become criminals."

"It's not silly at all. It's an excellent idea."

The praise warmed Keith's cheeks.

"Listen, Keith." Mr. Sharpe's stance changed subtly from relaxed to ready to pounce. Since Keith boxed regularly, he caught the tiniest muscle contractions. "You know Sir Howard's mansion here in Hertfordshire well, don't you?"

"I do, sir. At least I know the grounds, kitchen, stables, and barn. I've never been in the upper floor rooms."

Mr. Sharpe scratched his chin. "How far is the barn from the main house?"

Keith hesitated before answering. Mr. Sharpe didn't care about Sir Howard. Why the questions? "Not much."

"In yards."

"Four hundred, give or take."

"Any basement?" The tone sounded like that of a copper.

"Wine cellar. Why?"

Mr. Sharpe shrugged. The lines on his forehead relaxed. "The bastard is giving a party. His vile friends are crawling to his house from every part of the country. I'm worried something might happen."

The questions didn't sound like concern but like interest.

"Yes, the Fenians might get ideas."

"Stay away from his estate in the next few days."

"I will, sir."

"Maybe I'm being too apprehensive. Never mind. Good night, lad." Mr. Sharpe brushed past him but stopped. "You'll keep an eye on Violante, won't you? Make sure she doesn't go to Windy Ridge."

"Of course, sir."

"Good." Mr. Shape's smile tensed as a man entered the hallway.

His expression changed so quickly that even Keith stared at the man. He was someone Keith had never seen. No, he'd seen him the night of the Christmas ball at the town hall. The large scar crossing his nose gave him away. His long travelling coat covered him from neck to ankle but couldn't fully conceal the pistol hidden underneath it at his side.

"What are you doing here?" Mr. Sharpe gritted out. "Go to the barn."

"The front door was open," the man said, jabbing a thumb towards the entrance.

"My fault," Keith said.

"It's all right." Mr. Sharpe didn't sound pleased. "Keith, go to your room and stay there." He turned towards the man. "To the barn."

The man left with a quick nod.

"Is everything all right, sir?" Keith asked.

Mr. Shape's features softened a fraction. "Do not worry. Go to bed. It's quite late." It was an order.

"Good night, sir."

Keith went up the stairs towards his room, glancing behind him. Mr. Sharpe disappeared with the man in a hurry and shut the door firmly. Keith rushed up the stairs and stopped at the landing to look out of the window. Mr. Sharpe and the scarred stranger strode along the path that didn't lead to the barn but to the opposite side. Unless Mr. Sharpe meant the old, unused barn, the one that stood at the edge of the forest. No one went there. What was going on?

He tensed when Violante came out of her bedroom, wrapped in her lilac dressing gown. The garment was more covering than a nun's habit, but the fabric fell in soft waves around her, making her look like a lavender angel. He ignored his heart skipping a beat at the sight of her. He and she couldn't be more different. She was all creamy skin, golden hair, and fair eyes; he was dark and twice her size with rough hands and sharp features. He'd never felt tiny, especially since he ate and slept regularly and his body had grown. But standing next to her made him feel quite the giant, clumsy and inadequate.

Once she became a debutante, she wouldn't be allowed to be seen in her dressing gown at night.

"Good evening." She hurried towards him in a flutter of fabric, enveloped in a cloud of scent of lilies. "I was—ah, you made progress." She eyed the bookmark. "How's the reading going?"

"I love it." Too much passion slipped into his words. "Very much."

"I had no doubt." She rose on her tiptoes to glance towards the stairs. "I heard Papa's voice. Where is he? I haven't seen him since this morning."

"A man came, someone I don't know, and they left together."

She tugged at her long braid. "Papa must have one of his meetings with the local farmers. There's always some dispute to solve about a farmer trespassing in someone's field. I hope that no sheep went missing again. Papa walked for days up and down the hills the last time an animal got lost."

No, the stranger hadn't looked like a farmer. Besides, the farmers had never come here armed, and Mr. Sharpe had never asked questions about Sir Howard's basement.

Keith was about to say he knew almost every farmer who visited Mr. Sharpe regularly, but thought better of it, not wanting to worry her.

"Did you need anything?" he asked to change the subject. "A glass of milk? Tea? I can fetch it for you."

"No, it's the stove I need help with. The door is stuck again. I can't open it and add another log, and I'm freezing."

"I'll do it." He deeply inhaled her scent when he stepped into her bedroom. It was like holding her. Almost.

The fine drapes and delicate wallpaper gave him the illusion of being in the middle of a meadow in spring. Budding roses and half-closed buttercups crawled over the walls, perpetually about to blossom. A good metaphor for the feelings he had for her. They were in a state of everlasting stillness, not allowed to grow into something deeper, always held back.

He put the book on the bed and crouched in front of the cast-iron stove. The glow of the dying embers came through the grate. He gave a yank to the handle of the door. It didn't budge, and a rattling noise came from it.

"See?" She sat next to him. "I used all my strength but nothing."

"Either it's a case of bad design or the door is broken. I'll try again." He grabbed the handle and pulled with more strength.

The door flung open with a shot of sparks and the smell of dying wood. The momentum pushed him back, and he smashed against Violante with a hard smack. They both ended up on the carpet in a heap of limbs and fabric. Somehow, he found himself on top of her. Her braid filled his mouth, and her wide sleeves covered his head. Dammit. He must have hurt her.

"Violante." He brushed the braid aside and shoved away the layers of fabric until he found her.

She laughed, one hand on her belly.

He touched her chin. "Are you hurt?"

"No, no." She laughed so hard her words came out like a hiccup.

He didn't laugh. He couldn't. Watching her laugh so freely and feeling her soft, warm body while he was on top of her was no laughing matter at all. He dared to brush a wayward golden curl from her flushed face to tuck it behind her ear. She smelled of lilies and lavender, and he wished to drown in her sweetness.

She stopped laughing. Her violet gaze was fixed on him. She was so serious and quiet he swore he could hear her heartbeat thumping against his own chest. Or maybe it was his own heartbeat. She parted her plush lips as he stroked her chin with his thumb. None of them moved because something between them had changed forever in a split second. They were no longer playing. No longer joking. No longer friends.

This—whatever the flutter in his chest was—was serious. When had things changed between them? He couldn't tell. Or maybe they hadn't changed. Maybe it was he who started to notice something different. He'd always been attracted to her, but there was a new depth to his feelings, a new type of ache. Hellfire. He wasn't making any sense.

He stroked her cheek again with his fingertips. The delicate curve of her jaw was tempting as well. Every curve of her body was tempting. He could spend the night tracing each one of them with his fingers, lips, and tongue.

She drew in a breath that pushed her breasts against his chest, sending a jolt of heated sensations throughout his body. Their lips were half an inch away. He tilted his head and brushed the softest of kisses against her pretty mouth. The ache that had tormented him for weeks burned more fiercely. She kissed him back, pressing her velvety lips against his. A shiver went down his back as she caressed his jaw with gentle fingers. The tip of her tongue teased his bottom lip.

He wasn't prepared for the intense pleasure shooting through him. The shock was so intense it broke the spell. He shouldn't be here. He shouldn't touch her. He shouldn't be on top of her.

He scampered off her, careful not to hurt her with his knees and elbows. "I'm sorry. Sorry. I shouldn't…"

She put her hands on his biceps as if to stop him from moving. "Keith—"

"I'm sorry." He rushed out of her room and closed the door behind him for good measure. What the hell was he thinking?

He owed Mr. Sharpe his life. The least he could do was to respect him and his daughter in their own house. No more reading sessions. No more unchaperoned walks through the forest. No more time spent together alone. He would stay away from her. The thought was like a dark stiletto blade twisting in his soul, but he had no other choice. If Mr. Sharpe had entered Violante's room and seen them, he would have been furious, and rightfully so.

Restless, Keith thudded downstairs and left the house through the back door, not caring about grabbing a cloak. The chilly night air did nothing to lower his rising temperature. He sped up along the gravel path although he didn't have a destination. Any place that was far from Violante's scented bedroom and her warmth was fine. Mr. Sharpe would kick him out if he knew.

Whatever feeling Keith harboured for Violante needed to be restrained.

He slowed his pace when the orange glow of the oil lamps from the old barn flickered through the darkness. He hadn't realised he'd gone that far. Hearing about lost sheep and farmers' disputes sounded like a good idea to get distracted from the tingle in his body. He stopped as he spotted a cart burdened with barrels. It was odd that a farmer brought a heavy cart to a meeting. What was inside the barrels? Ale? The armed man and the loaded cart didn't bode well.

He paused next to a corner of the barn where two wooden boards formed a gap wide enough for him to see without being seen. Mr. Sharpe stood in the middle of a circle of men. All of them carried guns. All of them were strangers. Aside from Mr. Sharpe, Paul, and a few other men who worked on the farm, the others were men Keith had never seen. Paul sat in a corner. Deep worry lines marked his brow.

"This is an opportunity we can't let go," Mr. Sharpe said, shaking a fist. "It won't happen again. It's a risk, but we must act now."

The scarred man Keith had seen in the hallway rose. He had the same stance as Mr. Sharpe's, perhaps another former soldier. "Time is of the essence. Sir Howard will start the celebration at noon. Twelve members of parliament have confirmed their presence. The Duke of Devon and his family will be present as well."

Murmurs spread. The others nodded.

"We're delivering justice," Mr. Sharpe said in a hard voice Keith had heard only when Mr. Sharpe had talked about Sir Howard.

Keith inched back. The nagging feeling he'd experienced a few times when in the presence of Mr. Sharpe became a certainty. It seemed impossible, but it was the only explanation.

"How much are we carrying?" another man asked.

The scarred man took his time as if pausing from a dramatic effect. "Thirty-six barrels in honour of Guy Fawkes."

A round of raucous laughter spread. Thirty-six barrels. Guy Fawkes, the man who had plotted to blow up the parliament two centuries ago in the infamous Gunpowder Plot.

"Finest quality," the scarred mad added. "This is French white powder. Ten times more powerful than the normal gunpowder. Getting it has been difficult, but we have it now."

A round of laughter swept the barn as a chill dipped into Keith's bones. Ten times more powerful than normal gunpowder? He didn't remember his mother, but she would be alive and with him if it hadn't been for the Fenians and their obsession with blowing things up. They hadn't solved any of their problems with their bombs. They'd only fabricated orphans.

If he were going to be honest, he'd never really hated the Fenians. His mother's death had been a tragic fatality, and he'd been too young and too busy surviving to care about politics. But the situation was different now. These people planned to blow up a mansion full of people in cold blood, aware that innocents like his mother would die. The story of his life would be repeated for others. Orphans, widows, widowers, desperate parents, loved ones dead. The ripples of the consequences of a bombing reached places no one could foresee.

He didn't realise he'd dug his fingernails into his palms until blood trickled through his fingers. Murderers. These people terrorised England with their bombs and attacks. Whatever rightful claims they had, they'd forfeited the moment they started killing innocent people. But...Keith rubbed his eyes as if wanting to wake up. Mr. Sharpe would never, ever get involved with the Fenians. It wasn't possible. Mr. Sharpe wasn't a murderer. There had to be another explanation. Perhaps Mr. Sharpe was only pretending to support them.

Paul was the only one who didn't laugh. He stood up on trembling legs. "Gentlemen."

No one paid him the slightest bit of attention. The others were busy patting each other's shoulders for a job well done.

"Gentlemen!" Paul raised his voice.

"What is it?" Mr. Sharpe asked.

"Sir Howard..." Paul twisted the hem of his shirt. "He has two children. The girl is barely ten. There will be other children for the girl's birthday."

"And?" the scarred man asked, taking a menacing step towards Paul. "What about our children? All those children who died from starvation? My own children are dead because I couldn't provide for them after the government refused to grant me a military pension. Dying from starvation is a long, painful death. Blowing up will take a moment."

"What about the orphans of war?" Mr. Sharpe said. "The war Sir Howard and his friends promote produces an endless number of orphans and widows. And for what? So they can keep their seats in parliament and lecture us on what it means to be honourable. We must raise our voices to be heard."

Paul sat down again, his gaze on the rushes. Keith copied him, sitting on the ground with his knees bent. All his doubts had been vanquished. The rest of the conversation was a jumble of voices. The men—or rather, conspirators—discussed the details of moving the barrels, how many carts they needed, how to put the barrel in the wine cellar with the help of a few of Sir Howard's servants, and which route to the mansion was the best.

He raked a trembling hand through his hair. He was devoted to Mr. Sharpe. But no matter how many times he repeated that, his loyalty and gratitude for Mr. Sharpe paled when confronted with the indisputable fact that he was a murderer. Bloody hell. Perhaps Violante's mother had known. Perhaps Mr. Sharpe had got rid of her. Keith shivered at the thought of Mr. Sharpe killing his own wife.

When the meeting was over, he scurried to hide in the shadows. The men left one by one, vanishing into the dark lane that led to the town. Paul staggered towards the manor like a drunk man. The last one to exit the barn was Mr. Sharpe, and Keith couldn't help himself. He *had* to talk to him, persuade him to give up. Do something.

Keith stepped out of his hiding place while Mr. Sharpe locked the barn. He didn't need to say anything. He breathed loudly enough to be heard, and Mr. Sharpe was a fine soldier. He pinned Keith with a glare that didn't hold any surprise, only a hint of sadness.

"It can't be true," Keith said so low he wasn't sure Mr. Sharpe would hear it. "Please tell me you aren't with them."

Mr. Sharpe put his hands on Keith's shoulders in his usual paternal way. "Sometimes violence is the only way to start a change."

"Violence is never the answer."

"Really? Don't countries go to war to change things?"

"Yes, but this is different."

"How?"

Keith didn't recognise the light in Mr. Sharpe's gaze. It was hard and cold like a diamond. "Because soldiers are trained to fight other soldiers, and they're ready and prepared to fight each other. You're planning to kill innocents unaware of the attack, who didn't do anything to you."

Mr. Sharpe dug his fingers into Keith's shoulders. "There are no innocents in the parliament or among the *ton*. Those politicians' hands are stained with more blood than mine. They sent me to war. They killed thousands from the safety of their armchairs. Now they refuse to give the Irish the chance to create their own country while keeping all of us as slaves. Protests and petitions didn't work. We must stop them."

Keith was tall enough to stare straight into Mr. Sharpe's eyes. He'd been wrong. Those eyes weren't like Violante's. "What about Sir Howard's family? Or the families of the politicians he invited to his estate? The children and the servants?"

"Casualties are a sad part of every war. We can't wait." Mr. Sharpe sounded tired.

"As your wife was? Did you kill her?"

A ghost of a smile twisted Mr. Shape's lips. "I didn't kill my wife, for crying out loud. I'm not a monster."

Keith wasn't sure about that.

"I thought that you of all people would understand."

"Understand?" Keith shoved Mr. Sharpe's hands away. "My mother was killed by the Fenians."

The shock on Mr. Sharpe's face was genuine. "A tragedy, but as I said, casualties are part of every war."

"Not from my point of view."

Mr. Sharpe scowled. "Don't you hate Sir Howard for what he did to you?"

"I do." Why lie? "But killing him and his family is something I've never wanted, and it won't change anything."

Thirty-six barrels of gunpowder would blow up Sir Howard's entire estate, including the servants' quarters, the stables, and the farmers' huts. It'd be a bloodbath. Hundreds of people would die. The worst thing was that the bombing wouldn't change anything.

Keith closed his fists. "The prime minister will repress the anarchists with more strength. The repression will crush everyone. You'll never win."

Mr. Sharpe shook his head. "The message will be delivered, and they will listen."

"Mr. Sharpe—"

"I will not let more people die in a senseless war because those ancient barons are greedy. The sun never sets on the empire, they say. For how long shall we expand? What will we do when there are no more lands to conquer? How many soldiers have to bleed to satisfy these monsters' appetite? No more. Enough." Breathing heavily, he stepped closer to Keith. "The only question that remains is what are *you* going to do now? I love you like a son,

Keith. Don't stand between my battle and me. You're going to get crushed."

"I can't let you kill innocents. There will be orphans like me. Never. I can't." His voice broke with sheer fear and determination. He was angry for his mother, the people who had died in senseless acts of violence, and he was angry for having been betrayed by the only man he'd ever considered a father.

Deep lines of worry marked Mr. Sharpe's brow. "Then I'm really sorry, Keith."

The blow in the head was the last thing Keith felt before his eyes closed.

six

KEITH WOKE UP in complete darkness.

No, a distant, faint glow limned the wooden boards surrounding him. It had to be night still. He massaged his eyes, wondering what had happened. Touching around, he recognised the rough wooden planks and the smell of the wet soil in one of the garden sheds. Likely one of those that were far from the manor. He rubbed the ache out of the back of his neck where a swollen and tender spot throbbed. *Blimey*. Mr. Sharpe must have hit him and trapped him here, wherever he was. He hadn't even seen Mr. Sharpe hitting him. So much for being good at boxing. Keith agreed with what Mr. Sharpe had said. Yes, he understood every word. But he couldn't approve of the method.

He staggered to his feet. At least Mr. Sharpe hadn't killed him. Yet. He reached the door, but it didn't budge. When he shouldered it, dust rained from the ceiling. The walls shook, but the door remained closed. He thumped a fist on the walls. Dammit.

"Let me out!"

No one answered.

He opened his mouth to shout again, but footsteps

approached. He stepped back from the door, closing his fists, ready for a fight.

"Keith?" Paul whispered from the other side of the door. "It's me."

"Paul. Get me out." He slammed a fist on the door again.

"I'm trying."

The noise of metal clunking came then a rustling sound from the lock.

"I saw Mr. Sharpe taking you here. I waited for him and the others to leave before helping you," Paul said among metallic ticks.

After a sharp click, the door swung inwards, screeching on the hinges.

"You are—"

Keith grabbed Paul by the jacket, cutting off whatever Paul wanted to say. "You're one of them. How could you?"

Paul shoved him, glowering. "No. I've never hurt anyone. I only helped them find the horses and the carts."

"You're helping them kill people." His throat hurt with worry and fear.

Paul gazed away. "I didn't know what the carts were for until tonight. I promise. I mean, I talked with Mr. Sharpe about...you know, politics, and I told him I agreed with him, but I wasn't sure...I might have said something about a death penalty for the politicians..." He ran a hand through his hair. "Hell, Keith. I just opened my mouth and breathed. I didn't think he was serious."

Keith scoffed. "What did you think they needed the carts for?" He had to control his voice in case one of the conspirators was close.

"They have their reasons."

"We're talking about murdering children," Keith said among pants. "Servants, farmers, people who didn't do anything to you. How can this be right?"

Paul paced. "What do you want me to do? Stop them? They'll kill me and bury my body in gunpowder. They're too strong."

"We must go to the police."

"Are you mad?" Paul seized Keith's arm. "Do you think the Fenians will let us live if we denounce them? If they don't kill us, the police will arrest Mr. Sharpe, and what will happen to us? We won't have a job or a home anymore. All the people working for him will be thrown into the streets."

"We must do something."

"What about Violante?"

Violante's name was like a punch in Keith's stomach. She lived a lie, and it was a matter of time before Mr. Sharpe died in an attack or was arrested. She'd find herself alone and scared, as Keith had been when his mother had been killed. "Can you live with the blood of those children on your hands? I heard you. You told them the girl was barely ten. They didn't care."

Paul shivered and leant against the shed. "I owe my life to Mr. Sharpe. If he hadn't employed my mum, she would have died in poverty."

"I owe him my life as well, but he's with the Fenians." The air itself seemed to quiver when he pronounced the last word. "My mother is dead because one of their bombs killed her. I can't let him do this. It's wrong."

Paul thumped the wall. "Think. Do you believe Sir Howard is going to thank us for saving him? He doesn't care about us one way or another. We aren't human to him. You should know that. He treated you like vermin. Even if we save his life, we're going to pay the price. The police will arrest us as well. Whatever we do, we're going to get the short end of the stick. We'll lose everything, and no one will thank us or consider us heroes."

"I don't want the deaths of Sir Howard and so many others on my conscience." He pushed Paul aside. "You can stay here or come with me to the police station. Your choice."

"They'll lock me up too as their accomplice."

"Not if you tell the truth." Keith closed his fists in case Paul attacked him. The fact Mr. Sharpe had taught Keith how to box didn't lack irony. Even if his chest tightened at the thought of denouncing his friends, he would do it if it meant saving innocent lives. "Why did you let me out?"

Paul kept pacing, releasing a sharp breath. "I don't know."

"I'll tell you why. You aren't a murderer. You know what they're doing is wrong." He let his friend pace. "I know you have a good heart. You've taken care of me from the moment I came here. You aren't like them. You don't want to kill anyone. You won't be able to live with yourself if you do nothing."

Paul stopped, bending over as if his stomach hurt. He gazed up and nodded. "Let's go to the police."

NOT EVEN A WALK uphill could soothe the odd restlessness in Violante's chest. She'd promised not to go to Windy Ridge, and she'd obeyed. Papa had seemed rather worried. She didn't want to challenge him. But the path she'd chosen wasn't as exciting as she'd like. That wasn't the only reason for her distress.

Vivid dreams had troubled her sleep after last night's encounter with Keith. After their kiss. It hadn't been a proper kiss. Not like one of those she read about in novels. Those were savage and deep and led to tumbles. He'd barely touched her lips with his. But heavens. It'd been the most wonderful sensation she'd ever experienced.

When she'd woken up, a palpable tension had thickened the air. She hadn't found Keith anywhere, and even her papa had disappeared. No one knew where they were. The gymnasium was empty. Thus her lonely walk.

Maybe it was Keith who troubled her. Every time she thought about the moment she'd lain under him, feeling the delicious weight of his strong body against her, heat flooded her chest and face. He'd caressed her cheek with such sweetness her skin still tingled. She wouldn't know why he'd left so abruptly though.

Perhaps he'd changed his mind about kissing her, finding her lacking in some way.

No, she hadn't imagined the desire in his gaze, as she hadn't imagined her own. Or maybe the source of her distress was her papa. If Papa learnt about how close she and Keith had grown, he'd throw Keith out and send her to London.

She paused, a hand on her chest. What if that was the reason for Keith's and Papa's absence? No, Papa would have talked to her first before kicking Keith out.

Poppies and daisies nodded their pretty crowns under the breeze. Not a cloud obscured the sky. It was a perfect spring day, but a nagging feeling bit the back of her head. That would be the only instance when doing house chores would help her feel better. If she kept herself busy with pulling the weeds in the cabbage patch or grooming the horses, her anxiety would go away. Although she couldn't deny that Papa disappearing without a word and Keith vanishing as well worried her.

The sense of urgency growing within her didn't make sense until a commotion attracted her attention.

Many horses and carts approached the manor at breakneck speed. From the top of the hill where the trees didn't grow, she could see blue-uniformed men spreading through the grounds, holding rifles. The armed police. What was happening?

Some of the police officers rushed inside the manor. Others ran towards the stables. Their rifles glinted in the sunlight. She ran down the hill, losing sight of the manor as she rushed onto the flat land where the trees grew and blocked her view. The path seemed to never end. It took her too long.

She arrived at the manor breathless. The front door had been left open, and the marks of boots soiled the carpet. Pieces of broken vases lay scattered.

"Papa?" She searched around. The entry hall was empty, and an eerie silence lingered. The police must have searched for something and left, not caring about having destroyed doors and vases.

She rushed up the stairs to her father's study. "Papa, what hap —" She gasped.

Crouched in front of the open strongbox, Paul was emptying it. Judging by the way the door of the strongbox was contorted and dented, it'd been forced. Paul filled his satchel and pockets with banknotes, gold necklaces, coins, and rings. He froze upon seeing her, his hand grabbing a fistful of guineas.

She was so shocked she forgot about the police. "What are you doing?"

He stood up and closed the satchel. His arrogant expression wasn't that of a thief caught red-handed. "I can't lose everything because of your father."

"What are you talking about? You're a thief." She ran around the large oakwood desk to shove him away from the strongbox.

He let her do it without opposing any resistance, but the clenching of his jaw belied his anger. "If you have any sense, you'll grab some money and leave before the police confiscate everything and lock you up. I'm not going to prison for your family." He snatched her mother's star-shaped pendant and stashed it in his pocket.

"Give me that. It's my mother's."

"She's gone."

She put her hands on his chest and shoved him again. "Why would the police confiscate everything? And give me that satchel." She tried to snatch the satchel, but he was too tall and strong for her.

He blocked her at every move. "I need this. I must leave this place with my mother immediately."

The more he blocked her, the more frustrated she grew.

He went to leave, but she yanked his arm. "Answer me. You owe me."

He glanced at the hallway, holding the heavy satchel with both arms. "Your father is a Fenian—"

She slapped him. Hard. Her hand burned, and her wrist hurt,

but the shock of her moment of violence hurt more. "How dare you?" Tears and sobs of anger choked her.

He rubbed his cheek, his nostrils flaring. "Your father is a bloody murderer and a traitor to our country." He spat every word with venom. "He's responsible for the bomb at Whitehall and many others. I will not be locked up with him or pay for his mistakes."

"Liar." She couldn't raise her voice. The boy, who had grown up with her, had betrayed her family.

"Bloody hell, Violante. You're nothing but a spoiled little brat who doesn't understand anything of the world. You go around with your books and spouting nonsense about how kind your father is. You know nothing." Hatred dripped from his words as if he'd waited years to say them.

"You're nothing but a thief."

"Suit yourself. I won't let the police arrest my mother and me. We're leaving. I warned you. Your choice."

"Paul—"

Ignoring her, he strode out of the room and headed for the servants' stairs.

Violante stood motionless. Her brain couldn't cope with the absurdity of the situation. Her papa a Fenian? Impossible. Paul had lied. Someone hated her father so much to throw accusations against him. The room tilted, and she put a hand on the desk not to fall. Loud noises and shouts came from outside, but she was numb. She didn't know what to do.

"Violante." Keith swept into view. He took in the open strongbox and peered at her face. "You shouldn't be here. It's too dangerous."

She nearly sagged against him when he took her shoulders. "What's happening?"

Gunshots rent the air, jolting her.

"We must leave." Keith dragged her away from the study and down the stairs.

"Where's Papa?" She glanced around, but she didn't see anyone. The manor was seemingly empty. "Who called the police?"

"Violante." Keith's grave tone was like a slap. "I called the police."

"Because of what Paul did? He was here. He stole my father's money, our jewels, and even my mother's pendant. Did you call the police to arrest him?"

His fingers gripped her shoulders harder. He stared at her with an intensity that made her shiver. "Your father is with the Fenians."

A wave of sheer anger burned her chest. Her numbness was crushed under that wave. "That's rubbish. Not even you." She shrugged herself free. "How dare you."

He didn't flinch. "I saw it with my own eyes. He met with the Fenians last night to plan an attack on Sir Howard's house. Paul and other people who work here were there, too. When I confronted your father, he locked me up in the old shed. Paul let me out, and we went to the police."

"Don't be ridiculous. It must be a misunderstanding. Papa would never hurt anyone." A buzzing noise rang in her ears.

He shook his head. "I talked to him. He admitted to wanting to kill Sir Howard and his family. I'm sorry. I had to call the police."

"You're lying." She shoved him. Not that he budged. "Why are you lying?"

"It's the truth." His voice broke, and tears glistened in his eyes. "It kills me, but it's the whole truth."

Another gunshot rang out. Keith grabbed her hand and dragged her towards the rear of the house.

"Where are we going?" She tried to get free, but he didn't let her go.

He led her through the back door towards the path that led to the town. Another round of gunshots thundered from the barn.

He wrapped his arms around her, shielding her, and she couldn't see anything.

"Quick." He urged her onwards, almost hauling her up.

She shuffled, trying to understand what the heck was happening.

When he released her, they were close to the barley field.

She stepped away from him. Her head throbbed, and a sudden exhaustion took her. "How can you be so ungrateful towards us? Papa welcomed you here, fed you, and protected you, and you accused him of such a heinous crime." She pointed a finger at him. "You're in cahoots with Paul. You two want to rob my father. The police are a diversion to give you time to steal from him."

His muscles bulged as his face reddened. "No. I don't know why Paul stole from you, but that has nothing to do with what I saw last night. Your father met other conspirators in the barn. The meeting wasn't with the farmers." He grabbed her hands, his features hardening. "It hurts me. It really does. But I'm not lying, and I'm not mistaken. Your father gathered thirty-six barrels of gunpowder to destroy Sir Howard's house with his children and party guests in it. Please believe me."

"No." She slid her hands out of his. "I refuse to believe such a thing until I speak to him."

She turned towards the manor, determined to see her papa immediately. She wouldn't leave. She'd wait for him somewhere. Surely, he'd tell her it was all a big mistake, then laugh with his deep baritone, and they would have lunch together. And Keith would leave the manor.

"Don't go." He followed her, and she didn't care.

Where would her papa be? She was halfway to the stables when she spotted him. "Papa."

He waved her away. He carried a rifle, and a cut bled from his forehead. "What the hell are you doing here? Leave. Leave, dammit!"

She rushed to him, but his angry expression slowed her down. Keith tensed, following her.

She hugged her papa with desperation. "Papa—"

"You must leave." He gave her a shove, causing her to stagger. "Go to the town. Stay away from the manor."

"Keith says you're a Fenian." She hardly recognised him. The cold, hard expression of his face was foreign to her.

He ignored her and glared at Keith. For a split second, she could swear he was about to aim the rifle at Keith. Either she misunderstood his move or he changed his mind because he lowered the rifle and stepped back.

His jaw clenched. "Keep her safe. You *owe* me that." Something passed between them with a quick exchange of nods.

"Come." Keith pulled her towards the path to the town.

"Is it true?" She sank her boots into the ground, refusing to move. "Tell me the truth."

Her papa kissed her forehead. "I meant to build a better world for you." His face transformed into that of her lovely, sweet papa before returning cold and unforgiving. "If something happens to her, I'll kill you," he said to Keith.

She could hear her heart shattering. The agonising sound rang in her ears. She let Keith drag her wherever he wanted to while Papa ran towards the barn, rifle at the ready.

The day wasn't perfect after all.

seven

THE HARD WOODEN bench at the police station hurt Keith's back. He was sick of that place, especially since he'd been separated from Violante. Last night, after he and Paul had come here, the officers hadn't let them go until that morning, and now Keith was once again at the police station. He wasn't sure for how long he'd been sitting there, but his legs had grown numb, and an ache pounded in his head. A detective had interrogated him for hours, asking each question at least ten times. Then anonymous constables had asked him arbitrary questions about everything regarding Sharpe Manor. After that, they'd ordered him to sit in the lobby and not leave while the officers celebrated the huge success of their anti-anarchist operation.

He didn't feel any sense of triumph. People had died that day because of his actions. There was nothing to celebrate or be grateful for. He certainly didn't feel like a hero.

Yes, the attack had been foiled, the gunpowder and weapons had been confiscated, and Sir Howard, his family, and his guests were still alive. But Mr. Sharpe...Keith rubbed his chest where a different type of ache throbbed.

Mr. Sharpe had been shot dead after he'd barricaded himself in the barn with other Fenians. Paul and his mother were nowhere to be seen. Keith suspected they'd left with the stolen money, never to return. Even Violante had vanished. He'd lost sight of her when the police had snatched everyone in the manor and along the road to the town. Rowdy constables had stuffed Keith and other men in a cramped waggon. Violante and the housemaids had been shoved into a different coach. Not even the stableboys had been spared from being locked up in an interrogation room for hours.

He didn't care about being interrogated, but he had to see Violante. He stopped a passing constable. "I need to see Miss Violante Sharpe. Where is she?"

The copper shrugged and left.

"Excuse me…" He tried to stop another officer who ignored him.

"Please." He blocked the path of yet another officer. "I must see Miss Violante Sharpe. Where is she?"

The man pointed to the other side of the hall. "I have no idea. Take a look at the cell—"

"The cell? Was she arrested?"

"I don't know, but we locked a few people up in case we need to question them further and to prevent them from leaving. If she isn't there, I have no idea where she might be."

Keith made his way through the crowd of uniformed men and civilians. The journalists fought among themselves to interview the superintendent, who conceitedly talked about his excellent detective skills in understanding where an attack would take place. Yes, right. If it hadn't been for Keith and Paul, there would be a crater where Sir Howard's manor was.

Relatives of the arrested people yelled and threatened the officers. Someone cried in a corner. A man bumped into him. He had to shove people aside to reach the other side of the lobby. A short staircase led to a wide corridor lined with a series of cells. They were empty for the most part, but he found Violante in the last one. She sat on a bench between two of the maids of the manor and other women he didn't know. Her hair was dishevelled, mud stained her boots, and rips tore her dress. A bruise marred her cheek.

"Violante." He grabbed the bars, his pulse spiking.

She raised her head, but her face remained a mask of tired lines and hopelessness.

"How are you?" It was a stupid question, but he couldn't think of anything better to say.

"Go away, Keith." She stared at her folded hands on her lap.

He licked his dry lips. "I'm sorry about your father."

Fire flamed her cheeks in an instant, turning her violet eyes into a deep purple. She shot up to her feet. "Sorry? How dare you say you're sorry? My papa is dead because of you, because of your betrayal."

"Betrayal?" Dammit. He would take the blame for her father's death, but he wouldn't be considered a traitor. "What was I supposed to do? Let him carry on his plan?" Getting upset had to be contagious because he grew offended as well. "He betrayed *me*."

"You should have done something, dissuaded him, forced him to renounce his plan. You should have warned me. Not call the police." She closed her fists. "If you'd called me, talked to me, I would've convinced him to stop his plan. He would've seen reason. He would've listened to me. He would've done anything for me."

"This is absurd. Do you think I didn't try to persuade him? And you would have never believed me, and even if you had, he wouldn't have changed his mind. Too many people were involved. The barrels filled with gunpowder were ready. It wasn't the first time he'd blown people up. Hell, for all I know, he killed my mother, too."

"My papa is dead." Her voice broke with pain.

"My mother is dead, too," he said, shaking. "The Fenians killed her."

"So it was revenge. You denounced my father because you wanted revenge."

"I wanted justice." He slammed a hand on the bar. "I wanted to save people."

"Look at what a great job you did," she said. "Papa is dead. Six other people are dead. The manor is destroyed. My family is gone. Well done. You're a true hero."

"Shooting at the police was your father's choice." He gripped the bars harder. "If he and his men had surrendered themselves, they would be alive."

She kept staring at him with fire in her gaze. "Are you and Paul going to share? You should be proud of that, too."

"Paul and I aren't together in this—"

"I don't believe you."

"Paul left, and I don't know where he is." He didn't recognise her. But he forced himself to remember that the shock and pain had to be too much for her. He shouldn't judge her for that. "You lost your father today. I know how you feel."

"You know nothing." She sagged her shoulders as if she'd lost energy. "I don't know why you hate us so much, but we didn't deserve any of this."

"I don't hate you. How can you say that?" He stretched out his arm to touch her, but she stepped out of reach, hugging herself.

"Go away. Take the money. I don't care. I don't want to see you again."

His vision darkened at the edges, and his legs seemed to have turned into rubber because they didn't work properly. If the evidence the police had found had not convinced her that her father would have never listened to her, and that Keith had done the only decent thing possible, then he didn't have anything else to add. He understood her sorrow, but he couldn't have lied. He'd protected children who would have lost a loved one, as it'd happened to him. Violante needed time. She wasn't herself today. But he would do as she asked. He released the bars inch by inch. With each step he took away from her, his heart broke a little.

He returned upstairs. His chest hurt so much he was surprised it didn't bleed. He walked through the crowd, not caring about the shoves from strangers and loud voices.

Maybe Paul had been right about Keith wanting to be a hero. Not that he'd expected Violante to sing his praise, but her hate hurt. Although she had a point. He hadn't thought, not for one second, to talk to her first. It wouldn't have made a difference, but he should have talked to her before going to the police. Too late now.

He left the police station without anyone stopping him. Who cared? If the constables needed him, they would find him. Rain drizzled, soaking his jacket. He shoved his hands in his pockets and started down the pavement, not knowing where to go. Never mind. The only home he'd ever known didn't exist anymore. The only friends he'd ever had hated him. He was alone again.

"Keith," a familiar, grave voice said from behind him.

Turning around, Keith gazed up and held his breath. "You." He checked the street, ready to bolt away should Sir Howard attack him.

Sir Howard stood in front of him in all his arrogant authority and fine coat. He removed his tall hat and bowed to Keith from the waist. The shock nearly caused Keith to laugh.

"I have no words to express my deep gratitude for your courage." Sir Howard's face was ashen, but his voice remained strong. "Thanks to you, my family…" He sucked in a shaky breath. "My wife and children are safe. My guests' children are unharmed. The police found twelve barrels filled with French gunpowder hidden in my cellar, but the Fenians had planned to bring more. Just those twelve barrels would have destroyed my house and killed everyone in it. I will always be in your debt."

Of all the things happened so far, Keith hadn't expected that. "I simply did the right thing, sir." Although it had destroyed his life and Violante's.

"The right thing is always the hardest." Sir Howard straightened, his expression softening. "As it is admitting one's mistakes. I treated you beastly. You had every right to keep silent and let the Fenians kill me. Despite the way I behaved towards you, you saved my family. Why?"

"Because the Fenians killed my mother. Because I couldn't live with myself if I had let them kill again. Because your children are innocent." He exhaled. "Sir, I don't hold grudges against you. I'm not fond of you." He had to be honest. "But I don't hate you so much that I want to see you and your children dead. You owe me nothing. Now, if you'll excuse me." He didn't bother bowing and resumed his aimless walk.

Sir Howard wasn't finished though. He stepped in front of Keith. "I will show you what gratitude means and make amends for the pain I caused you. I'm sorry it took my family being in danger to understand that. But a lesson learnt is a lesson earned, and I've learnt from my mistakes."

Keith didn't know what to say but had an idea of where the conversation was going. "I don't want your money."

Sir Howard frowned as if offended. "Money? That would be like putting a price on the lives of my daughter and son. I'll do more than give you money. I'll give you a future."

eight

Five years later

FOR AN EXPERT thief like Violante, nothing was more exciting than a busy pavement in central London, filled with rich people. Very rich, judging by the silk, jewels, and fine coats around. Rich and distracted. They didn't pay attention to women like her who kept their heads down and brushed past them in a hurry. A little bump, a quick hand, and a wallet fat with banknotes would change the owner.

Violante pulled up her scarf over her face and her hat down to her nose, holding her basket more tightly. Rich people might be distracted, but covering her face was always a good idea. She inhaled the faint, mouldy smell of her scarf. No matter how many times she washed it, the worn wool stank. But then again, London's air was no better. Coal and horse dung formed a powerful odour that stung her nostrils.

Where should she start? The gentleman just come out of his fancy club? The lady followed by a footman who carried all her shopping boxes?

She was spoilt for choice, but she didn't want to get too greedy lest someone spot her. In the five years she'd lived on the streets, she'd had more brushes with the coppers than she would care to admit. Speed was good, but haste was dangerous.

Her stomach gave a loud roar, reminding her that the last thing she'd eaten had been a slice of pork pie two days ago. Maybe three.

She searched around, checking the jewels and the pockets. With that lady's bracelet, she could feed herself for weeks on end, and with that gentleman's pocket watch, she could rent a room. Something decent with a stove and clean bedsheets with no bugs. Not that dump she shared with rats and cutthroats. Her fingers itched for action. She wouldn't steal more than a couple of things. Besides, she was too tired and hungry to lift more than a wallet. Hunger interfered with her usual speed and efficiency. If someone noticed her, she wouldn't be able to run for more than a handful of minutes.

After all the years of struggling to survive, stealing, and cheating, the pang of guilt for committing a crime still bothered her. She'd only become a quicker pickpocket to push down the guilt and do what she had to. Although stealing from George the Blade, the rookery's mobster, hadn't brought her any guilt but instead a lot of trouble. If George found her, hunger would be the last of her problems.

A tall, broad gentleman in a fine dark suit caught her eye. His silk hat and gloves marked him as a rich one. A golden chain hung from the pocket of his shiny waistcoat. Surely, it was a pocket watch. Pocket watches were highly requested in the black market, sold for at ten pounds apiece. She might lift his wallet, too. Then she'd flee towards the gutter where people like her belonged.

Keeping her head down and her feet quick, she weaved through the crowd, careful not to make eye contact with anyone. Rich people didn't like meeting poor people's gazes. Those gazes reminded them of their humanity. Eye contact was also potentially problematic for her. The scandal around the Sharpe family had been long forgotten, especially since the Fenians had become less active. But she didn't want to meet someone who had lost a loved one because of the Fenians and had the brilliant idea of venting their anger on her.

The gentleman walked a few feet in front of her. Goodness, he was a broad and strapping one with bouncy dark hair and strong shoulders. Even his arms were thick. Better be quick. She didn't want to get caught by him. She might choose another target, but that lady's footman didn't look less intimidating.

The tip of her big toe appeared through a hole in her shoes, and she winced as the bitter cold numbed her feet. No, she wouldn't get enough from the watch to buy food, rent a room, buy new clothes, and also a new pair of shoes. She hadn't bought a new pair of shoes in years. At best, she could find a discarded one along the banks of the Thames.

Her target hurried on. She sped up lest she lose him. Taking a deep breath, she pushed onwards to perform her quick, bumping move.

"Careful, madam," the man said in a deep voice when she bumped into him.

"I'm sorry." She brushed past him, snatching the watch. She dropped it in her basket and strode forwards without looking back.

Madam. The man had called her madam. No one called her madam.

Her pulse thundered as she tried not to slip on the wet cobbles. Only a few yards, then she would vanish in a dark alleyway leading to a maze of side streets that only people like her knew. The gentleman would never know what had happened to his precious watch.

She cut through the crowd and paused only to inhale the delicious scent of freshly baked bread. Nothing was more mouthwatering than freshly baked bread, when a slice was so hot that the butter would melt on it, releasing all its fragrance. Another cramp of hunger twisted her stomach. She shouldn't think of food; it made hunger worse.

The street tilted for a moment. Nothing new. Her energy was

rather low. To safety now. She exhaled once as she slid into the alleyway. Finally, a moment of respite. She leant against the brick wall and rubbed the bridge of her nose. She was safe now. Thank good—

Quick footsteps thundered into the alleyway. "Excuse me."

She glanced behind her. *Drat*. It was the gentleman, striding towards her with all the power his strong legs provided. She ran, her scarf nearly unravelling.

"Stop." The man was in full pursuit.

She sped up, breathing heavily. Her stomach cramped again, and she had to take a breather. Gosh. The pain was like a stab in her belly.

"You stole my watch." The man hounded her. His heavy footsteps sounded dangerously close.

She turned a corner, but the brick walls closed in on her as her head became light. The world spun. A firm hand grabbed her arm, but she didn't have the strength to shrug herself free. Oh, not now. Not another fainting.

"You—" The man's face swept into focus. Harsh features delineated his male beauty. His intense dark eyes sucked her in. They were so dark the pupils weren't distinguishable.

There was only one man with such deep black eyes like a bottomless abyss.

He faltered, his grip easing. "Violante?" he whispered in disbelief.

She didn't know what to say, but it didn't matter because two men appeared from behind him. Her heart jumped to her throat. George the Blade and his henchman from the rookery were staring at her.

"There you are, Fleet-foot Vi." George cracked his knuckles. His completely bald head gleamed in the sunlight. "I've been searching for you for a while. Too long for my taste."

The henchman spat on the ground. "No more games, harlot."

Ha! Of all the things Violante was, harlot wasn't one of them. She wasn't desperate enough to solicit herself. Not yet.

Keith pushed her behind his back, forming a human shield in front of her. "What do you want?"

George stepped closer, scratching his short beard. "She owes me something, and I either get it back, or teach her a lesson and then get it back. Her choice."

Violante's instinct was to run and save her neck, but she wouldn't get far. And Keith...he could take care of himself. He didn't need her, did he?

"I can pay you," Keith said in a calm, cold voice.

George shook his head. "She stole my mother's ring."

And sold it without making much because it'd been a fake, or so the man who had acquired it had told her. Better to steal from rich people and feel guilty than from mobsters and remain poor. And risk her neck.

"No one steals from me," George added.

No one stole from him because he stole from everyone else. It was a circle of life of sorts.

"We can settle the situation—" Keith didn't have the chance to finish the sentence.

George lunged and aimed a punch at his head. Keith parried the blow and returned the favour, hitting George's stomach with one smooth move. The thug doubled over with a gasp, his eyes growing wide.

Goodness. Keith was fast. She remembered him being good at boxing. He still was.

Instead of helping George, the henchman grabbed Violante's wrist and shoved her against the wall. "Harlot."

She hit her head hard, and flashes of white light danced in her field of vision. The sounds of the fight between Keith and George receded as a buzzing noise rang in her ears.

"The ring," the henchman said. His putrid breath made her want to gag.

She turned her face away, fighting to stay conscious. "I don't have it."

The henchman raised a fist. "Liar."

She squeezed her eyes shut, waiting for the blow, but the pain never came. Only thuds and the sickening noise of a punch hitting flesh reached her ears. When she opened her eyes, George was on the ground, moaning, and the henchman staggered on his feet, waving his arms about like an acrobat wire-walking. Blood oozed from his nose. She would have laughed if she'd had the energy.

"Are you all right?" Keith cupped her face with gentle hands. A corner of his cheek was red, but aside from that, he was the same handsome man she'd met.

Her legs gave in and her eyes shut before she could say anything.

nine

KEITH PERCHED IN his armchair by the fire and rubbed the tight spot between his eyebrows. Not even the peace and quiet of his cosy sitting room could soothe his worry.

Of all the thieves in London, the last one he'd expected to catch that day was Violante Sharpe. Or rather, of all the people in London. Hell, he'd barely recognised her. Her face was haggard with her cheekbones protruding too much. Her skin was pale and covered in grime. Her body looked frail. Even her breathing sounded laboured. He'd lost contact with her years ago after the tragedy, but he could have never imagined that something so terrible had befallen her.

She'd fainted in his arms in that alleyway, and he'd feared she might have died so frail she was. Too many strong emotions too quickly had coursed through him—finding her again, worrying about her weakness, and fearing she was dead.

He stood up when the nurse he'd hired to look after Violante entered. Hired was the wrong term, though. Dragged her out of a clinic and offered her a hefty sum to take a look at Violante was a more correct description of what had happened.

"My lord." She bobbed a quick curtsy.

He had still to get used to being called 'your lordship' or 'my lord.' "How is she?"

"Exhaustion and starvation are what afflict her. I helped her take a bath and gave her a rich broth. She'll recover after a few good meals and plenty of rest."

"Does Violante need a physician?"

The nurse shrugged. "If Miss Violante's health doesn't improve in a few days, I'd suggest Your Lordship take her to the hospital, but otherwise, I don't think she needs particular medical attention. Rest and good food are what she needs. Aside from her physical weakness, her health isn't compromised."

He opened and closed his fists aching after the fight with those two thugs. "May I see her now?"

"She's awake."

"Thank you." He forced himself not to run to the bedroom he'd given to Violante.

He waited for the nurse to leave before dashing out of the sitting room. He wasn't sure of the reception Violante would give him. The last time they'd talked, she'd been clear about not wanting to see him ever again. After that, she'd disappeared. Sharpe Manor had been confiscated by the authorities. Mr. Sharpe's servants—those who hadn't been involved with the Fenians—had found other employment, and he knew Paul and his mother had moved to the Americas. Some of Mr. Sharpe's employers had vanished as well. He'd searched for Violante for years and hadn't found her. But the situation was different now, wasn't it? She was in trouble and weak, and he wanted to help her.

He knocked and held his breath until a feeble, "Come in," came from the other side of the door. He inched it inwards and paused on the threshold. He'd fantasised about seeing her again, and in all those fantasies, the current situation—Violante robbing him and him fighting two thugs—had never been part of it.

She propped herself up on her elbows upon seeing him.

Her violet eyes were too big in her thin face but held the same fierce light as ever. What the devil had happened to her hair? It'd lost its shiny golden quality, and it looked like rough wool.

Keith and Violante stared at each other for a long moment in silence. The crackling of the flames in the hearth was the only sound. He wanted to say many things; he had many questions but didn't know where to start. Her violet flame didn't encourage him to talk.

She pushed the cover aside. "I'll leave in a moment. Don't worry."

He blinked. "What?"

She staggered to her feet. She wore one of his nightshirts that covered her to her knees. Her too-slender silhouette was visible through the fabric. "You want me gone. I understand."

But he hadn't said anything. "I…"

She tottered on her feet, her knees buckling.

"Careful." He strode to her and caught her by the waist before she fell.

She was too light. Her bones pressed against his palms. Aside from her fragility, she felt the same in his arms—soft, warm, and lily-scented. She didn't sag against him, her muscles tightening like ropes.

"You aren't strong enough." He helped her sit on the bed and released her. "I don't want you to leave. Why would I have taken you here otherwise?"

She touched her forehead. "I can leave. I'm fine."

"I beg to differ. So does the nurse." He poured her a glass of water. "You need to eat and rest."

"And after that?"

Now he recognised the determination in her fierce expression. Answering her took him a moment because he got lost in the power of her strength, something he hadn't experienced in a long time.

"Listen, let's start from the beginning. What happened to you after that day?" he asked.

She let out a bitter laugh, taking the glass of water with a quick gesture. "What do you think happened? The police took everything, the house, the horses, even the sacks of barley grown in my father's fields. They confiscated the land and the money in the bank. They even took my friends. All the people who had worked for my father left. I couldn't blame them. There was nothing for them. Nothing for me. So I left too."

He exhaled. "I'm sorry."

She sipped the water. "Are you really?"

"I searched for you after the incident. The manor was empty. No one knew where you were. I was worried, but I couldn't find you. Everyone had left, and you'd vanished."

She stared at the glass. "People who live on the streets disappear quickly."

Another long silence stretched between them.

He fought the urge to hold her hand. "You're welcome to stay here for as long as you need to. I don't want you to leave. I'm glad I found you."

She pressed her lips hard, and a lonely tear trickled down her cheek. But she didn't say anything. He had no idea why she cried. Was it relief? Exhaustion? Or she hated him so much she couldn't bear to stand close to him. Whatever the reason, he still wanted to help her. If she didn't want to stay there, he would pay for a room for her. If she didn't want his money, he would find another way to sustain her. He'd find her decent employment. Whatever was going to happen, she would never, ever starve again.

He handed her his handkerchief. She hesitated before accepting it.

"What happened to you?" he asked again in a gentler tone.

She put the glass down. "The people in the town hated me. With my father dead, their anger was directed at me. No one would offer me a job or a room to stay. Not that I had any money. I left Hampstead and moved several times, finding odd jobs. But whenever people realised who I was and my involuntary connection with the Fenians, they threw me out at best and tried to stone me to death at worst. Giving a false name didn't help. Every newspaper in the country had published my father's picture and mine. Sooner or later, I'd meet someone who recognised my face, and the persecution would begin." She talked in a flat monotone as if what had happened didn't touch her.

"Hell." The sorrow flaring inside him was like a creature trying to claw its way out of his chest. If he'd known what she'd been through, he would have helped her.

She lifted her chin as if realising she'd said too much. "I had to fend for myself. I'm not doing a great job, as you can see." The moment of fierce confidence disappeared, and she hung her head. Her shoulders were hunched under the burden of her story.

He couldn't resist and took her hand, but she snatched it away like a scared animal. Her eyes flared wide in outrage.

Right. He wouldn't touch her again. "As I said, you can stay here."

She cocked her head towards him. "You don't mean that."

"I do. I don't regret having gone to the police that night, but," he hurried to add when she opened her mouth, "my actions brought you where you are now. I take full responsibility for that."

Her expression became guarded. "I'm not your responsibility."

"I contacted the police. What happened to you after that was caused by my actions. Yes, I feel as if you're my responsibility. I'm in a position to help you. Let me." He had the chance to make amends and to repay her generosity when she'd offered him a home.

She folded the handkerchief on her lap. "What happened to you? It seems that we've exchanged our lives." Obviously, she avoided giving him an answer, and he didn't want to pressure her.

"After I left the police station, I met Sir Howard. He apologised for the way he treated me and thanked me for saving his life.

From that moment on, he took good care of me. The scare about the foiled attack changed him, touched him deeply. He wasn't the same man I knew."

"Is he dead?" she asked.

He nodded, remembering the good moments he'd shared with him. Sir Howard hadn't been as charismatic as Mr. Sharpe, and to be honest, Keith's affection for Mr. Sharpe had been deeper than what he'd felt for Sir Howard. But the affection had been there.

"He died last year. I grew fond of him, something I wouldn't believe could be possible. But he truly changed. He provided me with an education and financial support. I travelled with him around the world. I built my own company, and I even hold a title."

Her lips parted. "A title?"

"Viscount." It sounded odd to his own ears.

"How did you get a title?" Her voice was stronger. Good. "The queen bestows titles only to those who commit a noble gesture."

Well, not exactly noble. It'd been a matter of being in the right place at the right time. "I was with Sir Howard and some of his peers in Hyde Park when an anarchist tried to stab the queen."

She let out a muffled sound, staring at him. "You're the mysterious man who saved the queen's life. I read it in the newspapers." The hint of admiration in her voice made him prouder than he should feel.

He scrubbed the back of his neck. "I actually didn't know she was the queen at that time. She was incognito, taking a walk with her ladies-in-waiting. I didn't do anything heroic. I saw a man running towards a lady, wielding a knife, and stopped him. But the queen was so grateful she granted me a title, and Sir Howard interceded for me as well. Without his help, I'd probably be only a baronet."

"That explains the luxury of this house. Foiling conspiracies is your call." The ghost of a smile graced her lips, making her radiant.

Although he couldn't understand if it was a sarcastic smile. Never mind.

He held onto that shadow of a smile with desperation because he wanted to believe that deep down she was the same happy, strong Violante he knew. They'd both changed, but he would hate to know that the hardship she'd endured had broken her spirit.

He wanted to hold her and never let her go until she was strong again. "I meant it when I said that you can stay here and take your time to recover. Then you'll decide what you want to do. You don't have to talk to me if you don't want to. You don't have to see me either."

The hint of happiness was gone from her face. "Why do you want to help me? You could have called the coppers but didn't. Why?"

Why? The question was a little insulting. What kind of bastard did she think he was? She was a victim as much as he was. "I don't forget what you did for me, and despite what happened, I still owe you my life. I always settle my debts." He sat next to her, glad she didn't recoil at his closeness. "What do you want to do? If you don't want to stay here, I'll rent a room for you anywhere you want."

Her bottom lip trembled, but she trapped it between her teeth, stopping the quivering.

"Why are you crying?" He touched her hand, glad to find it warm. "Is it because you hate me?"

She didn't deny nor confirm his greatest fear but moved her hand away from his. "I didn't expect to see you today. Too many emotions all at once." She glanced at him. "I'm confused and tired, especially after that thug hit me."

Speaking of which. "Who were those men?"

She released a breath. "George the Blade and his henchman. George is the head of the Waterdeep gang in St. Giles. Nasty, powerful thug."

"Did you really steal from him?" He hoped he didn't sound

judgemental because it wasn't his intention. But he was surprised and shocked by her state of misery.

A flush crept to her cheek. "I stole a ring from one of his mistresses. I thought that stealing from a thug would be more bearable for my conscience than stealing from honest people. I sold the ring but didn't earn a lot. Now I don't have it."

He would do everything in his power to make sure George wouldn't bother her ever again. "You shouldn't feel guilty. You stole to survive."

Her eyes became two narrow slits. "Don't tell me how I should or shouldn't feel."

He held up a hand. "I've been desperate, too."

She twisted the handkerchief. "But you've never broken the law."

Actually, he had. He'd better change the subject. "I have to admit you're quick. I barely felt it when you took my watch."

She kept tormenting the handkerchief. "Years of practice, and when your life depends on one skill, you hone it to perfection."

She wouldn't need that skill anymore if he had something to do with it.

"Will you let me help you?" He would never grow tired of asking her.

She stopped fiddling with the handkerchief, and he feared she would say no. Moments passed, and she didn't say anything.

He cleared his throat. "If there's something I learnt from that snowy day in Windy Ridge, it's that there's no shame in asking for help. You taught me that. I understand I'm the last person you'd accept help from, but if you accept my help, you won't need to think you owe me something. We'll be even. Consider my help as overdue compensation for what you did for me."

Her long, silent moments would drive him mad. He had no idea what she was thinking. "Violante, the choice is simple."

"Don't force me." There was ice in her voice.

"I didn't mean to." *Bugger*. He'd better shut up.

"You're right, though," she said so low he barely caught the words. "I need help."

Good. He exhaled, realising only now how worried he'd been for her, how much he wanted to help her. "I'm glad you said yes. Do you want to stay here or go somewhere else?"

"Here is fine," she whispered. Also, she didn't look at him. Her long eyelashes fanned her cheeks, and her bony fingers clenched.

He wouldn't embarrass her further. She was a proud woman, and likely, the whole affair stung her honour, and her prejudice against him didn't help.

He gave her a nod and stood up. "I'll let you rest." A jolt of surprise went through him when she gently took his hand.

She released him immediately. "I won't be a burden. I promise."

"You could never be." He tried to catch her gaze, but she didn't look at him again. "Violante—"

"Please. Don't say anything. I'm grateful, but it's difficult for me."

He waited for her to say more, but she remained still and silent. What was difficult for her? Accepting his help or thanking him?

He left the bedroom and shut the door behind him, wondering if maybe they'd both changed too much to be friends again.

ten

VIOLANTE HAD FORGOTTEN what it meant to sleep in a soft, warm bed and to eat until her belly was full. Or not to be constantly afraid of being attacked by either rats or thugs.

A week had passed since Keith had welcomed her into his house, and she hadn't seen him once. She'd only caught glimpses of him entering or leaving the house. He'd meant it when he'd said she wouldn't need to talk to him, which made her feel guilty.

If she was going to be honest, she'd accepted his help because she was desperate, and that hurt her pride, or what was left of it. She'd got better at stealing, but selling the booty and negotiating its price afterwards was her bane. Otherwise, she wouldn't be in this predicament.

Getting a good deal and a lot of money from stolen jewels and watches wasn't a skill she possessed. She tried to negotiate a price, but the dealers at the black market were more expert than she was and never backed down from their offers. She needed the money. Any coin was precious. It was difficult to think straight with an empty stomach, and she didn't want to return to that life.

On top of that, George's gang would kill her—or worse—the

moment she returned to the streets. Staying at Keith's house would allow her to vanish from the streets for a while and recover her strength. Pride was useless when it came to surviving.

A pang of guilt bit her again. A different type of guilt. She was in the house of the man who had denounced her father and started the chaos that had destroyed her life. She wasn't sure how to feel about that. On a cold, logical level and after five years, she understood that Keith had done the right thing by going to the police. Her father had been guilty. No point in denying that. The evidence had been overwhelming.

But on an emotional level, she was a complete disaster. One moment, she wanted to yell at Keith to leave her alone. The next, she wanted to weep and beg him to forgive her for what she'd said that day.

Oh, well. Her predicament didn't have a quick solution.

But then again, the first thing she'd learnt in the streets was to take advantage of whatever she could without hesitation. If Keith wanted to help, she would let him, and then she would...she had no idea. Should she leave, stay, or ask him to help her find a job? Did she want to ask more from him? Goodness, her head ached.

She rolled up the sleeves of the oversized shirt. It was *his* shirt. She was sure of it. The thought started a stirring in her belly. A stirring she hadn't experienced in years and that had no business bothering her.

Many things had changed in the past years, but Keith's fresh citrus scent hadn't. Even the blue dressing gown belonged to him. She'd worn nothing but his shirts and dressing gowns for days now, and she didn't mind. They were warm, comfortable, and in a better state than her frayed clothes.

She inched open the door of her bedroom and listened to the noises of the house. Keith was likely out again. Only two servants worked for him. Mrs. Collins, the housekeeper, who also prepared the meals, and Murray, a man who worked as a footman, butler, valet, and whatever else the house required. Not a sound came from downstairs. Perhaps the housekeeper was in the kitchen and Murray was out on some errands. She wouldn't know. She'd slept so soundly in the past days that not even a thunderstorm had woken her up.

For a lord, Keith didn't surround himself with a staff of maids and footmen.

She tiptoed out of the bedroom. Boredom, curiosity, and restless energy urged her to take a tour of the house. She didn't plan to steal anything and wasn't doing anything wrong, but she couldn't help but feel like an intruder. She'd been cooped up in the bedroom for a week, eating and sleeping. There was nothing wrong with her exploring her new environment, was there?

Rich-brown wood wainscoting panelled the walls, and a thick carpet covered the polished floor. But there was an astonishing lack of decorations. No porcelain vases, paintings, or frills. She appreciated it, and it fit Keith's spartan personality. She knocked on the door to his bedroom. No answer. She pushed the door open, wondering if she would find him sleeping in his bed.

The townhouse didn't have many rooms, but Keith's bedroom was bigger than hers. She stepped inside, pausing. *Tarnation.* She hadn't asked him if he had a wife. She would have noticed a woman coming and going by now, wouldn't she? No, in the state of unconsciousness she'd been, she wouldn't have noticed anyone, and since the house was equipped with modern plumbing and a water closet, she didn't even need a personal maid or a chamber pot.

No, her heart didn't pound faster at the possibility he could be married. She didn't care one way or another. Her juvenile infatuation for him was long gone, buried underneath years of starvation and humiliation.

The hem of the dressing gown brushed the floor as she walked further into the room. From the looks of his room, if she wanted to steal something, she would be disappointed. He didn't keep anything precious in his room aside from yet another watch and fine clothes. But then again, he didn't come from money. He understood the real value of life. So did she. She'd loved pretty trinkets and gowns years ago. Now she felt rich when she could have dinner.

The writing desk in the corner was overwhelmed with documents, bills, and letters. Some letters were in Italian, and she couldn't help but take a peek. Since she hadn't seen him for the whole week, she hadn't had the chance to ask him any questions. Her curiosity was justified. Yes, it was.

Keith had gathered information about an Italian aristocrat. She wondered why.

Who was this Paul with whom he corresponded regularly? Could it be Paul Wellington, the stableboy who had stolen from her father? Just thinking about that traitorous, false friend made her blood boil.

"Did you find anything interesting?" Keith's voice jolted her.

"Gah!" She dropped the letter and gripped the chair, ready to use it as a shield. Sloppy of her. The good food and comforts had already softened her senses.

"I'm sorry." She straightened the stack of documents from where she'd taken the letter, her face heating. "I didn't mean to steal anything. I know I shouldn't have come here."

He folded his arms over his chest, straining the fabric of his jacket. "I wasn't accusing you of stealing."

"I was curious. But I shouldn't have snooped around. Forgive me."

"Apology accepted." His gaze flickered over her exposed bare leg for a moment.

The shirt covered her to her knees, leaving her ankles and calves naked, and the dressing gown was gaping open on the front. Not appropriate. She pulled the lapels and tied the sash to stop the show. Well, a meagre show, that is. She doubted he considered her ravishing. Her father had always said that only dogs liked bones.

She stepped away from his desk. "I thought you were out." Ouch. Too late she realised what she'd said.

"Clearly." He walked over to her, not menacingly, but a little shiver of fear went down her back.

He'd always had that rough, pirate-like charm she found alluring, but now that charm was ten times stronger, fuelled by a certain swagger that suited him.

"My Italian correspondence," he said, glancing at the letters she'd displaced.

"I shouldn't have...I'd better leave." She went to brush past him, but he took her hand gently.

He still had calluses on his palms and fingers.

"I gather you feel better," he said with kindness.

"Rested and stronger." His warm fingers around her wrist distracted her from whatever else she wanted to say.

"Is the food to your liking?"

She let out a derisive scoff. "My liking? It's perfect. I have eaten things you wouldn't look at when they were alive." She meant it as a joke, but it came out serious.

His expression darkened. "I was where you are. I understand what hunger can do to a person's mind and soul." His voice held a gravity that didn't leave room for any replies.

She tugged at the lapel of the dressing gown again. The garment was too large and her body was too thin; the fabric kept slipping off her shoulders.

"I can arrange a visit to the modiste." He released her wrist, and she almost missed the comfort of his hand.

"It's not necessary." She folded her arms over her chest to block the view of her cleavage. "If Mrs. Collins returns my clothes, I'll wear them. She said she would launder them. I feel strong enough to leave your house. No need to worry about me." She didn't know why she wanted to leave. But if he gave her some money, she wouldn't have any reason to stay.

He leant against one of the bedposts and regarded her from

underneath his long black eyelashes. "When I said I wanted to help you, I meant it. Helping you means making sure you have a secure position and earn your own money without breaking the law. Simply offering you a few meals and a hundred pounds isn't helping you."

It sounded great but..."What job could I ever find?"

"Translator, for starters. You speak Italian, don't you?" He nodded at his documents. "I'm dealing with an Italian count who is also a denizen of the British Empire. He was granted the privilege of buying land here, and he owns several properties, including a building close to St. Giles he now wants to sell."

"Do you want to buy it?"

"Yes, for a project of mine." His tone softened. "I don't really know him, though. A bowing acquaintance, but he has the reputation of being a very strict, traditionalist man. I bought every Italian journal and magazine I could find to get information about him. Nobility is often at the centre of this or that Italian magazine. I also received several letters from an Italian merchant I met a while ago during one of my travels with Sir Howard. He knows the count intimately and gave me clues on how to behave with him, or at least so I hope. I'm spending a fortune to have the correspondence translated. You could help me."

"Do you mean that I should work for you?" She couldn't remove the incredulity from her tone.

"Why not?" He lowered his voice. "Are you too proud to work for the man who once was your servant?"

"No." She tilted her chin up. "Trust me, living on the streets cured me of any arrogance I had. Pride is a useless commodity when one is desperate. I was merely surprised by your offer." Living on the streets had also cured her of anger. Anger was useful only when she had to fight. Otherwise, it was a waste of precious energy.

His frown relaxed. "I understand. You said I'd never broken the law. But that's not true." He shot her a glare as if in challenge.

"What do you mean?"

He paced, which drew attention to his strong legs. "I've never told you what I'd done because I was afraid you would have asked your father to kick me out, but I stole food, clothes, and money when I worked for Sir Howard and he sent me out for errands. I wasn't as fast as you, but I was never caught."

She wasn't surprised, not after the things she'd seen in the rookery. "Not that it matters, but did you steal from my house?"

"Never." He shoved his hands in his pockets. "I couldn't, and I didn't need it. Your family gave me everything I needed and more."

She didn't regret having helped him. Despite everything, she was glad her papa had taken care of Keith.

"Do you accept to work for me then?" he asked.

What did she have to lose? She'd agreed to stay in his house. In for a penny. Besides, she'd be stupid to refuse the offer of a warm bed, regular meals, new clothes, and even a job.

She stretched out her arm. "I do."

He shook her hand and held it, closing his other hand over hers. "You'll have to get stronger first. Another week of rest."

"I'm sure I can start working without fainting." She wasn't sure, but inactivity was something she wasn't used to anymore.

"No. You rest." He sounded bossy. He even looked bossy.

"May I take a walk in the park?" she teased.

He frowned. "Maybe, if I think it's all right."

Goodness, he hadn't caught her sarcasm.

"You're too strict."

"Concerned." He released her hand.

"Just a walk in the park. A bit of fresh air. As much fresh air as one could get in London. It'll refresh my mind."

He smiled, and his smile was contagious. "The park it is."

"Great."

His smile disappeared. "But I'll come with you."

eleven

I N THE SUNLIGHT, Violante's pallor was more evident than indoors, but Keith was relieved to find her cheeks less hollow. Her dress, on the other hand, was a different matter. He wasn't a fashion expert, and his housekeeper had done an excellent job of mending and cleaning Violante's worn clothes, but they added an air of desperation to her thin figure he didn't like. She resembled a character in one of Dickens's novels. Her steps remained slow and guarded as she walked next to him, but her slowness might be due to her shoes. He'd given her a pair of old boots because Violante's were too worn.

He hadn't talked to her about their last conversation years ago at the police station. He desperately wanted to, but she needed to be stronger and more comfortable when in his presence. Their clarification could wait.

He offered her his arm. "Beautiful day, isn't it?"

She hesitated before hooking her arm through his. "A bit chilly though."

He wasn't surprised. Her cloak had more holes than a slice of Swiss cheese. "We can return home."

"No." She gripped his arm harder. "It's all right. I need the walk although..." She gazed at him. "Someone might recognise me, and your reputation might be questioned if your peers see you with someone like me."

"It's a good thing my peers know where I come from and who I really am. Besides, I'm rarely seen with other aristocrats. I'm considered an arriviste who had a stroke of luck and easy money. Not exactly the type of men the gentlemen invite to the club to smoke expensive cigars with."

He couldn't completely remove the disappointment from his voice. Not because he was desperate for the *ton*'s approval, but because he wished his business didn't suffer because of the aristocrats' snub.

"There's something I'd like to ask you," she whispered.

"Anything." He meant it.

"What happened to Paul? I couldn't help but notice that you correspond with a man called Paul who's from New York City."

He exhaled. He should have told her. "He's Paul Wellington."

She came to an abrupt halt, her fingers clenching around his arm. "You're still his friend? He stole from my house when the police were attacking my father. He took my mother's pendant."

"That was despicable, and no, I'm not his friend. Not really. I searched for him because I wanted to know if he knew where you were."

"He's nothing but a scoundrel."

"Try to understand, though. He stole from you because he was afraid that he and his mother would starve."

Anger flushed red in her cheeks. "Please don't defend him."

"I'm not defending him. I'm only saying he was scared."

"As everyone," she said. "Anyway. What happened to him?"

"He started over." Keith felt as if he were walking on eggshells. No matter how lightly he moved, he would crush something. "It won't please you, but he invested the money he took from your strongbox."

She scoffed. "Great."

"He moved to the Americas with his mother, and he's now a businessman, dealing in shipping as I do. I met him in London months ago. He does business with the Italian count as well."

"So he's rich thanks to my father's money." Her facial lines tightened, enhancing her flaming cheeks. "He stole from me and became a successful businessman while he left me with nothing, forcing me to become a thief. Fate doesn't lack irony."

"Paul is very sorry for what he did. He told me he tried to find you. I don't approve or forget what he did, and as I told you, we aren't really friends, but eventually, anger and disappointment are tiring for the soul."

"I want my mother's pendant."

He could relate to her sentiment. Paul had disappointed him, too. "I can contact him on your behalf. He should come to London soon. We might do some business together."

"What's this project of yours?" She stumbled on a stone on the gravel path, and he coiled an arm around her waist to steady her.

They stood so close her flowery scent teased his senses.

He withdrew his arm when she stiffened. Right. She didn't like too much closeness to him. "I can show you if you want. It's not far from here."

"What's not far?" Her tone was guarded.

"You'll see." He headed for the exit of the park.

She didn't talk for the rest of the promenade, but he could bet she was pondering how to deal with Paul.

Sitting in the hansom cab next to her, Keith changed his mind. What if she got angry once she saw his gymnasium? His project was a copy of what her father had done. Even Paul had started a similar project in New York City, influenced by Keith. She might not appreciate it. He shifted on the seat, running the possible outcomes in his mind.

"Is something the matter?" She narrowed her gaze. She already hated him—or at the very least, disliked him—it was better if she learnt the whole truth about him. If she decided to leave his house, so be it. He'd find a way to take care of her anyway.

"I wonder what you might think of my project. You might not like it."

A golden eyebrow rose. "Why? You will make me think the worst. What's your venture?"

The cab rolled to a stop in front of a red brick building. The front door gleamed with freshly applied timber polish, and the sunlight glinted off the windows.

"Here we are." Keith climbed out first and helped her out.

Mistrust radiated from her in waves. If she hated his project, there wouldn't be much he could do.

He pushed the set of double doors open, and the smell of sweat, worn leather, and beeswax wafted in the air. Young people sparred or threw shadow punches around the training hall. Punching bags, benches, weights, and a sparring ring competed for space. The loud chatter and laughter covered the noise of the punches. Several heads turned towards him as he stepped inside.

"The viscount."

"His Lordship is here!"

"Lord Ashford."

He smiled at the small crowd of young men and women surrounding him. Curious glances were thrown at Violante.

"Sir." Matthew, one of the youngest boys, wrapped his short arms around Keith's legs and gave him a toothless smile. "I'm learning to swim."

"Well done." He ruffled the boy's dark curls.

Matthew released him. "Once I can swim, I can work at the docks. My mum wants to learn to swim, too."

"She's welcome here any time." Keith patted the boy's shoulder.

"Some people came to St. Giles," Matthew said. "They said they'd take our home and demolish it. They said we must leave. I don't want to leave. We don't have anywhere else to go."

Alas, Keith knew about that. The count's building was highly desirable, and many businessmen—including Sir Howard's son—had already started planning and getting ready to invest in it; they wanted to renovate it and turn it into some type of establishment, even though the count hadn't decided to whom he wanted to sell. Seizing the shacks around the building was what many investors wanted to do first. Not Keith.

Other boys nodded. Mutters spread. Violante threw Keith a puzzled look.

"I'll do everything I can to help you," Keith said. "For now, you have work to do."

After a loud round of greetings and handshakes, he walked around the hall. Violante had remained silent while he'd chatted with his charges, praising them for their small and big triumphs. The people he'd hired to teach these children to spar, swim, and exercise came from the streets as well. Like him.

When he and Violante remained alone in a corner of the hall, he shoved his hands in his pockets, waiting for her reaction.

She cleared her throat. "You built a gymnasium."

"This is only the first. I'm planning to build a new one in St. Giles." He waved to gesture at the wide hall. "With the title came land and buildings. This is one of my properties. This gymnasium turned out to be a success. These children and young men don't spend time in the streets, stealing or joining gangs. I provide food and clothes for them while they learn to box and swim. Many of them want to become police officers. Others will find employment at my shipping company. I receive donations from businessmen and a few peers. I have more than enough funds to expand."

"My father's idea," she said in a low voice.

That was the moment of truth. His heart gave a quick kick. "Yes. His gymnasium helped me more than I can tell, and I want to do the same for other children. The building in St. Giles is perfect for my second training centre, and if I own it, no one will be kicked out of their homes. Surely, someone who has very different plans from mine paid a visit to St. Giles to scare the people living there."

She pressed her lips together, her cheeks flushing. Not a word left her mouth.

He inched closer. "Violante, does the idea bother you?"

"Does it matter?"

"Yes." He dipped his head to meet her gaze. "Very much."

Unshed tears glistened in her eyes. "I'm not sure how I feel. Too many things have happened in a few days, and I didn't expect this." She waved a hand towards the hall.

"Despite everything that happened, I firmly believe your father's idea was a noble and effective one. Paul started a couple of youth centres in New York City as well."

She wiped a tear quickly. "What you're doing here is important. You should continue, no matter what I think."

That wasn't the whole truth. "But?"

She inhaled. "There's no but. You're doing the right thing."

"I understand you hate me—"

"I don't hate you!" she said so loud her voice ricocheted off the high ceiling.

A few chaps stopped boxing to turn towards her.

"Can we leave?" She moved towards the doors, her eyes rimmed with red.

"Of course." If that wasn't a complete disaster, he didn't know what it was.

VIOLANTE ALMOST RIPPED her worn cloak when she removed it once in Keith's house. The drive back to his house had been one atrocious moment of silence. She was mostly to blame for that. But the swell of emotion in her throat had prevented her from saying anything.

She paced in the bedroom. Her nervous energy fuelled her

hunger. She wasn't sure why she was so upset. What Keith had built was good and noble. She'd seen firsthand what poverty and desperation did to children. Creating a space where poor children could learn a trade and be safe was the best solution to keep them off the streets.

Her father had believed in the same venture. It didn't matter where a good idea came from. Keith had taken her father's project, expanded it, and perfected it.

But in her heart, seeing the gymnasium and those happy faces brought her back years and reminded her of what she'd lost, of the good deeds her father had done, and of what her life could have been. It hurt.

If her papa had been a terrible parent, beaten her, and behaved beastly to his employees, having lost him wouldn't be so devastating. But knowing he'd possessed a very good side, that he'd been loved and admired even by the very man who had denounced him, pained her so deeply she couldn't breathe. Why had Papa chosen violence? How could someone with such a good heart also be a murderer?

Try as she might, she couldn't reconcile the two aspects of his life. Had she known him at all? She couldn't tell. She'd grown up with a stranger. The five years she'd spent thinking about that had led to no solution, no explanation, and no closure.

"Violante." Keith touching her shoulder caused her to gasp.

She hadn't heard him coming. "What are you doing here?" It came out harsher than she meant.

"I heard you sobbing from the other room." He raked a hand through his midnight hair. "I'm sorry today's visit upset you. It wasn't my intent." He offered her a handkerchief.

Bother. She should start carrying one around if she kept crying. She hadn't realised she'd been sobbing loud enough for him to hear it.

She plonked down onto the bed. "Thank you." She wiped her

face, taking her time to postpone the moment she would have to talk to him.

"You can tell me what you really think," he said. "Or if you want to leave."

She licked her lips, tasting her salty tears. "I admire what you're doing. I really do."

"Why are you so upset?" He sat next to her on the edge of the bed. The mattress dipped under his weight.

"Seeing the gymnasium brought back all the good memories I had of Sharpe Manor. I forgot about them. Only the bad memories kept me company for a long time." She couldn't meet his gaze. "After all this time, I can't reconcile the good man I loved with the cruel anarchist who killed people for his principles. How could he be so sweet and good to me and his employees and so cruel to those he considered enemies? It's this contrast that rips me apart. I want to remember only the good things about him, but I can't. Every memory is tainted, and I feel like I'm choking with his lies. The more I think about that, the less I understand him."

He hugged her, gently wrapping his arms around her. Maybe she was too weak, but she couldn't fight the need to be comforted and feel protected. She rested her head on his chest and exhaled, inhaling his scent in his handkerchief.

"How could I have been so wrong about him? How couldn't I see who he was?" She shut her eyes tightly. "The last time we talked..."

He tensed immediately. His arms around her became stiff.

"I was angry with you," she said, leaning against him. "I believed that I could have changed Papa's mind and saved lives if I had talked to him. If you'd warned me before going to the police and I'd talked to him, I was sure Papa would have seen reason because he'd always told me he would've done anything for me."

"I'm sorry I didn't talk to you." He caressed the top of her head.

"No, I am sorry. It took me a while, but all that thinking made me realise that he wouldn't have changed his mind, not even for me. It hurts. He taught me all the values I believe in today, yet he disregarded them, and in the end, my opinion didn't matter to him."

She relaxed as he kept stroking her hair. "My mother, I think she knew. She must have understood, but why did she leave? Why didn't she come back? I wonder if he..." She couldn't finish the sentence. The possibility was too horrible.

"I don't believe he killed her. When I asked him if he had, he replied no. He sounded honest."

"Really?" Her mother could be alive. "Where is she then?"

"I don't know. You should accept the fact your father had a very good heart." His caresses calmed her uneven pulse. "He was loved and admired by many. That part of him was real. It wasn't a lie. He meant to help others. He believed in his principles of justice and equality. You shouldn't take that from him."

"But he was also a heartless murderer." It was the first time she'd said it out loud, and it was as if she'd been stabbed.

"Yes." He held her closer. "His ideas were noble, but his methods were too extreme. He had both light and darkness within him, as has everyone. He loved you more than anything else. That love is pure and authentic and all yours. Nothing will ever change that. It's for you and you only to cherish."

She shamelessly snuggled closer to him. Unburdening herself made her breathe more easily. "How did you become so wise?"

"I have to thank your father for that. I have precious memories of him, too, and I keep them jealously away from the darkness."

"That's wonderful."

They sat in silence as she sagged against his hard chest and he caressed her back. In a way, they were mourning her father together for the first time, and she didn't mind.

twelve

KEITH FOUND IT difficult to focus on his work when Violante sat next to him in his study. He hadn't had time to arrange a visit to the modiste yet. Violante still wore one of his dressing gowns and nightshirts. Thank goodness his servants were limited to two people, or she would appear regularly on the scandal sheet.

Glimpses of her slender ankles flashed through the folds of the fabric. Her creamy skin seemed to glow from within; something he suspected had to do with her improving health. Her little pink toes held some fascination too. He'd never paid any attention to a lady's toes also because he hadn't seen many of them, but Violante's made him want to take her feet, put them on his lap, and stroke them. How odd.

"Did you hear me?" She lowered the document she was reading and arched her blonde eyebrows. A few curls caressed her cheeks, and he discovered her toes weren't the only part of her to hold him captive.

He pinched the bridge of his nose. "I was distracted."

The modiste had to be called as soon as possible, and a shoemaker as well. Violante couldn't keep walking around his house in such revealing clothes. All right. They weren't so revealing. In fact, he couldn't see anything. He guessed he was to blame for his wandering thoughts. Still, she needed proper clothes and shoes.

She tilted her head to catch his attention, but she didn't know she'd already had all his attention. "I was saying that your translator did a very poor job. See, Count Bassini-Verdelli uses mostly his own language from Rome."

"Isn't it Italian?"

"Not really. The Italian language was, let's say, created after the unification of the Italian peninsula. They chose an old dialect spoken in Tuscany to establish a common language for every Italian, but people still speak their own local language. My mother was from Rome, too." She paused before continuing. Every time she mentioned her mother, she turned serious and silent. "According to this latest communication, the count is coming to England in a few weeks."

"Is he?" He perked up. How had he missed that information? "I must see him."

She worried at her bottom lip with her pearly teeth, and he had to focus on the count not to get distracted again. "That might be a problem. He owns an estate in Bakewell and wishes to spend the spring there to conclude a few of his business deals. He isn't staying in London."

"Is there anything about the count selling his house in London? I know he received many offers."

"He did, and he's considering them very carefully." She lowered the letter. "According to your friend and the newspapers, the count is a very strict man with rigid principles. He won't sell the house to someone he considers unworthy."

"Good. An honest seller is ideal."

"Exactly. He shares your sentiment, but from what I read, I guess the count won't believe you're a worthy buyer."

"Excuse me?" He scoffed. "Is it because I don't come from

wealth? Is he another of those snobs who don't believe a man of humble origins can't be a good person?"

"Not really." She cleared her throat and read from a letter. "Your friend wrote that the count heard rumours of your rakish behaviour, specifically of your frequent visits to the poorest areas of London."

"For charity, not for pleasure." He grunted. "The count makes assumptions."

She flashed a quick smile. "Your contact is sure that your being a bachelor bothers the count deeply. He has some rigorous morals. Quote: *A man must take his responsibilities seriously, and a man who refuses to commit himself to a proper relationship is untrustworthy. Unmarried men commit a crime in the eyes of propriety.*"

"This is spectacularly unfair." Keith propped his chin on his fist. "I don't refuse to commit. I haven't found a wife yet. That's all."

She clicked her tongue. "He sounds adamant. No wife, no trust, no respect."

"No deal." He crossed his arms behind his head and stretched out his legs. Bloody count. "What does my marital status have to do with anything? How annoying."

"Is it true?" she asked.

"What? That I'm annoyed? Yes, very." He shook his head. "The count would rather sell to a married man who wants the house to build a gaming den, but he wouldn't be comfortable selling it to me because I'm a bachelor. Absurd."

"I don't think he'd sell to someone who has a not-so-honourable plan for the house either." She folded the letter. "I meant if it's true that you don't have an intended."

Was there a hint of interest? Wishful thinking on his part.

"Yes, I don't have an intended or a sweetheart." Because he wasn't interested in having one. Although from the moment he'd seen Violante again, the embers of his passion had been stoked. Hell, he kept noticing everything about her.

"Why, if you don't mind my asking?" She avoided looking at him again.

He shrugged. "I haven't spent time in society unless it was for business. No lady caught my eye or my heart." There had been a time when his eye and heart had belonged to her. Judging by the warm, fluttery feeling in his chest, that might still be the case.

The air between them stiffened after his small confession.

"Even the count should consider you a hero after you foiled two anarchist attacks." A corner of her mouth pulled tight at the mention of the attacks.

"I don't come from aristocracy. The *ton* consider me a social climber without scruples. My title only caused more mistrust and embarrassment. Some say I'm behind the attack on the queen, that I hired the assassin only to stop him and become a hero."

"That's ridiculous."

He liked how indignant she sounded on his behalf.

He bowed his head. "I'm glad you agree with me for once."

She was flustered. "I agree with you rather often."

"That brings me some comfort."

"Who spread the accusations about the attack on the queen?"

He exhaled. "Dear old Nigel, Sir Howard's son. Sir Howard helped me build my shipping company at the docks. His son fiercely disagreed with his father's decision. He accused me of ingratiating myself with his father only for money. He wasn't happy about his father's interest in me."

"I thought Sir Howard's family were grateful to you for saving their lives."

"Sir Howard was. His wife and daughter were very kind to me. Nigel is another matter. In fact, Nigel means to buy the count's property, throw out the people who live in that area, and build something new. I'm not sure what, but I'm sure the last thing those people need is to lose their homes. I'll do my best to stop Nigel's project."

"Good on you." She rolled a pencil back and forth.

The wide sleeve of his nightgown slipped back, revealing her elbow. She had a nice elbow as elbows went, that is. Oh, hell. There was something wrong with him.

"I'm sure the count will find your project worthy of his attention," she said. "You have only to find a wife."

"Where? How? I wouldn't know where to start to find one." Actually, he did, but the timing wasn't the best. She needed time before he could court her properly. Yes, sod it. He couldn't pretend he wasn't interested in her. He wanted to woo her. There. He'd said it.

She stopped tormenting the pencil, for which he was grateful. Her lovely arm distracted him. "Surely, you must know a lady willing to marry you. There must be a debutante eager to find a titled, rich husband."

"A debutante?" He unfolded his arms. "Some slip of a girl still wet behind the ears? Hell, no."

"I understand. What about a widow? You must know a grown woman looking for someone to share her lonely life with."

"No, I don't know any widows." He scratched his stubble, raking a glance over her. What if he proposed? That wasn't a bad idea.

"I can't believe that you don't have any lady friends."

"Violante," he said, still watching her. "It's not easy to find a woman I like enough to ask to marry me. I need someone whom I trust and who understands who I am and the current situation." He raised his eyebrows.

"Whom do you have in—" She straightened, a hand on her chest. "Oh, I see. You're thinking about me. Clever."

"Exactly." After she recovered fully, she'd be ready to meet the count as Keith's wife. He was glad she didn't recoil at the possibility of marrying him. Unexpected, but who was he to complain?

"Although there's a problem." She touched her chin. "The count values honesty and honour above everything else, and lying to him and deceiving him is a risky strategy. I mean we can do it, but we must be careful."

"What are you talking about? I have no intention of lying. I'm against deceiving, especially in business."

"Well, introducing me as your wife is an obvious lie. I can make it work, though. Once, I impersonated a nun to steal from a dowager viscountess. I'm sure I can play the role of your wife well." A mischievous gleam lit her eyes.

"Actually." Keith thrust his chest out. She'd misunderstood him. "What I'm clumsily trying to say is that we could get married. For real. Not a deceit. We could ask for a special licence and get married in a few days. That way, I won't be lying about who I am. I can commit to marriage. I share the count's values of honesty and respect. That's what I offer to you."

He wished he sounded more determined and not scared. But he was ready to take care of her, and it was true he didn't have any love interest. He hated to use her poverty as leverage, but she needed to be taken care of properly, and he would fully commit to her. Making her happy was a worthy pursuit. He couldn't forget her kindness when he'd needed help. She'd taught him to read and write. She'd saved his life. The tenderness he felt for her was too strong to be ignored.

"You can't be serious." She leant back in the chair in shock.

"I'm very serious. Think about how your life would change."

"Uh-uh." She wiggled her finger to say no. "I don't think it'll work."

"You're perfect."

Violet fire flashed in her gaze. "It sounds like a compliment, but it actually isn't when you're simply desperate to find a wife."

"Desperate? I'm not desperate. People arrange marriages all the time. Listen." He held up a hand to silence a protest. "You're half Italian and speak the count's language. Who better than you?" No, he shouldn't have said that. Her fluency in Italian had nothing to do with his proposal.

"No." She pouted, and she looked stunning. "Do you really want to marry me because I speak Italian?"

"No. I'm ready to provide for you. You'll have financial security and all the freedom you want. I won't force you to do anything you don't want to do." Hopefully, that was a better argument. "We get married, make this deal, and then you can do what you want. I won't expect you to live with me if you don't want to."

She wouldn't starve or steal again. She wouldn't return to the streets. If she didn't care about his affection, it would hurt, but she would be safe.

"We're talking about marriage. Marriage is forever," she whispered.

"Exactly." He stared at her without blinking. He was bloody serious.

"No." She rose. The fabric of the dressing gown flowed down her legs. He couldn't stop himself from catching another enticing glimpse of her ankles. "I appreciate your help, but I can't marry you so I can live a comfortable life. It'd be an awful thing to do, and I have an already long list of awful things on my soul. I can pretend to be your wife, but I won't marry you."

He rose as well. "Will you think about it? Please?"

"Keith." Her shoulders sagged. "I'm sure you can find another woman, someone better than I am to be your hastily arranged wife. If you'll excuse me, I need to rest." She left the room in a swish of fabric.

No, he couldn't find a better woman. Not in a million years.

VIOLANTE KEPT REPEATING to herself she'd done the right thing by refusing Keith's mad plan. As much as she needed money and safety, she wouldn't be his wife so he could make a deal with an Italian count. Ridiculous idea. They would be shackled to each other for the rest of their lives, share their bed, work together, maybe have a family...no, what was she thinking?

She adjusted her skirt as she sat at Keith's desk, reading more articles on the infamous count. Mrs. Collins had lent her a gown, tired of seeing her scandalously dressed in Keith's dressing gown. She didn't mind wearing his clothes; they were comfortable and smelled divine, while Mrs. Collins's dress smelled of mothballs. She wasn't sure what Keith's opinion on the matter of her clothes was. Oftentimes, he frowned when she wore his dressing gown. Maybe he disapproved.

"Violante?" Keith called from the door.

"Come in."

He eyed her new gown with disappointment if the way he narrowed his gaze was any indication. Had she been wrong about his dislike for her previous attire?

"You changed." That sounded like an accusation.

She smoothed the bodice. "I didn't steal it if that's what you're implying. Your housekeeper gave it to me," she quipped.

"I didn't think you stole it." He shed his coat and sat next to her. "Did you think about my proposal?"

Goodness. He was persistent. If she was going to be honest, the idea tempted her. No more feeling her stomach empty. No more freezing nights. No more stealing. She believed him when he said he'd give her all the freedom she wanted. He would never force her. But marrying him wouldn't be right.

"I can't be your real wife." She rearranged the pencils. "It wouldn't be fair to you."

"Fair to me? It'd be more than fair. We know each other well. I trust you."

She rubbed the aching spot between her eyebrows. "I can't believe we're discussing marriage. We know each other, but we've been separated for years, and we changed deeply."

"There's something else you need to know." He stapled his fingers together, causing the fabric of his shirt to ripple over his biceps. "I've just received a wire from Paul. As I told you, he's doing business with the Count Bassini-Verdelli. They have a deal on a shipment for the Americas. Anyway, chances are that Paul will be in Bakewell too. Paul doesn't know about your presence here yet, but he's coming to England soon."

"Oh." She froze. Yesterday, she'd been eager to see Paul. Now she wasn't sure she wanted to.

"Do you want to meet him? I'll do whatever you say. I can inform him or not of your presence. I can help you convince him to repay the stolen money to you, or not. It's up to you."

Dash it. If Paul compensated her for the money he'd stolen, she wouldn't need to marry anyone. Not to mention getting back her mother's pendant. If Paul had sold it, she might trace it somehow. At least, she'd know what had happened to it.

"I can come to Bakewell with you, pretend to be your new secretary, and meet with Paul." It sounded like a good plan that didn't involve any weddings.

He chuckled, lowering his eyelashes. She'd forgotten how mesmerising his deep eyes were. Between his impossibly black irises and long eyelashes, he acquired more charm than should be humanly possible. "Do you think the count will believe you're simply my secretary? One look at you and he'll understand I'm lying, or worse, he'll believe you're my mistress."

"Why would he think that?"

Every trace of amusement disappeared from his face. "Because...he won't be fooled." His jaw muscles bunched. She could bet he meant to say something else but changed his mind. "I don't want to use my deal with the count as a weapon to force you to do something you don't want. That wasn't my intention when I told you about Paul. If you want to see Paul, I'll organise the meeting with him here in London, whatever you decide. He might refuse, though." He stood up, seemingly defeated. "I'll leave you now. And by the way, the modiste is waiting for you in your bedroom."

"The modiste?" The news distracted her from giving an answer.

"No more borrowed clothes." He gave her a shy smile. "You'll have a new wardrobe."

Too much sadness laced his voice. Something cracked in her chest. He wanted to take care of her, and now he gave her a new set of clothes. From the moment he'd taken her into his house, she'd done nothing but cry and treat him with coldness while he'd been kind to her. But then again, if she got Paul to repay her, she'd have enough to live decently and wouldn't need to marry Keith.

"Good day, then." He put a hand on the knob.

"Keith, wait."

He turned towards her. "Yes?"

"Listen, you really should consider my plan. I can pretend to be your wife." She ignored the flutter in her stomach. It was surely hunger again.

"But I agree with you that it'll be risky. The count would be furious if he knew."

"I'm good at pretending, and I've done many despicable things in my life." She opened and closed her hands. "I want to see Paul and help you with your project. It's a noble enterprise. Lying for a few days isn't anything worse than what I've done in the past. The difference is that this time it's for a good cause and for helping those in need, not myself. Trust me. We'll create a story about how and when we met, and the count won't be the wiser."

"We could get married." He said that as if getting actually married were easier than lying. "There wouldn't be any reason to lie."

"I don't want to marry you." It came out with an aggressive tone she regretted. But she had to be honest.

His pain worried her. She hadn't expected him to be so hurt by her rejection. His plan was madness, for Pete's sake.

"We know each other well, yes. But it'd be wrong to shackle you to a hastily arranged marriage you wouldn't have proposed to start with," she said. "Marriage is a serious commitment. I can't take it lightly."

He strode to her so quickly she tensed a little. Old habit.

He took her hand in his. "It'd be no shackle."

"Please." She shook her head. "I can't do it."

A tendon in his neck ticked. "Fine. I respect your choice."

"Does it mean we can pretend to be married?"

He kissed her knuckles, and a shiver went up her arm and straight to her heart. "If this is what you want." Why did he sound so sad?

"It is." She couldn't believe he really wanted to marry her.

Surely, he felt a misplaced sense of guilt or protection towards her, and that had pushed him to propose. He felt guilty for what had happened to her and wished to make amends. There couldn't be a worse reason to marry than guilt. Theirs would be a miserable marriage if guilt was the premise.

He breathed hard and seemed about to say something but remained silent.

She couldn't take her gaze off his hand holding hers. There was something fascinating about watching his strong fingers close around her pale hand. The way his thumb stroked her knuckles started a funny ache between her thighs.

He kissed her hand again before releasing it. "It's going to be a great marriage of convenience," he said in a forcibly cheerful tone.

She chuckled. "We're deceiving a count. Inconvenience is more likely."

thirteen

THE MARRIAGE WAS only a pretence. A ploy. Nothing else. Unfortunately.

It didn't matter how many times Keith repeated that, the stupid flutter in his chest didn't want to stop. The ring he'd just purchased for Violante had a violet stone that would match her eyes, and the gold band was the same shade as her hair. She'd wear his ring but only to make her performance more real.

I don't want to marry you.

He couldn't blame her. His proposal had been hasty and unconvincing, but if he'd told her he really wanted to marry her, she would have run for the hills. Obviously, she didn't feel what he felt. She might not hate him, but she didn't care for him either.

He closed the lid of the velvet ring box and resumed walking along the busy pavement. The warm sunlight didn't do much for his foul mood, and the ladies and gentlemen promenading and crowding his space didn't help either.

His heart gave a kick at the thought of seeing the ring on Violante's finger, of her smile when she put it on. Count Bassini-Verdelli would never believe Violante was Keith's secretary because the way Keith looked at her would betray him. He hadn't told her that. She would have understood how much he wanted her.

Before going home and offering her the ring, he stopped at Mr. & Mrs. Beresford Private Investigators.

The visit to the renowned private detectives could be either the best idea he'd ever had or the worst. A bell chimed when he pushed open the glass door to the investigators' office. The sound of clerks beating the keys of the typewriters filled the room. The smell of tobacco rose from a corner where another clerk smoked.

"Sir?" A young woman walked towards him along the aisle formed by the rows of desks. "May I help you?"

"I have an appointment with Mr. and Mrs. Beresford."

"Your name?"

"I'm Lord Ashford." The title still sounded pompous to his own ears.

The secretary curtsied. "Follow me, my lord." She showed him to a quiet study where filing cabinets took up half of the space.

"Lord Ashford." Mrs. Beresford dropped a quick curtsy as her husband bowed. "Please take a seat."

"What can we help you with?" Mr. Beresford asked.

"I want to employ you for a case, although, I don't have much to share, unfortunately." He patted the ring in his pocket before taking a seat in the stuffed chair in front of the desk. "I need to find a woman, Mrs. Marina Sharpe."

As Keith went up the stairs with the velvet box in his hand, he wondered if the private detectives would find anything. What he knew about Violante's mother wasn't much. A letter for him lay on the console table. It was from his Italian friend, and of course, Keith didn't understand a word. Thank goodness Violante was here.

He sidestepped a silk slipper on his way up. The modiste's visit had left a trail of empty boxes and scraps of fabric on the stairs, landing, and corridor. Empty cups of tea were piled on a tray with squeezed half lemons and sugar cubes. His housekeeper wouldn't be happy when she came the next morning.

He knocked on Violante's door, clenching the precious box. "Violante?"

"Come in." Her voice held a hysterical note.

"Is something the matter?" He walked around another frilly box with a silk ribbon to enter her bedroom.

She paced, surrounded by gowns of every colour, fabric, and shape. Shoes, hats, silk sashes, and reticules were scattered around in a riot of colours. There were chemises, fine unmentionables, stockings, and corsets as well. The pink corset with satin roses on the neckline would look great on her. Not that the chances of him seeing her in that corset were good.

"Look at this." She spread her arms. Her dishevelled curls bounced over her reddened cheeks.

Yes, he looked at the glorious display of intimate garments and enjoyed it. "You don't like the clothes?"

"I do. Very much." She selected a light-blue capelet rimmed with velvet. "Look at this. It's beautiful."

"What is the problem then?"

"It's too much." She lowered the capelet carefully. "Too expensive. Not even when I lived with Papa, could I afford such beautiful gowns. Half of these are from Paris. The other half is from Milan."

He didn't know what to say. He understood nothing of fabric and gown values, and money wasn't a problem for him at the moment.

"I see," he said, although he didn't see at all.

"I'm borrowing these garments. They aren't mine." She pointed a finger at him. "I would never be able to repay all this."

"You don't have to repay me."

"But you can't possibly spend all that money on me." She

closed her fists, underlining her point as if he were the unreasonable one.

Yet he'd been in her position when he'd owned nothing and had relied on her family's generosity to survive. The sensation of being at the receiving end of compassion was bittersweet; it warmed his heart but troubled his mind. He wouldn't force her to accept his money.

"I'll clean up the mess." She gestured at the boxes and cups of tea. "Your housekeeper will have a fit. Why don't you have an army of servants, as every lord in town?"

"Oh, please." He patted the box in pocket again. "At first I had the lot, a butler, two footmen, a valet, countless maids, and a cook, and I was going mad. I didn't have a moment for myself. There was someone cleaning or tidying in every room, and to be honest, I felt ridiculous. It's only me here, and I can take care of myself as I've always done. I dismissed them except for Mrs. Collins and Murray, who, thank goodness, don't live here. I'm not a child, and they're more than enough."

"Right." She worried at her bottom lip. "I'll tidy up then. It's not a problem."

"I'll help you."

"No." She balled her fists on her hips. "So? Do you agree to take everything back after our mission is finished?"

Mission. He wanted to laugh. "If you don't want the clothes, it's your choice."

She exhaled and flexed her fingers. "Thank you."

He grinned. "You're thanking me for not giving you the clothes?"

She rubbed the deep lines on her forehead. "Er...yes, I guess I am."

Hell, she looked adorable, all flushed and bothered.

He handed her the velvet box. "Then I guess this is borrowed as well." Despite his efforts at joking, a quiver crept into his voice.

"What is that?" She hesitated before taking the box.

"Open it." He didn't realise how much he wanted her to like the ring until now.

A gasp left her when she opened the lid and the light hit the violet stone. Silence stretched to the point where he had to say something.

He cleared his throat. "I thought it matched your eyes. And it'll complete the disguise," he added in a hurry in case she protested again.

She seemed to freeze, and a flush coloured her cheeks. "It's beautiful. It's the most beautiful jewel I've ever seen."

An awkward moment thickened between them. He shifted his weight. She avoided his gaze. He hoped she wouldn't reject the ring only because it was expensive. It was, but he wanted to see it on her finger.

"May I?" he asked, stretching out his arm towards the ring.

She nodded, lifting her trembling hand. He slid the ring onto her elegant finger. That damn flutter in his chest started again. It was as if a hummingbird were trapped inside him. The violet stone glittered in the sunlight. The ring was indeed perfect.

"Is it too tight?" He found it difficult to release her hand.

"No. It must have cost a fortune." She admired the stone. "It must have been expensive."

"Only the best for my wife."

She whipped her head up. "Keith—"

"It completes the pretence." He closed his hand around hers. "Please accept it. Please."

She gave him a nod that lacked confidence.

He let go of her hand reluctantly. "I've just received news." He handed her the letter. "Would you mind translating it?"

"Of course." She drew her eyebrows together as she read the letter, looking adorable. "Your friend says that Count Bassini-Verdelli will be at Rochefort Teahouse tomorrow. He arrived in London earlier than expected. The house in St. Giles hasn't been sold yet. The count won't stay in London, though. He'll leave for Bakewell soon. If you want to see him, you'll need to be quick."

"Thank you." He cradled his chin. "I hoped I had more time to talk to him."

"The next step of our mission is to get an invitation to Bakewell from the count," she said.

"How?"

She eyed the pretty capelet she'd shown him. "By introducing your new wife to him."

fourteen

VIOLANTE LOVED HOW wearing nice, clean clothes that fit properly felt. She wore a completely new set of fresh garments from her chemise and drawers to her brand-new capelet, silk stockings, and embroidered kid gloves.

The scent of lilies wafted from her afternoon gown, and she had styled her hair in soft curls, shiny with scented argan oil. The rouge was a must. Her skin had improved, but a ghostly pallor lingered, and while today's fashion favoured pale cheeks and liquid eyes, she preferred a bit of colour.

Maybe she was the vainest woman in London, but she couldn't stop staring at her reflection in the mirror. Her own papa wouldn't recognise her. The dark-red gown hugged her body and made her look more shapely than she was. Glossy layers of velvet formed a small bustle that enhanced the small of her back. Another light touch of rouge coloured her lips, and the black velvet hat added a few inches to her height. It was the first time in the recent, difficult years that she hadn't worn patched clothes and broken shoes. Or that her stomach hadn't cramped from hunger. Goodness, even her head was clear.

She was aware this moment wouldn't last. Once Keith got

what he wanted and she demanded Paul compensate her for what he'd stolen, her life would return to its lonely reality, like a beautiful spell broken by a curse. Yes, breaking the spell had been her decision because she couldn't marry Keith only to live in comfort. That would be even more lonely, and he didn't deserve that. He deserved true love and genuine commitment.

But exactly because the dream wouldn't last, she wanted to savour every moment. The ring...heavens, the ring was perfect. Every time she wiggled her finger, the gem sparkled, and a little flicker of excitement teased her belly. Another spell that would be broken. She wasn't Keith's wife. He shouldn't marry someone like her, a woman who had lost everything and survived by stealing, not now that he was a titled gentleman.

She glanced at the mirror again before leaving her room. Keith came out of his bedroom, dressed in a dark suit that complemented his sable hair and strong build. The silk waistcoat stretched over his broad chest nicely. She couldn't avoid thinking about those times she'd seen him half-naked working with the other lads. He'd looked handsome then. Now he was simply magnificent.

He raked a slow glance over her, a heated one if she was still capable of judging such matters. Another thing she hadn't experienced in the past years was attraction. She'd been too busy trying not to die from starvation or infections to care about what men thought of her or to find men attractive. Keith was different.

"You look beautiful." His serious tone didn't leave room for doubt. He wasn't being nice. He told her exactly what he thought.

Her face warmed. "It's the gown. Excellent quality."

He offered her his arm. "I beg to differ. I mean, the gown is lovely, but you seem different in it, more confident."

True. "It makes me feel pretty."

"That's the point of nice clothes." He smiled when she accepted his arm. "Shall we?"

She mentally rehashed the story they'd agreed to tell. "So we met at a ball given by Sir Howard, before that, I spent a few years abroad in Italy, and then we had a regular one-year engagement."

"I hope the count won't ask too many questions. I'm not a good liar."

Yes, she knew that.

He kept looking at her when they went down the stairs. While she had to focus on not tripping on the hem of her skirt, he didn't need to see where he put his feet not to fall.

He stared at her even when he sat in front of her in the carriage as if he were under a spell. There was no escaping his presence, scent, and warmth in the confined space. The lightest of brushes of her knees against his sent a thrill of sensations up her neck. Another jolt of the carriage sent her forwards, and she hit his legs.

"Sorry," they said together.

She moved back to her corner of the seat, her pulse thundering. How silly of her. It had to be the gown.

She didn't know what to make of the fact she still found him attractive. The attraction could be gratitude for his generosity. Or simply, it could be due to the fact she was eating regularly. Or he was indeed too handsome and kind to be ignored. If he'd been only handsome, she wouldn't have thought much of it. But she had to admit he'd been nothing but compassionate to her.

On the awful day at the police station, she'd ordered him to leave her alone. Yes, she'd been harsh and wrong to send him away. In her defence, at that moment, she'd been in shock and couldn't have imagined they wouldn't have seen each other again.

She shook her head to get rid of those dark thoughts. She'd spent many a night obsessing about that day. If the count invited them to Bakewell, she'd have the opportunity to speak with Paul and be compensated. She wouldn't have to rely on the generosity of anyone and would build something for herself. Once she was independent, she would examine her feelings for Keith without her gratitude and guilt misleading her.

"I know what you're thinking." Keith reclined his head,

exposing his Adam's apple. She was developing a fascination with it all over again.

"I doubt it, but pray do tell."

"What are you going to do if Paul refuses to compensate you for what he stole?" His tone didn't lack kindness, but it worried her all the same.

"If that's the case, I will..." She would be utterly lost. No money, no job, no future. "The thought I would catch Paul one day sustained me through my dark days although it was only a vague dream. If I have to be honest, I didn't do anything to find him. I didn't have the means to do that. I asked around, but obviously he'd never spent time in the poorest rookeries of London. I clung to the possibility of seeing him again, only to give myself something to dream about, something to survive for. Now that I'm close to achieving that goal, I don't have anything else left." She stroked the smooth fabric of her brand-new reticule. "It probably doesn't make any sense to you."

"It does. I understand the need to have a goal to survive. I was the same when I lived with Sir Howard before he changed. The only thing keeping me going was the thought that my mother had died while working to feed me before the Fenians—" He clenched his jaw. "Apologies."

"It doesn't hurt me," she whispered. "You can be honest. I thought about that as well. What if the attack that killed your mother had been organised by my father? The possibility causes me more pain than I can handle. At least you got justice."

"At great cost to you."

"That day at the police station," she said, gathering her courage, "I treated you horribly. My papa's death and the truth about him were a terrible shock. I denied the truth. But that's not an excuse for the awful things I said to you. I haven't apologised yet."

"I don't want your apology." He sounded offended, even hurt. "I don't care about your apology."

"What do you want then?" It came out more bitter than she liked.

He gave her one of his soul-searching stares. "I want you to be happy."

"I don't think I can be happy. Not as I was before the tragedy." Her voice cracked. "One needs to practise happiness in order to be happy, and I haven't exercised being happy in a long time. I didn't have the energy."

He took her hand in a tender gesture that surprised her. "You say that because you endured years of hardship. That life is over. If you want to. If you let me."

He withdrew his hand and didn't press her for an answer, which she appreciated because she hadn't decided yet what to do with herself. Maybe she was too proud, but if she could rebuild her life with her own devices, she would.

She pondered her next words carefully. "You must admit that your generosity towards me comes mostly from your guilt. That's why I'm reluctant to accept it."

"It's not guilt. I understand what it means to live on the edge of death and desperation. If anything, you should ask yourself if it's your anger towards me that prevents you from accepting my help."

She pressed her lips together. Nonsense. She'd accepted his help, had she not? She wasn't angry with him. Not anymore.

They didn't talk for the rest of the trip. She used the silence to collect herself or try to. The carriage lurched to a stop in front of the gleaming Rochefort Teahouse. She had only heard about the luxurious tea parlour where the members of Parliament and the higher echelon of society met regularly. They said the Rochefort was where every important decision in the empire was made; the discussions at Parliament were a formality.

Keith helped her out of the carriage, taking her hand gently. Tension still darkened his face, but she had no idea why he was still bothered. She'd done everything he'd asked. Well, aside from marrying him.

She closed her eyes for a moment. If she wanted to retrieve what was hers, she had to start the show and be a convincing wife.

The Rochefort lived up to its reputation. Elegant but not ostentatious. Imposing but not overwhelming. The white walls shone so much she wondered how many people worked to keep them clean from the coal dust that covered everything in London. Her shoes sank into the plush carpet covering the marble steps to the entrance. Uniformed servers bowed at her passage, and she nearly stopped to look around to see whom they bowed to.

Keith thrust out his chest, his arm tensing under her hand. "Where is that bloody count?"

"You're too nervous."

He fiddled with his silk cravat. "I've never felt at ease among these people. I might have acquired a title, but I'm a stableboy at heart." He gave her his secret boyish smile that caused her to shiver and brought her back to those years when she and Keith read under the sycamore tree. "I have to thank you for having taught me how to read. That was the beginning of my success."

"Which includes catching the Fenians." She regretted the words the moment they left her lips. Stupid, stupid mouth.

He tensed further and led her to a table at the end of the hall.

She tugged at his arm. "I'm sorry. That was an uncalled-for remark. I didn't mean it in that way. It came out wrong."

"It doesn't matter." It sounded like the opposite. He held a chair for her before sitting in front of her.

"I hurt you. It wasn't my intention."

"I'm all right."

"Keith—"

"Don't worry. Please choose your order."

She didn't press the matter. If he didn't want to talk, she wouldn't pester him. She focused her attention on the menu. The

list of types of tea and delicacies was shocking for two reasons—
the variety and the ridiculously high prices.

"Eight shillings for a cup of Earl Grey?" she half-whispered,
half-hissed, lowering the menu. "I could rent a nice room for two
weeks for that price."

"The king's tea is one pound per cup."

"Ridiculous."

"It's worth it. Don't you want to try it?"

She checked the menu again. Did she want to drink the most
expensive tea in the world? Actually, she was curious. "It's too
much."

"Just this once. My treat." He smirked.

Smiling, she shot her gaze skywards. "Obviously."

"I'll add some *langues de chat*." *Cat's tongues.*

She put a hand on her chest. "Half a pound each? Robbery."

"I want to try them."

"They'd better be good, or I'll steal their silverware."

He laughed, and she smiled. Hearing his deep rumble was like
a caress that washed out the tension.

After a server took their expensive order, Violante swept the
room with her gaze to understand who the other customers were.
Old habits die hard. Her thief's eye searched for sloppily latched
bracelets, open reticules from where to steal wallets and guineas,
and easy-to-unfasten gold brooches. She found plenty of targets.
But then again, who would spend a pound for a cup of tea if not
the ridiculously rich people?

Keith's hand over hers stopped her search. "Now it's you who
are nervous."

He brushed her knuckles with his thumb, and the simple
gesture transported her back to Windy Ridge where she and Keith
had spent lazy afternoons walking up the hill and reading, their
fingers stealing furtive touches. The contact was familiar and
strange at the same time.

He removed his hand with a snappy move as if just realising

he'd touched her. The server came with their tea and biscuits, breaking the moment.

She inhaled the intense, rich aroma of the tea. "Goodness. Just the smell makes me feel better. If it tastes half as good as it smells, it has to be the best tea I've ever had."

He took a sip and nodded. "It's excellent. Worth every penny."

She tried it, and the luxuriant, full taste filled her mouth. A tad smoky and fully aromatic. Even better than she'd thought. The *langues de chat* melted in her mouth, leaving a sweet, buttery trail on her tongue. She might have moaned a little.

"How do you like it?" he asked, taking another biscuit.

"I'm pleasantly surprised. When I had enough money to buy tea, I would use the leaves at least a dozen times until the brew was simply dirty rain. This tea is a dream. Really. I dreamed about these delicacies when I slept under a heap of rags in the street. Although slept is a big word. You can't sleep when it's so cold your teeth chatter and the icy rain—" She drew in a breath at the way he watched her.

He stared at her with fire in his dark gaze. His eyebrows set low on his forehead, and it seemed the white in his eyes had disappeared.

She wiped her mouth with the napkin. "Did I say something wrong? Was I speaking too loudly?" Their marriage was a pretence, but she was a viscountess now. Ladies didn't raise their voices.

He gave her the slightest headshake. "I hate that you had to endure such hardships for years while Sir Howard pampered me. If I had known, I would have helped you."

"I wouldn't have accepted your help." She closed her suddenly cold hands around the warm cup of tea. "At first, my anger and denial, fuelled by hunger, were so strong that I believed you were the cause of all my troubles." She took a fortifying sip of the magical tea. "I hated you," she whispered.

She chanced a glance at him, worried to see his intense stare burning her. But no. Once again, pain flickered over his tight features.

"You said you don't hate me now. Is it true?" he asked.

"Five years is a long time to hate someone."

"That's not an answer." Even his voice darkened.

"I don't hate you. Truly, Keith, you must believe me. If anything, I never have, not even when I believed I did. I directed my anger at you because I was a coward." She sipped her tea again, needing comfort. "I hated my father." The confession burned the back of her mouth. She'd never said that out loud, and saying it now didn't make her feel better. "I hated him for what he'd done, for betraying me, for being a murderer. But, at the same time, I couldn't hate him because I loved him. I still love him. Everything was so confusing." She drew in a deep breath. "Sorry. I shouldn't have said that. Not here. Not now."

He stroked her hand gently. He didn't say anything but didn't need to. The devotion lighting his gaze said it all. He drew slow circles over her knuckles until her breathing returned to normal. It was amazing how his touch soothed her.

"I don't hate you, Keith," she whispered to him only because she didn't want anyone else to hear it. "Quite the opposite."

"Thank you." He showed his special smile again, and she acknowledged the turmoil in her chest. He straightened, his expression returning guarded. "The count is here. The man with the tall hat and the dark cloak."

She threw a casual glance around. A tall, lean man smiled and shook hands with other peers. She would have understood he was Italian even without Keith telling her. The bias cut of his long dark jacket and the type of waistcoat ending with two pointed edges marked him as an Italian, or at least as someone who followed Italian fashion closely.

As a thief, keeping up with international and local fashion was a good way to spot tourists in a crowd. Alas, tourists were the best targets. Once robbed, they'd leave the country, and the police didn't care about their stolen goods.

The beautiful woman next to him had to be his wife. Now that Violante paid attention to the sounds, a few Italian words reached her ears.

"I expected someone different," she said, glancing at the glamorous young couple.

"How?"

She lifted a shoulder. "I expected someone older. He seems to be in his thirties. Quite handsome as well. His wife is a stunner."

"Handsome?" He glanced at the count. "A rather normal chap, I think."

"No, he's elegant and very handsome."

He scoffed. "If you say so."

"Are you jealous?"

"My wife is admiring another man. I can't say I'm pleased." He rose, straightening his jacket, his brow furrowed. "We should say hello." He gave her his hand before she could say anything.

After her confession about whom she hated and didn't hate, touching his hand sent a different type of shiver down her back. There was a generous dose of regret because if she hadn't been so angry and proud, her life would have been different. Thoughts for another moment.

She forced a smile as they approached the count's table. "Are we going to just introduce ourselves? Isn't that rude?"

"I've already been introduced to the count a while ago."

The closer they went, the more her smile became forced at the thought of pretending to be a viscountess. Goodness. Stealing caused her less anxiety.

"Count Bassini-Verdelli." Keith bowed his head. "Countess. I hope you remember me. We met briefly at the latest Great Exhibition of London last year."

The count stood up. "Lord Ashford. Of course I remember

you. You were with Sir Howard." His accent brought back memories of her mother. "What a coincidence."

Ha! He had no idea.

"May I have the pleasure of the introductions?" Keith asked. "My dear, this is Count Bassini-Verdelli and his wife, the Countess Bassini-Verdelli. May I present my wife, Lady Ashford." He added a touch of possessiveness to the word wife. He gripped her hand more tightly.

She curtsied. "It's a pleasure to make your acquaintance, my lord, my lady."

"My lady, a pleasure." The count bowed but tilted his head towards Keith. "I had no idea you were married, Ashford."

Keith remained deadpan. "Violante and I met at a ball two years ago. Our marriage is a recent event."

Very recently. She smiled again. "It seems like yesterday, doesn't it, darling?"

Keith gave her hand a light tug in warning.

The count smiled so widely she could see his back teeth. "If I may be bold, Violante is an Italian name."

"It is. My mother was from Rome."

"Wonderful. My home." He stretched out an arm towards his wife.

The countess rose with the grace of a panther and gave a shallow curtsy. Her deep amber eyes had a feline quality that made them stand out in her olive skin. Violante had to confess to a hint of envy at how she moved and at her beauty.

"Why don't you sit with us?" Lady Bassini-Verdelli asked.

"A splendid idea," Violante said.

She perched on the edge of the stuffed chair as she and Keith enjoyed their tea with the count and countess. Drinking tea together was the easy part. Now she and Keith had to find a way to be invited to Bakewell. She smiled and nodded politely while the count talked about their trip to London from Rome.

"The trains in France were excellent," he said with enthusiasm.

"The food was delicious," the countess said, "but too heavy for my tastes. The French add cream everywhere. Do you prefer French food, Lady Ashford?"

Cream. Hmm. Violante wouldn't complain about too much cream. "Violante, please, and yes, I love French cuisine."

"Then I am Diana," Lady Bassini-Verdelli said.

Violante smiled and turned to the count. "Are you planning to stay here in London, my lord?" she asked.

"No." The count waved a hand. "We're here only to rest after the trip. We will go north to the country. I own an estate in Bakewell, fully immersed in nature. No coal smoke or traffic."

Keith arched a brow, feigning surprise. "A holiday, I presume."

"No, no." Lady Diana laughed. "My husband never stops working. We are going there for business."

An idea struck Violante. "But next week is Saint Joseph's Day. The day you celebrate both Saint Joseph and Father's Day. Surely, you are resting on that day, my lord. I haven't celebrated Saint Joseph's in years." She sighed dramatically. "I don't remember anymore how a good broad bean stew tastes with the roasted breadcrumbs on top, or the delicious pastries filled with cream and custard."

"And the braided bread," Lady Diana added.

"With the sesame seeds on top," Violante and Lady Diana said in chorus before bursting out laughing.

The count stared at her with such sympathy she nearly felt guilty. "What a shame, Lady Ashford. By all means, you should come to Bakewell. We'll have a proper Saint Joseph's Day celebration for you."

Lady Diana nodded. "With the flowers and the lovely food. It's also dear Giuseppe's name day." She smiled at her husband.

The talk about Saint Joseph's Day had started as a joke, but now Violante longed for the celebration. "That would be wonderful." She wasn't lying.

"Ashford?" The count angled towards Keith. "What do you say?"

Keith took her hand. "How can I refuse such an invitation when my wife is so happy?"

"Excellent." The count tapped the table to underline his agreement. "The more the merrier."

"Besides," Violante said cheerfully. "I'm sure you gentlemen will find the opportunity to talk about work and business deals. Is there any particular deal that preoccupies you, my lord?"

The count's smile faltered. "Ah, there is, my lady. The property I mean to sell seems to be the business deal of the moment. Even your husband is interested. I recall receiving a letter from his solicitor."

Keith bowed his head in acknowledgement. "That building is a great opportunity for many."

"I'm not surprised," the count said.

"Please no talking about business." Lady Diana frowned. "Not here and now."

The count kissed his wife's hand and turned to Keith. "We'll have time and opportunity to discuss your interest, Ashford."

fifteen

EXHAUSTION WEIGHED VIOLANTE down when she and Keith finally left the Rochefort and sat in the carriage. Maybe pretending to be someone she wasn't required more from her than she'd expected.

Shadows crossed Keith's face, and the tension radiating from him was palpable.

She stifled a yawn. "You got what you wanted, but you don't look happy."

"Yes, I've got what I wanted." He flexed his fingers. "You were great. The idea of celebrating Saint Joseph's Day was a stroke of genius."

"But? I sense a 'but' coming." She removed her hat. It was lovely, but the hat pin bothered her scalp.

"You sounded honest."

Was there a note of reproach in his voice? She couldn't tell.

"Because I was. My mother loved to observe Italian celebrations and share them with all the members of the household. Papa pretended to be outraged by the fact we were always celebrating something." She smiled. "He was right, I guess. There was always a saint to celebrate or a holiday to observe. I loved Saint Joseph's

Day. Toasted breadcrumbs are in every dish. They symbolise the sawdust because Saint Joseph was a carpenter, and the broad beans are—" She laughed. "I'm sorry. I keep chatting about things you don't probably care about."

"Quite the opposite. You've never told me about your mother's traditions."

"After she left, my father and I didn't talk about her, despite the fact I had very good memories of her."

"But when you talked to the count, you sounded sad," he said.

"I miss her, especially since I realised she might've known about Papa. I wonder what happened to her."

He seemed about to say something but remained silent for the rest of the trip. She'd never had problems reading him, but things had changed deeply between them. She couldn't tell if he was angry or simply thoughtful, if he was happy or bothered.

When he helped her out of the carriage, he didn't let go of her hand until they were upstairs, and she didn't mind it.

"My lord." Murray, the butler, bowed when he opened the door. "Miss."

"Actually," Keith said, "Violante is now Lady Ashford. If someone asks, Violante is the viscountess. It's a long story. Suffice to say as far as anyone is concerned, Violante is my wife."

Murray cast a sceptical glance at her. His thick grey beard didn't hide his confusion. "Of course, my lord, my lady."

"Thank you, Murray," Violante said.

The butler muttered, "Welcome, my lady."

"I'll need a word with you and Mrs. Collins before you leave for the day. Thank you."

"My lord." Murray bowed again, but she didn't miss the displeased twitch of his mouth.

Keith stopped at the door to her bedroom. "Thank you for today. The count would have never invited me without you."

"We have a deal." She opened the door and paused.

He rubbed the back of his neck. "If the count learns we tricked him, his wrath will be intense."

"Then we'll be careful." She loitered. "Is something the matter?"

"What do you think happened to your mother?"

The question caught her by surprise. "If she's alive, I don't know why she didn't contact me in all these years. Maybe she's dead. Maybe she fled somewhere. I have no idea. Why do you ask?"

He shrugged. "We'd better prepare our luggage. We leave by train tomorrow. I have to talk to Murray and Mrs. Collins about the trip." He kissed her hand with a delicate brush of his lips. "You need to rest. The trip will tire you, and you haven't fully recovered." He released her hand slowly, staring at her fingers touching his palm. "Good night, Violante."

A fierce tingle crawled up her arm, preventing her from saying anything.

He headed to his bedroom, leaving her with an odd ache in her chest.

∼

KEITH COULDN'T HELP but smile at Violante's enthusiasm.

The train to Bakewell wasn't particularly fast or luxurious. Hell, he'd travelled on board the recently developed Orient Express, the most lavish and comfortable train in the world. In comparison, this modest train was a hay cart, especially considering that it was crowded and their compartment was so narrow that Mrs. Collins—now officially Violante's lady's maid—and Murray had to travel on another train.

But Violante couldn't sit still and kept sticking her head out of the window, touching the hard wooden seats, and watching the green fields stream past with wide eyes.

"Look, sheep!" She pointed at the white dots in the middle of a pasture.

He laughed. "There are more sheep than humans in this part of the country."

"I won't complain." She giggled. "It's been so long since I saw the country that it's like seeing it for the first time."

He loved it when she giggled. Her whole body transformed and radiated happiness. It was a joy to look at her. She returned her attention to the field, placing her hands on the glass.

It was funny how he'd become accustomed to wealth in a matter of a few years. Until Mr. Sharpe had employed him, he'd known nothing but deprivations and pain. Yet money and a title had made him forget about the nights he'd spent awake because hunger wouldn't let him sleep. He was glad Violante reminded him of his humble past. It was his turn to make her forget hers.

"It's so fast." She propped her elbows on the lowered window and let the gusts of wind ruffle her hair. She closed her eyes, seemingly in ecstasy.

He would immortalise this moment if he could. "Fast? Tosh! You should see the Orient Express."

She whipped her head towards him. "You have been on the Orient Express?"

"Yes, I have. The entire route from Paris to Constantinople. I met a few investors in Constantinople. Amazing city, great food, lovely weather, and friendly people."

She sat in front of him, her eyes larger than the stars. "You must tell me everything. I'm so envious. I'd love to see the world. I'd love to travel on the Orient Express." A delightful colour like that of a spring dawn coloured her cheeks and lips.

He wished he could immortalise this moment, too.

"I'll be happy to take the Orient Express again with you and eat some dolmas in Constantinople. They're vegetables stuffed with rice and spices..." He must have said something wrong because all the light radiating from her vanished. "What is it?"

She shut the window and sat stiffly in front of him. "Travelling with you would be impossible."

"No, it wouldn't."

"Keith." She exhaled. "Why would you take *me* to Constantinople?"

Why? It was obvious, wasn't it? "I think it's clear why."

"We were friends. Now it's different, even if we might consider ourselves friends," she said. "We're accomplices. Once each one of us gets what we want, we'll go separate ways."

No. *That* would be impossible. He'd found her. He wouldn't let her go. "What if I want to employ you?"

She pulled the lapels of her coat closer as if she were cold. "Do you think if you become my employer, the situation will be different?"

No, likely more complicated and awkward, but he was desperate. Desperate to keep her close. He'd make sure she wouldn't starve again. She might still hate him deep down or not want to be close to him. He would help her anyway. But she was right. They weren't friends as they'd been before because he didn't feel the urge to kiss and hold his friends, take care of them, and protect them from any discomfort life might throw at them.

"I don't care," he said, touching her hand. She seemed to like it when he touched her hand. "I'd love to take you to Constantinople. I'd love to be with you. The rest is your choice. Would you accept?"

He got lost in the way the tip of her tongue darted over the plush pink flesh of her bottom lip. The view was rather arousing, judging by how much his body tensed.

When she stopped tormenting her bottom lip, he exhaled.

"I guess I would." She flushed again. "I'd love to see the world."

He grinned. "Excellent."

Her answer lifted his mood for the rest of the journey, even though she didn't talk.

The carriage trip from the train station to the count's estate was less exciting and more bumpy. The uneven road caused the carriage to shake and jolt so hard he hit the roof with his head a couple of times.

"Bloody hell," he muttered, rubbing the top of his head. "Where does the count live?"

"Not a smooth beginning—" The rest of her sentence was cut short by yet another jolt that shoved Violante straight into his arms. Not that he'd complain.

She let out a whoop that would be comical if his mouth didn't suddenly fill with the feathers of her hat.

"Ouch," he mumbled as her elbow dug into his ribs.

"I'm so sorry." She started to scurry away from him, but another jolt had them both jumping on the seat.

He shielded her from hitting the wall by wrapping his arms around her. She was practically sitting on his lap in a froth of skirts, fluttering feathers, and her flapping cloak. Her lips parted in mute shock. Lips that were an inch from his. She must have applied a layer of rouge because they were rich, full, and shiny with a glossy hue. If he tilted his head a little, he'd kiss her as it'd happened years ago. He wondered if she tasted the same. He wondered if she'd let him.

He ought to release her, but if he held her, she wouldn't get hurt, would she? Her breath came out faster. He didn't know if it was a good or a bad thing. Perhaps a bad one.

He released her and inched away from her as much as the damn seat allowed. She stared out of the window, straightening her dress and hat. Between her reddened cheeks and his dishevelled clothes, they looked exactly like a couple madly in love, who had dirty-puzzled in the carriage. Good. Or maybe not.

"I prefer the train," she said, swatting a wayward feather away from her face.

"You might change your mind after you see the world. Once, I took a train to Wales that derailed because of the mud. It was raining so much that half of a hill slid down the railway with a terrifying rumble. Not enjoyable, believe me."

She stared at him as if he were a hero. "I do envy your travel experiences. I haven't seen anything of this world. I'd like to live an adventure."

"My offer still stands." He braced himself when the carriage bounced up and down along a steep road going downhill. "As my secretary, you'll travel with me. Think about it. Besides, you're living an adventure right now, which is a fancy way of saying a miserable, horrible trip."

She threw her head back and laughed. "Then I might change my mind about adventures."

He laughed as well, hoping she'd decide to stay with him.

It was a relief to arrive at the count's estate both because the rocking and jolting ended and because Keith would get away from Violante's intense presence and the temptation to kiss her. Except that he was supposed to be her loving husband. Their closeness was expected and inevitable.

He climbed out of the carriage and offered her his hand. He acknowledged the quickening of his heartbeat as she slid her soft hand into his.

"What a journey," she said, glancing up at the tall building.

"Indeed." It was just the beginning.

sixteen

KEITH WENT TO take one of their bags stashed on the top of the carriage, but the coachman and a footman were faster and threw a curious glance at him. Right. He was a viscount. He didn't need to fetch his own luggage.

Violante hooked her arm through his as they walked to the manor's front door. Tall trees and hedges enclosed the estates. The thick vegetation formed a green wall around the garden and the driveway. The scent of pine trees and wet soil thickened the air. Only the birds' song could be heard. One would believe they were in some remote forest and not a few hours away from London. Previous carriages had left a few marks on the ground. It was amazing no one had died driving there.

"Stunning place," Violante said.

"The road is anything but. Mrs. Collins and Murray will have a hard time."

The coming and going of servants to carry their luggage continued when they entered the manor through the wide set of double doors. The servants' footsteps echoed off the cavernous entry hall, which fit the trip—a bumpy, dangerous road like that could only end up in a gloomy cavern.

A uniformed butler welcomed them. "Lord and Lady Ashford, I trust you had a pleasant trip. I'm Fletcher, at your service."

Yes, as pleasant as being bitten by a snake. "Lovely."

Violante hid her chuckle behind a polite cough.

"Follow me, please."

The butler showed them to their bedroom upstairs. Like the entry hall, the room was wide enough to be considered a ballroom with a domed ceiling, dark wainscoting, and heavy dark drapes. At least the floor-to-ceiling windows offered a spectacular view of the garden. Intricate garden. The hedges and bushes formed a maze pattern disturbing to look at. He'd get dizzy from staring at it.

"His Lordship will receive you in half an hour for a repast when the other guests arrive," the butler said. "If you need to find the drawing room or need anything, ring the bell, and a maid will come."

"What other guests, may I ask?" Violante asked, removing the feather-covered hat.

"Mr. Wellington and Sir Nigel, my lady," the butler said.

Keith spun around from the window to face the butler. "Sir Nigel Glenister?"

"The very same, my lord."

Keith tried not to scowl at the unpleasant news. The fact Nigel was after the count's land wasn't new, but his presence here was unexpected. "Thank you, Fletcher."

The butler bowed and shut the door behind him.

Peace at last. And stillness. Keith dropped himself onto the bed and exhaled. Violante paced the room without touching anything as if worried she might break the glass vases or the golden lamps.

"Is it a problem that Sir Nigel is here?" she asked.

He rubbed his aching forehead. "It might be. Does he know you? Have you ever met him in Hampstead?"

She shook her head. "I don't think so. Papa never wanted me to go to Sir Howard's house, and from what I know, Sir Nigel attended a boarding school away from Hampstead. Sir Howard and his family didn't spend the whole year at their manor. I've never met Sir Howard's sons."

"His presence here is upsetting, but then again, Nigel wants to deal with the count as well." He propped himself up on his elbows. "Please don't tell anyone Paul was your former stableboy. It might cause trouble."

She came to a screeching stop and spun towards him. "Cause trouble? What about the truth about him being a thief?"

He held up his hand. "I understand. That came out wrong. What I mean is that it'd be to your advantage to keep your relationship with him quiet lest he decide to leave, and the count might ask questions about you we don't want to answer."

She pressed her lips. "Never mind. I don't care about causing Paul trouble. I only want to get back what he owes me."

She yanked her bags open and rummaged through them like a police officer would search the luggage of a suspect. She selected a few garments and disappeared behind the screen on the other side of the room. He should change, too. Dust covered his clothes and shoes. The next few days promised to be exhausting. He slid behind the other screen on the opposite side of the room and removed his boots and breeches. He exhaled in relief when he washed himself with the warm, soapy water in the basin.

"Why do you care about Paul, anyway?" she asked as the swish of silk came from her side of the room.

He chanced a glance through the louvred panel, only to catch a glimpse of her silhouette. She had a pretty silhouette. Nice hips. And legs. Elegant neck as well.

"He's a good man who made a huge mistake."

Her silhouette stilled, and he wondered if she stood in only her chemise. The thought ignited an annoying stirring in his chest and lower.

"What mistake? Stealing from my father or abandoning him like a rat when the ship is sinking?"

He towelled himself dry and buttoned up a fresh shirt still stiff with starch. "Paul was devoted to Mr. Sharpe. The whole affair destroyed him. That day, he panicked. I find it hard to forgive him, but I understand he was worried about his mother."

"His choices didn't destroy him as much as they destroyed me." The sound of fabric being tugged came.

"It's not a competition." His voice rose.

"It's not a happy collaboration either."

He didn't say anything else. It was her battle with Paul, and he'd already got into the middle of it too much. Yes, he tended to forgive people. Otherwise, he wouldn't have called the police to protect Sir Howard. But Violante had gone through terrible years. He respected her pain. Years of living on the streets would make anyone bitter.

He stepped out of the screen in a clean suit and soft leather shoes. Bugger, he was tired. His muscles ached. He wanted to shut those ugly curtains and take a nap. Sod the count and his guests.

He gazed up and hitched a breath. The lemon gown Violante wore exalted her golden hair, and with the sunlight lighting her from behind, she looked like an angel with a glowing halo. The mauve dressing gown hanging from a hook and fluttering behind her completed the picture, giving her a pair of wings. Energy rushed back to him.

"You look beautiful." So much for being tired. Damn.

"The modiste is an artist. She would make a hag look pretty." She flushed, fiddling with her bodice. "Since Mrs. Collins isn't here, I need help with the buttons, if you don't mind. I don't want to ask for a maid."

She turned around, showing him her half-naked back. Not really naked. Her chemise and corset covered most of her skin. But the flimsy fabric let him see her shoulder blades. Her neck was fully exposed as well. Lots of creamy, smooth skin to enjoy.

His mouth grew dry. The temptation to run a finger over her inviting back shook him. The tiny fabric-covered buttons slipped through his fingers, but he managed to fasten a few of them. The closer he came to the naked part of her skin, the slower he went. He wasn't to be blamed. The temptation was too strong.

"I don't want to argue with you about Paul," she whispered.

"Neither do I." The frilly hem of the chemise was too pretty not to touch it. Sod his resolve to be controlled. It wasn't working.

"I'm stuck." A swift shiver left a trail of goosebumps on her spine.

"Stuck?" He paused, leaving the dress half-buttoned.

"You moved on, built a life, and became someone different. I live in the past, still trying to understand who my father was and why I didn't see the truth. I feel guilty about my mother. For all these years, I thought she didn't care about me and ran away with a lover. Now I'm worried about her. I have so many questions. Did she leave of her own volition? Did Papa kick her out? Why didn't she write to me? If she knew what Papa was doing, why didn't she take me with her?"

If the private investigators he'd hired found Violante's mother, that might give her some peace of mind. But he didn't want to give her false hope.

"I can't move on," she said, "and I know you think I'm ridiculous and stubborn, but my papa was my entire world. He was taken from me, and Paul stole from him. At the same time, I want to be the master of my destiny, not live on your generosity or stealing. I did that, and it's not living. Not really."

"I understand. I genuinely do."

She glanced over her shoulder, her golden eyelashes fluttering. "Thank you."

"You're welcome." He resumed buttoning the dress up.

He stifled a groan when he brushed her silky skin. Another shiver went down her back, and he wondered if his touch caused it. Or maybe she didn't like having him so close.

She tilted her head forwards when he reached the last button. A little golden curl of her hair kissed the curve of her neck. He'd never envied a curl as much as he did now. It was only by sheer determination and discipline that he buttoned the dress without touching her.

"Done." His voice sounded all husky and low.

She turned around, standing inches from him. She was so close her breasts almost touched his chest. "Let's face the count, husband of mine."

He shouldn't like the word *husband* so much.

They went down the stairs together, their fingers brushing. He tried not to make anything out of that, but a shot of desire rushed through him unbidden, no matter what his logic said. Loud voices and the clink of glasses came from the drawing room, shocking him back to reality.

He paused in the hallway. "Ready?"

"Ready." She slid her arm through his, and he wished the way she snuggled close to him wasn't only a pretence.

"Lord and Lady Ashford." The count waved them in. His bright smile reached his eyes. "How lovely to see you here. I hope the trip wasn't too bad."

"Bumpy, my lord." Keith couldn't keep smiling as he spotted Nigel who glared at him.

The countess walked towards them in a green gown that made her tiger eyes stand out. "Lord Ashford, Lady Ashford, Violante, I'm so glad to see you've arrived. This is Sir Nigel Glenister, one of my husband's business partners."

"Lord Ashford and I know each other," Nigel said with a strained note. "My father took the viscount under his wing."

"Indeed," Keith said.

There was a round of bows and curtsies at the introductions, followed by remarks on the weather. Keith didn't avert his gaze from Nigel.

"Unfortunately, Mr. Wellington is going to be late," the count said. "His ship from New York City arrived in Liverpool one day later than expected. He'll join us tomorrow."

"I'm sure we'll find a way to amuse ourselves in the meantime." Nigel flashed a smile that was all teeth and no joy. "Lord and Lady Ashford. How interesting."

"Did you know the viscount was married?" the countess asked.

"I had no idea." Nigel didn't add anything else. Good.

Not that Keith's past was a secret. The count knew he came from humble origins, and Keith's role in helping to foil Fenians' attack against Sir Nigel's father was public knowledge. But the fact Nigel didn't know about Keith's wife sounded suspicious, considering the relationship between Keith and Sir Howard.

The count raised his glass of brandy. "I have to tell you, Ashford. Sir Nigel is as interested in my property in St. Giles as you are. I've always enjoyed healthy competition. Competition is the soul of business."

"Oh, that dreadful building and horrible area." Lady Diana waved a hand. "Nothing but awful smells and darkness. I'm surprised so many people are interested in buying it. We bought it only because it's located in the Italian quarter. Terrible mistake."

"The building only needs a bit of work," Nigel said. "The area is going to be excellent. Once all those decrepit houses around the building are demolished, I'll develop a grandiose hotel with a spa and a swimming pool, like one of those in Paris."

"A hotel?" Keith asked. "What for?"

"An exclusive hotel for exclusive travellers." Nigel's tone challenged him to say more. "The building is close enough to the docks to be easily reached by rich travellers, who arrive at the port on the Thames, and it's well-placed enough to be at a comfortable distance from the City. Once the area is cleaned up, the building will be profitable. My hotel will host prime ministers and dignitaries, competing with the prestigious Brown's Hotel, mark you."

Violante shifted on the armchair. "But what will happen to the people who live in the *decrepit* houses?"

Nigel lifted a dismissive shoulder. "They'll find somewhere else to live."

Bloody bastard. "How—" Keith's protest was cut off by Lady Diana.

"What would you like to do with that building, Ashford?" she asked.

"Start a new youth centre," Keith said. "A place for youngsters to train and learn how to box. The idea is to take them off the streets and give them a purpose, direction, and a future."

The count drew his eyebrows together. "Your enterprise won't make a profit then."

"It absolutely will, my lord. I firmly believe that investing in a better, safer society and its youth is the best profit we could ever make."

"A philanthropist." Lady Diana raised her glass at him. "I really admire those who care for others."

Keith bowed. "My lady."

Nigel shot his gaze towards the ceiling. The count remained deadpan. Difficult to say if he approved or not.

Violante touched Keith's arm. Her violet ring caught the light. "My husband has another gymnasium in East London. Those children adore him. He's their hero."

The count didn't appear impressed, which worried Keith. What was better, another hotel only a few people could afford, or a place to help people in need? Wasn't the count supposed to support charity?

Nigel scowled. "I'm sure of that. Lord Ashford seems to have been born a hero. Where would we be without him?"

"You in a coffin six feet under," Keith gritted out.

The air between them snapped like a rope pulled tightly.

"Unless," Nigel said with a charming smile that was a stark contrast to his tone, "there was no danger to start with and the whole incident was made up."

Keith took his time pondering all reasons why he should stay silent and not argue with Nigel in front of everyone. The list was rather short.

Violante touched his arm again. "My husband is very eager to fight the rising criminality in the streets."

"A useless fight. Lord Ashford can't win against crime," Nigel said.

"*Crime is a rigid, unbending master, against whom no one can be strong except by total rebellion,*" Violante said.

The count brightened in a moment. "This is a quote from *The Betrothed* by Alessandro Manzoni."

Violante blushed. "Manzoni is my favourite Italian author."

"Heavens, I hate him." The countess huffed. "Flowery prose and preachy monologues."

"*One of the advantages of this life is that you can hate someone without knowing him.* Manzoni again," Violante said.

The count burst out laughing. "I love Manzoni, and I love the fact the viscountess knows him so well." He clapped both Keith's and Nigel's shoulders. "Do not worry, gentlemen. We'll have plenty of time to discuss the details of your projects. You must be hungry after the trip. Let's have dinner."

seventeen

T HE DINNER WAS a dull affair, at least for Keith. Violante was the only ray of light. She chatted with Lady Diana about the typical food served for Saint Joseph's Day while the count discussed his passion for an Italian game of cards with Nigel who pretended to be fully invested in the conversation. Perhaps Keith should learn to pretend as well before Nigel ingratiated himself with the count. On second thought, bugger it. He wouldn't pretend to be someone he wasn't. His fake marriage of inconvenience was already a burden on his heart. He wouldn't lie about enjoying a stupid conversation when he didn't.

It was with relief when he said his goodnights to the others and climbed the stairs to his bedroom with Violante by his side.

Mrs. Collins and Murray waited for them in their bedroom, stifling yawns.

"Have you recovered from the trip, Collins?" Violante asked, closing the door.

Mrs. Collins rubbed her pale forehead. "Not quite Miss...I mean, my lady. The carriage was a nightmare."

Even Murray's face was ashen.

"You may retire then," Violante said. "We'll be all right, won't we, Keith?"

"Of course."

Murray didn't bow to Violante, saying, "Good night."

"My lady," Keith added. "You should address my wife appropriately." Someone might hear them.

Murray was flustered. "With due respect, but we're deceiving an Italian count, risking a diplomatic incident, and to be quite honest, you're barely a lord yourself."

Mrs. Collins nodded. "We don't even know who this woman is. We have principles."

Violante lowered her gaze, her cheeks reddening.

Keith didn't want to make a scene. Not to mention he couldn't hire anyone else. He lowered his voice. "I don't give a bloody toss about what you think of me, but you will not be rude to my wife."

"She isn't your wife," Murray said. "This deceit is dangerous."

"Two hundred pounds, each, to behave as proper, devout servants." Keith wouldn't ruin his chances with the count for these two people.

Violante stared at him, worried.

Murray exchanged a glance with Mrs. Collins before bowing low. "I wish you a good night to my lord and my lady."

"Should you need anything," Mrs. Collins said, opening the door, "don't hesitate to call us, my lord, my lady."

Don't hesitate his arse. "You both can go now." Keith shook his head.

Mrs. Collins curtsied, and Murray bowed again before leaving.

"I apologise," he said to Violante when they were alone. "That was inexcusable."

She shrugged. "Don't worry."

No, he did. "I've never paid too much attention to the way they address me, but this situation is different, and you deserve respect."

"It's all right. Really. I don't care." Yet she looked forlorn.

"Disappointed by Paul's absence?" he asked.

"Yes. But I can wait another day, and I loved chatting with the countess. She reminds me of my mother. I didn't realise how much I missed talking about my mother's culture until I met the countess and the count."

What a damn beautiful smile she had.

There was a sharp knock on the door. Not Murray and Mrs. Collins again.

"What—" Keith fell silent, staring at Nigel in front of him.

"A word, Keith." Nigel slid inside the room.

No my lord, or Lord Ashford. Not even Ashford.

"Lord Ashford," Violante said.

Nigel huffed.

What did Keith have to do to have a moment of peace? "What do you want?" If Nigel was rude, so could Keith.

Nigel shot a glare at Violante who returned the hostile stare. "I told you I was after the count's building."

"And I told you that so was I." He coiled an arm around Violante's waist and pulled her closer.

Nigel narrowed his sharp black eyes. Everything about his features was sharp. Sharp cheeks, sharp chin, and a sharp nose that looked like the dorsal fin of a shark.

"The deal is mine," Nigel said. "You aren't going to steal it from me as you did with my inheritance. Mark my words."

Keith forced himself to keep his voice low. "I didn't steal anything. Your father made a decision you disagreed with. Your problem, not mine."

"Exactly." Nigel strode to his bedroom without saying goodnight or bowing at Violante. Ass.

"What did he mean by that?" Violante asked when she shut the door.

"Bloody idiot." Keith yanked at the knot of his cravat. "Sir Howard left me a share of his money. It was a complete surprise for both his family and me. I think his generosity had a lot to do with his guilt. Anyway, Nigel didn't like it. He expects me to renounce the money and return it to him. Not bloody likely. And he wants to build a hotel. Nonsense." He removed his jacket and waistcoat. The nerve of that man. It wasn't his fault if Sir Howard hadn't had a great opinion of his own son, who was a lazy worker and a vain man. Keith had worked hard for Sir Howard, and that money would go to his project. "I don't understand the count at all."

"Why do you say that?"

"He behaves all haughty, looking down on gentlemen who aren't married, but apparently, he's happy to sell his house to Nigel to build a ridiculous hotel while evicting honest people from their houses." He unbuttoned his shirt, almost ripping the buttons. "There's more to his choice of Nigel's project. I want to know what it is."

"Er, what are you doing?" Violante asked, looking petrified a few feet from him.

"What?" Damn. He was undressing in front of her. "Apologies."

He marched behind the screen and finished changing.

"I wasn't...never mind," Violante said.

"What?"

"Would you unbutton me, please? I can ask Collins. I reckon she won't complain if I call her now that she'll receive your two hundred pounds."

"No. I don't want to challenge her." He hastily slid on his dressing gown and strode to her. He wanted to help her.

She turned around. "Only the top buttons. I'll do the rest."

Too many emotions bothered him. There was frustration, concern, and now desire. His clumsy fingers ripped a button. "Dammit. Sorry."

"Don't worry. I'll stitch it back."

He was too agitated not to do something stupid, like kissing her neck. On impulse, he dipped his head and almost brushed a kiss over her tempting, scented skin. Hell, the temptation was strong enough to cause his abdominal muscles to contract. No, he couldn't, shouldn't steal a kiss in such a fashion. He might not be a lord by birth, but he considered himself a gentleman.

Likely sensing his breath on her skin, she inhaled deeply. The top of her breasts appeared from above her neckline. If she was scared or disgusted, she didn't show it. Or maybe his judgement was impaired by his worry. Curse him. He had no idea.

"Done." He stepped away from her and marched behind the screen again.

She might have said, "Thank you." He wasn't even sure of that.

The water in the basin was cold, but he didn't care. Served him right for having dismissed Murray. He scrubbed himself with the soap and the sponge, staining the floor with water and suds. Bugger it. His sprays of water had missed the rug completely. There was a pool on the floor.

He dragged on his nightshirt and slid into bed. Only then did he remember something. His wife. Supposed wife. She stood behind the other screen, lit by candlelight. The scent of lilies wafted as she washed herself, judging by the sound of sloshing water.

As absurd as it sounded, he hadn't thought about the moment he would share his bed with her. Or maybe he should sleep on the floor. It wouldn't be the first time although he hadn't slept on the floor in years. He hadn't slept with a woman in years either.

He tried and failed not to stare at her when she came out of the screen in a delicate mauve dressing gown that, alas, didn't show anything inappropriate. His pulse wasn't concerned though. It thumped faster the closer she came.

She stopped at the edge of the bed. "We haven't discussed the sleep arrangement."

He swallowed hard. "We could ask for separate rooms. All the toffs do it."

"At this hour? We should have asked earlier. It'll sound suspicious. Everyone will think we argued and decided to sleep separately."

"Right." He drummed his fingers on the cover. "I think we should share the bed. If a maid comes in and sees me sleeping on the floor, there might be rumours. My position with the count is already at odds without a maid gossiping about Lord Ashford not sharing the bed with his wife. I promise I won't behave appropriately. I mean..." He rubbed the bridge of his nose. "Inappropriately. With the '*in*' that makes the difference." He ought to shut up.

She darted her tongue out over her bottom lip, and he found himself incapable of averting his gaze or thinking about anything logical.

"You're right. And I don't mind. I have slept squeezed between other people. Sharing this large bed with you won't be a problem." She removed the dressing gown, revealing a lovely, matching nightgown.

No frills or ribbons, only a simple layer of mauve satin. The light betrayed her this time. It showed the shape of her curves through the fabric. But while earlier the sunlight had made her look like an angel, now she was a temptress, all enticing curves and a delicious scent. She tugged at her long braid and lifted the covers. As she bent forwards to slide into bed, the neckline of her nightgown dropped enough to give him a spectacular view of the top of her breasts. He wasn't enough of a gentleman to look away. The narrow valley between her breasts had to be all soft skin. He wished he could—she stared at him, her eyebrows high and her expression pinched.

He cleared his throat. Great. He'd been caught staring like a lad. She lay next to him and pulled the cover up to her chin.

"Good night," she said, putting out the flame from the oil lamp.

"Good night." It wasn't going to be a good night.

Between his worry about the deal and Violante lying inches from him, he was restless. The bloody bed wasn't that big after all. He tossed and turned, tormented by her sweet scent and warmth. He should take a walk and return when he was cold and tired, but he didn't want to. Perhaps he enjoyed the torture. A cold bath wouldn't be bad.

"Keith." She touched his shoulder in the dark, and he almost jolted.

"What is it? Are you unwell? Do you feel cold? Let me fetch a hot cup of tea for you." He started to get off the bed, but she touched his arm again.

She shifted under the covers. "I was about to ask you the same thing. You keep moving. Is something the matter?"

"I'm fine."

Her hand stroked his arm through the sleeve. "You're burning up."

Yes, he was. "I'm restless. Too many thoughts."

The blankets lowered as she lit the oil lamp. The quick flash of the match gave him a glimpse of her lovely profile.

"What thoughts?" She propped herself up, blinking.

She looked so beautiful right now he couldn't think straight. With her hair dishevelled and her eyes sleepy, she was ravishing. He wanted to kiss her pouty lips and ran his fingers through her hair until she sighed on his chest while he dragged her nightgown down her shoulders to see where that valley ended.

"Nigel, the count, and you," he said. *Mostly you.*

"Me?" She brushed a curl from her face. "Did I do something wrong? Should I have talked more? Less? Was I too loud?"

"No, it's not that. You were perfect." He exhaled. "Don't worry. It doesn't matter." He ran a hand over his face. Yes, he was burning.

"I want to know." She touched his shoulder again.

She had no idea what she did to him, did she? But what was he supposed to say? That he'd never stopped thinking of her? That in his heart, he was still that boy who longed to spend an hour reading with her under the sycamore tree? That her copy of *Wuthering Heights* lay in the trunk a few feet from them? That he hadn't found love because his heart had stayed in Sharpe Manor? No. He wouldn't tell her any of that, not unless he understood if there was hope for him. She'd told him she didn't hate him. That was a start, but he longed for more, for everything. Her respect, companionship, and love.

He sat up as well. "I'm not used to sleeping with someone next to me."

She reclined her head on her arm, carelessly lovely. "Surely, you must have slept with women before."

"I don't sleep with women."

She frowned. "Do you mean you have a tumble with them and then vanish, leaving them in the bed? Or do you kick them out when you're done?"

"No, that's not what happens." The conversation was exhausting, and he did a poor job of expressing himself. "I don't lie with women."

She twisted a curl of her hair around her finger. He felt the same way as that curl—wrapped around her finger. "I don't see what being honest has to do with being rude."

He released a breath through his teeth. "Not lie to, lie with. I mean, I don't chase women. To be honest, I happened to have a lover a while ago, but..." Where was he going with that? "Enjoying a tumble is one thing. Committing to something serious is another. Sleeping next to someone is an act more intimate than a tumble. It's a shared vulnerability, and I won't do it unless I deeply care for that person."

"Didn't you have a sweetheart?" Maybe it was his imagination playing tricks on him, but he could swear he heard an interested note in her voice.

"No. I didn't have time for distractions, and I didn't find anyone I fell in love with."

She tilted her head, and the candlelight kissed her cheek. "Never?"

"Never." Because his heart was already taken.

"Not even when you travelled?" She rested her cheek on her palm, causing his heart to give a solid kick. It seemed everything she did was a cause of torment for him.

"I had to work hard to achieve what I wanted. A romantic liaison would be a distraction. Sir Howard helped me, and the title was a blessing, but people didn't trust me. I had to earn their respect. Certainly, sleeping around wouldn't have made me feel worthy."

She nodded, causing her golden curls to bounce over her beautiful face.

"What about you?" he asked. "Should I worry about a jealous darling wanting to stab me because we're sharing the bed?"

She smiled, but it didn't last. "No. I didn't have time for love either. Surviving was the priority, and it drained all my energy."

He pinched the bridge of his nose. "You're right. Stupid question."

"Not at all." She stroked his shoulder again. "Do you feel better?"

No. "Yes."

"What would make you feel better?"

A kiss. "Nothing. Don't worry about me."

"I have to worry. Unless you feel less restless, you'll keep tossing and turning, and I won't sleep either." She touched him again with a finger. "And you're lying."

"I'm not. About what?"

"I don't think you're well at all. Your skin is feverish. The trip exhausted you more than you want to admit. I can fetch you a cup of tea." She shoved the covers aside.

"No, please." He closed his hand around her wrist. "I don't want a cup of tea." *I want you.*

Any trace of amusement disappeared from her face as she

stared at him as she'd done earlier when he'd been caught ogling her. It was a stare that pierced his soul.

He was sure she could see every dark corner of his mind. He stroked her inner wrist with his thumb, trying not to show his eagerness to touch her too much. Her pulse kicked faster under his fingers. The temptation was too strong, and after all, the only way to get rid of a temptation was to yield to it. He drew slow circles over her silky skin, hesitant to take the next step. She took in a breath that pushed her breasts up and her neckline down. His gaze dipped to her lovely skin again, unapologetically this time.

"I can't stop touching you." His honest statement wasn't original or even poetic, but he couldn't find better words at that moment.

Her lips parted, and the tip of her tongue darted out a moment to lick her bottom lip.

"Keith." She sounded breathless.

He couldn't resist. He released her wrist to run the pad of his thumb over the curve of her bottom lip. It was softer than he imagined or remembered. When he pressed it lightly, her small white teeth made an appearance, and he wondered how they would feel on his skin. He traced the curve of her jaw so delicate yet so devastatingly beautiful. Her lines must have been drawn by an angel.

A sigh left her, and there was no mistaking the fact his touch pleased her. That didn't mean he felt confident enough to pull her down for a kiss. She would likely reject him, and he'd be damned if he did anything she didn't want. He was content to caress the slender column of her neck down to her chest. He paused to touch the top of her breasts. The neckline adorned them with its simple but loose hem. A single velvet ribbon sloppily guarded her cleavage. He ran a finger along the hem, feeling her velvety skin. The food and rest had restored her health and beauty and, more importantly, her inner fire. He'd helped with that, and he couldn't be prouder.

"You're the most beautiful thing I've ever seen," he whispered as if confessing a sin.

But it wasn't a sin unless he considered he was the son of a violent drunkard and a laundress. He wasn't ashamed of his origin, much less of his mother, but Violante came from another world. He could understand her if she saw him as beneath her. The title and money didn't count, especially since his good fortune came from her ruination.

She inhaled deeply, following the journey of his fingers across her skin. He lowered the neckline an inch before pausing to gauge her reaction. She watched his every move. Her spectacular eyes glowed from within.

He uncovered another inch of her until her taut nipple was bare for his hungry gaze. He paused again. She thrust her chest forth in encouragement. Despite every instinct inside him urging him to rip her nightgown off her body, he forced himself to go slowly. He stroked her nipple with his thumb, only a light brush, even though he wanted to close his mouth around it and suck hard until she cried out his name. A shuddering breath came out of her as he rubbed her nipple again, tearing a moan out of her. Her gaze never left his fingers. She stared at his thumb with fascination. He tweaked and pinched the puckered tip until it hardened further. She writhed, arching her back.

His pulse racing, he edged closer, waiting for her permission. Her reply was to pull down her nightgown another inch. Still, he forced himself to be slow and gentle, despite the desire consuming him. That desire had burned inside him for years, and now it clawed its way out of his chest.

She moaned when he tongued her nipple and sucked it into his mouth. Her thighs squeezed together, and he fought the urge to slip a hand between them to pull them apart and see how much she was enjoying his attention. He drew the tip of her breast deeper into his mouth, gently grazing her skin with his teeth. Little moans escaped her, the most beautiful sounds he'd ever heard. She dug her fingers into his hair. He scattered kisses on her breast and up her lovely neck as he kept rubbing her nipples. He fondled her breast, groaning at its softness. She was all soft, scented skin, and he longed to explore every inch of her with his lips and tongue.

Quivers went through her. They went through him too. Her breath feathered over his cheek as he kissed a tender spot under her ear. Her hand rested on his shoulder, and he wasn't sure if she meant to stop him or encourage him. He pulled back, needing to see her eyes. They were wide open, the pupil devouring her violet irises.

He cupped her cheek. It was heated. "Are you all right?"

She nodded.

"Was I harsh?"

"No," she whispered.

"Did you like it?" He tucked a wayward tendril behind her ear.

"Yes."

Right. A few more words wouldn't harm though. Had he shocked her? Hurt her? Before he could ask her more questions, she hugged him and squeezed him tightly, burying her face in the crook of his neck. It wasn't a simple hug. She clung to him with desperation.

He hugged her, caressing her hair and back. "You're worrying me. Please tell me that you are all right."

"I am." Her voice came muffled because she pressed her face against his chest. "Just hold me, please."

He obeyed without questions.

eighteen

VIOLANTE WOKE UP with her cheek resting on something warm and solid.

She blinked the sleep away and touched around. No, underneath her wasn't the bedsheet, but taut muscles and—Keith! She bolted upright.

Goodness, she remembered now. His smouldering gaze, his tender touch, his lips on her nipples. Above all, she remembered the scorching sensations burning through her body, the ache throbbing between her legs, and the all-consuming need to do more, feel more, to wrap her legs around him and beg him to take her.

Her cheeks heated all over again. It'd started with him chastely touching her wrist and had turned into something deliciously wicked from there. She would have never imagined that his touch would make her feel so powerful, beautiful, and happy. Her head reeled at the memory. Yes, powerful and a bit scary. Then she'd sagged against him and fallen asleep. A sweet, deep sleep on his chest, lulled by his steady heartbeat.

His nightshirt was open, and her hand touched his naked skin.

He opened his eyes and took in her wandering hand and her closeness.

"Oh, dear." She scurried away from him. "I'm sorry."

He scowled, rubbing his forehead. "It's all right." It didn't seem all right, judging by his harsh tone.

"You might not be used to sleeping with someone, but I am." She realised too late what she said. "I mean, reluctantly sleeping with others. I didn't want to." Goodness. That sounded even worse. She blamed it on his confusing touch.

That scowl of his turned into the flaming, fierce expression of a man ready to defend her. "Were you forced?" His voice was all but a chilling growl. "Did someone attack you? I swear to God, you'll be avenged. I'll find whoever hurt you and—"

She pressed a finger to his lips, meaning to simply shut him up. But once she touched his soft, sculpted lips, she didn't want to remove her finger. He didn't look less fierce. Corded tendons stood out in his neck.

She withdrew her finger. "I..."

He sat up. The blanket slipped down his body, revealing his half-naked chest. The dim light of dawn was enough to make out the sharp ridges of his chiselled muscles. The view distracted her from his palpable fury.

"Tell me the truth," he said in a low tone. "Give me a name. If someone hurt you, if someone touched you, I'm going to chase them down." It wasn't a threat but a vow. The air itself vibrated with the intensity of his determination. "Was it that thug, George?"

She pulled up her nightgown. The fabric chafed her tender nipples in the most delightful way. "No, no. It's not what you think."

His black eyes seemed to turn darker. "What do you mean?"

She held up a hand. "No one forced me. I mean, there were a few times when I was close to being—"

"What?" He didn't raise his voice, but the cold determination in it scared her more.

"I was lucky, and nothing happened to me. Ever. No one forced me. I expressed myself in the wrong way." She waited for him to breathe normally again before continuing. "I usually slept in a room with a dozen or so other girls. We squeezed ourselves together, both because of the lack of space and because it was cold. I have to say not being alone was comforting. The first time I'd slept surrounded by other people, I didn't like it, but it had its merits."

"No one attacked you." His eyebrows lowered over his glacial eyes.

"Never." She was about to say something else, but his fierce hug cut her off.

His strong arms wrapped around her as he crushed her in a bear hug.

"I'm glad of that. You endured such a hard life that having been attacked would be too much." He brushed his lips against her temple, and she suppressed a moan.

His warmth and scent engulfed her. The closeness was better than being squeezed between those other desperate souls. As he caressed her back in slow circles, she sagged against him. She should be careful. She should keep her distance because she had no idea where their closeness would lead. But only for that moment, she wanted to enjoy the safety of his arms.

"About last night," he said, holding her.

"Yes?" she prompted when he didn't add anything else.

"You seemed shocked."

"I was."

He took her face, rubbing her cheeks with his thumbs. Worry lines marred his forehead. "I..." he stammered the rest of the sentence, and she couldn't understand it. "Will you ever forgive me?"

"What for?" Besides, his big, warm hands on her cheeks made her feel peculiar. Peculiar as in needing his kisses again.

"I wanted you to enjoy it, not shock you. I should have stopped."

Oh, he had no idea. But it was her fault if he'd misunderstood her reaction.

"Tell me how I can make amends. I'll spend the rest of my life making amends." He breathed hard.

"No, no, Keith." She put her hands over his. "There's a misunderstanding here. You have nothing to make amends for. I enjoyed it, every moment." Saying it out loud caused her voice to quiver. "I was shocked because I liked it so much," she whispered. She couldn't say that aloud. "It was sweet and beautiful. You did nothing wrong. I wanted it, too. Truly. I've never experienced anything so beautiful. All new, wonderful sensations."

"You barely spoke to me when I asked you how you were faring." A hint of hurt crept into his voice.

"If I'd been uncomfortable, I would have told you." She ought to encourage him lest he decide not to touch her again, which would be a tragedy. "I liked it."

The lines on his brow smoothed. "I was worried."

"Sorry if I didn't express myself better." She leant against his palm.

Great. Now that the misunderstanding had been cleared, she didn't have the courage to ask him to do it again. He caressed her cheek with such adoration her spine wilted. If she initiated the intimacy, he'd likely follow. But where to start? From a kiss? Should she simply touch him?

"I'm glad you enjoyed it." He hugged her again, but this time the hug tasted differently.

It was sweeter than the first. He hugged her to protect her, to let her know he'd shield her from anything that might hurt her. His heartbeat slowed, and his caresses stopped as her stomach groaned in hunger. Not the best moment for her bodily functions to make themselves known. Besides, she wanted to feel more of those lovely sensations. Her stomach groaned again. They burst out laughing, and the tension left her shoulders.

"We should go to have breakfast." He kissed her forehead.

Actually...oh, well. "You're right." She missed his warmth when he released her. Before he left the bed, she held his hand. "Thank you."

"For what?"

"For the respect and the kindness. And the kisses."

He brought her hand up and kissed it. "Always."

She hitched a breath. What a wonderful way to start the day.

IN THE PAST HOURS, Violante had learnt so much about shipping goods she could start her own company. The count, Keith, and Sir Nigel had done nothing but talk about the advantage of using schooners against different types of brigades. No, it was frigates. Who cared?

The highlights of the conversation were Keith's heated glances at her. Every time their gazes met, a corner of his mouth quirked up in a fleeting grin she adored, and his eyes would become smouldering with desire and the promise to do more. The flutter in her belly went on and on, intensifying when he angled towards her. She no longer cared about how her body reacted to him. The reaction was well justified, especially since she knew where that reaction would go—to immense pleasure.

"Enough talking about business." Lady Diana huffed, throwing a hand up. "You always talk about work even when ladies are present."

Her husband kissed her hand with devotion. "You're right, darling. I'll make amends with the flowers."

Her eyes sparkled as she turned towards Violante. "We ordered flowers for the celebration. You'll love them."

If the florist managed to deliver them without breaking their neck along that awful road.

"Flowers are the secret of a happy marriage because they speak a language of their own," the count said. "What about yours, Ashford? What's your secret?"

Keith froze, his cup of tea halfway to his mouth. "Hugs. That's our secret."

"Oh, that's nice," Lady Diana said. "A hug is always a good idea."

The count nodded sagely. Violante's cheeks warmed at the memory of their long, sweet hug.

"And you, Glenister?" the count asked.

"I'm engaged to be married." Sir Nigel shot a fleeting glance at the countess. "My knowledge of successful relationships is limited."

"But what was your secret to wooing your bride-to-be?" the count insisted.

The corners of Sir Nigel's mouth curved down for a moment as if he were annoyed by the question. "I don't have any secrets, I'm afraid. I was simply honest and told her she captured my heart."

The count nodded. "Honesty, then. Good choice. Honesty is the best virtue. I don't trust men who lie and..." He drummed his fingers on the table. "How do you say it? Are unfaithful. Rakes. If a man can't take a vow seriously or commit to respecting his wife, how can I trust him with my business and friendship?"

Violante sipped her tea while Keith found his teaspoon suddenly charming. If the count knew of their ruse, he would kick them out, and it would be because of her. The idea of deceiving the count had been hers.

She changed the subject. "I find compassion to be a rather charming trait in a man. Don't you agree, my lady?"

Lady Diana's smile took a moment to develop. "Absolutely. What are we without compassion?"

"You should stop in London on your way to Italy," Violante said. "We'd be delighted to show you Keith's gymnasium." She put her hand over his, the gesture no longer awkward but very much thrilling. "He takes such good care of those young men. How many of them have found employment, darling?"

Keith flashed a knowing grin. "Since I started the project, more than a dozen. The idea is to take them off the streets and keep them busy while they learn a trade. That's what I want to establish in St. Giles."

Violante tilted her head towards the count, searching for his reaction. He frowned as if displeased. Keith had been right when he'd said the count didn't seem enthusiastic about helping children.

"Is something the matter, my lord? Don't you approve of the charity project?" she asked.

Sir Nigel rolled his eyes but didn't say a word.

"It has its merits," the count said. "My concern regards the success and consequences of such an enterprise."

"What do you mean?" Keith asked, stiffening.

Lady Diana pressed her lips in a flat line. "There was an incident," she said when the count didn't speak. "In Rome. A generous, good-intentioned soul, as you are, Lord Ashford, started a similar enterprise to yours, gathering poor young men from the most dreadful areas, but one of them revolted against their benefactor and killed him."

"Goodness," Violante said.

Keith clenched his hands around the cup. "An isolated incident. Every community contains a bad apple. It's important to understand the whole story before judging."

"I think you miss the point." Sir Nigel wiped his mouth with the napkin. "These people you're so eager to help are brutes by nature, no better than wild beasts. You want to domesticate them, but it's a useless, dangerous exercise. They can't change. They come from the gutter. They'll always be savages. You can't teach them to be civil."

The change in Keith happened in a second. One moment, he was hunched. The next, he straightened, the lines around his mouth tightening. "You forget I come from the gutter, too."

Sir Nigel lifted his cup. "Exactly."

"Sir Nigel." Violante let her indignation into her voice.

"I've met more humane and honourable people among the most unfortunate ones than among the aristocrats and rich," Keith said.

Sir Nigel opened his mouth, but Keith cut him off.

"You have no right to judge those young men who seek nothing but respect and compassion." He became more passionate. "They only ask for the chance to find a decent job and feed their families."

"Keith." Violante touched his arm, feeling the tense muscles underneath. She was no expert in manners, but she seriously doubted that raising his voice while having tea with a count, a countess, and a baronet was appropriate.

"People can change if given the chance, guidance, and opportunity to do so. Men aren't born evil," Keith continued. "You can't blame a hungry thief for stealing food."

"Why is he hungry in the first place?" Sir Nigel's tone sounded frosty. "Perhaps because he didn't want to work hard to earn money. Perhaps because stealing and murdering are quicker choices. Many of these *poor souls* you want so eagerly to help are only lazy cowards who find an easy living in crime and have no regrets or morals. Your nice suit doesn't make you a civilised gentleman. You are and *always* will be a man from the gutter. A savage. A beast."

Keith stood up so quickly that his chair scraped backwards. The table was shaken in the process, causing the cups to rattle. His chest heaved, and the harsh lines on his face gave him the expression of a...well, a wild man. Sir Nigel instead stared at Keith with a challenging expression as if daring him to go on.

"Well?" Sir Nigel asked.

"I'm not a savage," Keith hissed.

"Oh, really? That's all you have to say? Shock me, Ashford, say something clever." Sir Nigel rose as well. "When did you learn to read? Three years ago?"

"That's none of your bloody—"

"Keith." Violante shot up as well among Lady Diana's whispers and the count's mutters of disapproval. "Leave it. Please. For me."

That did it. Shaking, Keith stepped back from the table. His black eyes were two bottomless abysses that sucked in the light, fixed on Sir Nigel who seemed to wait for Keith to do or say something reckless.

"We'd better go to our room." Violante gently tugged at Keith's hand. "Apologies to everyone, and thank you for the tea."

Sir Nigel smirked. "Well, you've just proved my point."

"How dare you." Keith seemed on the point to start arguing again, but Violante stopped him.

"Enough. We must leave." This time, she gave a firm yank to his hand.

It would seem Keith needed more help than a fake wife could provide.

nineteen

KEITH CLENCHED HIS fists hard enough to hurt his palms. He strode out of the dining room, wishing he'd said something more clever instead of standing there like an oaf. Perhaps Nigel had a point.

Violante followed him as he marched towards the front door and outside. He headed for...he wasn't sure. He only needed to clear his head and don't think about Nigel's words.

The tall hedges of the maze in the middle of the garden cast their shadows over him, a fitting metaphor for how he felt.

"Keith, wait. You're too fast." Her quick footsteps sounded closer.

He slowed his pace as he turned around a corner of the maze to find himself in a long green aisle covered in gravel. His chest ached with hurt because deep down, he believed what Nigel had said. He stopped, unclenching his hands.

Violante swept into view like a ray of sunlight breaking free of the stormy clouds. "Why did you make that scene?"

He wished he were in his training hall, boxing and being with people like him.

"Keith." She searched his gaze.

Damn. "I apologise."

"It's not me you should apologise to." She put her hands on his biceps. "Sir Nigel was trying to provoke you."

"I'd say he succeeded." His voice sounded rough to his own ears.

"Who cares about what he thinks? I'm sure it wasn't the first time he'd provoked you."

"The count cares about what Nigel thinks, obviously. He doesn't care about my project and thinks I'm a savage. Perhaps I truly am a savage." He resumed walking. "We'll leave now. There's no point in staying here."

"You're giving up so easily." She matched his strides. "Do you want to help those children or not? We must stay."

He came to an abrupt halt, digging a groove in the gravel. "Do you want to stay because you believe in me or because you want to get money from Paul? He made a mistake, but he took that money because he was desperate. Move on, Violante. Leave the past behind. If you need money, I'll give it to you."

She gasped and stepped back from him, staring at him in horror. "You know nothing of me if you think that greed is my only motivation. I thought you understood me." She marched down the aisle, heading for the way they'd come.

Shit. He was a bloody idiot. He rubbed the bridge of his nose and chased her. "Violante."

She rounded a corner, speeding up.

"I'm sorry." He went faster.

She didn't stop.

"I really am. That was uncalled for." He overtook her and stopped in front of her, blocking her path. "I was upset. I wasn't thinking. Forgive me."

"Papa always said that when people are upset, they say things they don't have the courage to say when they're calm." She jutted out her chin. "You do think I don't believe in what you're doing to help those unfortunate children and that I place getting my money back from Paul above everything else. You're wrong and unfair towards me."

"You're right."

"Glad we agree on that point." She sidestepped him.

"I was upset," he said again because he didn't have any other excuse aside from his foul temper.

"If you leave now, your chance to make a deal with the count will be lost forever, but that's not the worst of it." She marched on with determination. "The worst of it is that Sir Nigel will build his exclusive hotel, kicking poor people out of their houses in the process and creating more desperate people. All because you couldn't let go of a provocation. What a shame."

"In my defence, I had a good reason. Didn't you hear what Nigel said?" He exhaled. "The nerve of him. He refused to travel with his father for work because he considers anyone who lives outside England a savage. Well, he considers even those who live in England savages. I worked with Sir Howard for years while Nigel enjoyed his soirées, parties, and horse races. He has never worked hard in his life, but he feels the need to preach to me about being civil. He spouts judgements on everyone he considers beneath himself when he's the real beast."

She stopped next to a lovely bush of begonias that matched her pink gown. "I understand he struck a nerve, but that's what he wanted. You played his game, and quite honestly, you seemed unhinged."

"I just wanted to say something that shut him up, but I couldn't think of anything. I'm not as clever as you are. Nigel is right about that."

"Keith, stop it. You aren't stupid or savage."

"I've had enough of people looking down on me because I didn't inherit my title from my father, or because I don't come from a wealthy family. He thinks he's better than everyone else because he's a rich boy. For years, he taunted me, made fun of me because of who I am. My patience has a limit."

Her pinched expression relaxed. "That's all understandable, but we can't leave now. You must speak with the count and apologise."

He worked his jaw. What a bloody mess.

"Keith? You'll apologise," she insisted.

"I will." He shoved his hands into his pockets. "I apologise to you again. I was an ass."

"Yes, you were." She folded her arms over her chest.

"Am I forgiven?"

"We'll see." She smiled though.

He shifted his weight. "The accident in Rome must have shocked the count."

"At least we know why he isn't enthusiastic about your idea." She craned her neck towards the fountain behind him. "Where are we going? I don't remember the fountain."

"Bloody hell." He gazed around. "I don't remember the begonias either."

"Great. We are lost."

"Isn't everyone?" He sat on the marble edge of the fountain.

Behind him, a giant cherub sprayed water from a cornucopia. Next to the fountain, tiny yellow roses grew, forming a heart-shaped pattern. Actually, their colour was saffron with red dots, and he didn't know why he cared about some flowers that looked like smallpox.

Violante sat next to him. "You were right, though."

"I usually am."

She laughed and gave him a playful shove. "Braggart."

He laughed too. "Right about what?"

"About me wanting to stay because I want to see Paul. But that's the second reason. The first one is because I truly believe in your project." She smoothed down her skirt. "Yes, the past haunts me. In a way, seeing Paul will give me closure, or so I hope. I'm not sure about many things. I think I'm lost, too."

He kissed her hand and held it, stopping her from fiddling with her skirt. He was glad she let him do it.

They didn't talk. The only sounds were the dripping of the water and the birds' songs. A gentle breeze caressed her hair, carrying her lily scent to him.

"I think you're helping me find myself again," she whispered, her gaze on her lap.

He took her chin and tilted her head towards him. For years, he'd dreamt about kissing her, but his fantasies couldn't hold up to reality. Because she was sweeter and softer than he could have ever imagined. Her mouth opened when he ran his thumb over her bottom lip. He had no problem admitting that he had a fascination with her lips.

She drew his thumb in her mouth and swirled her tongue over the pad. Not what he expected her to do. He sucked in a breath. A curse died on his lips.

An ache spread throughout his body, focusing on his groin. He leant closer and shared a breath with her before kissing her. The onslaught of emotions was expected. The sheer fear following them wasn't. He feared to do the wrong thing, to drive her away as it'd happened years ago, to be an ass, and to lose her again. He pressed his mouth against hers with desperation.

Please don't leave me.

He stroked her lips with his tongue and slid it past them as she invited him in. A shiver went down his back when she caressed his tongue with hers. She tangled her fingers through his hair and pulled him towards her in a possessive gesture that cracked something within him. The kiss turned furious. He devoured her mouth with long lashes of his tongue and gentle bites on her lips. All his repressed desire came unleashed. This kiss might be their first and last, and he'd create a great memory out of it to sustain him in a future without her in it.

She placed her hands on his neck, urging him closer. He held her by the waist, feeling the enticing curve of her hips. He moved his hand up to cup her breast. The layers of fabric didn't allow him to feel her warmth, but she moaned all the same. They fought for control over the kiss until they stopped, needing to breathe. Her kiss-swollen lips were the same colour as her cheeks.

He touched his forehead to hers. Her chest rose and fell quickly. "That kiss is the best thing that has ever happened to me," he said among pants.

She kissed his lips quickly. "Promise me you'll do it again."

He took one of the saffron roses and slid it in her hair. "Anytime. But not here. I'm sure the count won't appreciate seeing us here kissing."

"Soon." She sounded as desperate as he was.

"Soon."

She caressed his cheek with a tenderness new to him. "Now we have only to find a way out of this maze."

He wasn't sure he wanted to.

KEITH HAD LEFT the maze with Violante reluctantly, and even more reluctantly, he'd entered the manor with her and gone upstairs to the count's study. Apologising was the right thing to do, but he'd be lying if he said he didn't prefer sitting next to the fountain and kissing Violante. He paused about to knock on the count's door.

Violante nudged him with her elbow. "Come on. Don't be shy."

"I'm not shy. I'm pondering what to say. Perhaps I should return later, after I prepare a proper speech."

"Just do it." She knocked quickly and hurried away from the door, leaving him alone. She paused to wink at him and wave.

He feigned outrage. "I can't believe—"

The door was flung open, and the count came into view. "Ashford." He regarded Keith with solemn eyes. "I trust you're calmer now."

"I am, my lord. May I have a word, please?"

The count held the door open. "Be my guest." He shut the door behind them.

"I wanted to apologise for my behaviour." Keith paced to the window overlooking the maze that held one of the best memories of his life. "Being rude was inexcusable."

The count bowed his head. "I'd say unnecessary."

That was another word. "Sir Nigel and I have disagreed in the past. This wasn't the first time he'd expressed his opinion on my humble origins. I lost my temper. I'm sorry to have upset you and the countess."

"I confess I don't know much about you. I know your queen awarded you a title and that you were involved in foiling a terrorist attack, but I don't know much else." There was no reproach in the count's voice, only curiosity.

"My mother was a laundress at the late Sir Howard's service. She died during a bombing by the Fenians in London." Keith had never told his story to the count because he hated using his mother's death to draw compassion to himself. But he needed to make himself clear.

The count's stance slackened. "I'm sorry to hear that."

"My lord." He hesitated. A movement in the garden caught his attention. Mrs. Collins and Murray were talking with Nigel. Whatever they discussed, the conversation was brief. Mrs. Collins and Murray walked towards the manor, while Nigel strode towards the maze, glancing around as if checking if someone followed him. He disappeared after a turn.

Keith returned his attention to the count. "I believe my centre for the street children will improve lives. The Fenians often recruit desperate ones, taking advantage of their need for money. I have my first centre to prove the next one will be successful. Your building in St. Giles is strategically placed to attract the youth of the rookery in Seven Dials, one of the most problematic areas of London. Helping them is my only goal."

The count dropped himself onto the chair. "It's not that I don't approve of your idea. I think we should leave these sorts of social experiments to experts because when men like you, who have nothing but good intentions, meddle with complicated social problems, the result is oftentimes unexpected. Even dangerous."

"I work with people who have more experience than I do. I don't take the matter lightly."

The count straightened a few pencils on his desk. "The person who died in Rome was my brother."

"I'm sorry for your loss."

"He, too, believed his project was effective and had only good intentions. Despite my trying to persuade him to be careful, he kept going. When he realised the boys he'd rescued were rebelling against him, it was too late." The count sighed. "I'm not sure I share your enthusiasm for such an enterprise. I think only physicians and law enforcers should do that job."

"Do you think Sir Nigel's project is better? A luxurious hotel? He plans to force out the modest residents of that area to *clean* it, as he said. How is that better?" He couldn't completely remove the frustration from his voice.

The count pressed two fingers to his temples. "I need to think, Ashford."

"My lord—"

"I admire your passion, but I don't want to be the cause of another death. If I support you, and then someone dies, it'll be on my conscience. You must understand my position."

No, he didn't. The choice should be obvious. He was about to protest when the butler entered.

"Apologies, my lord," Fletcher said, "but there's an urgent message for Lord Ashford." He handed an envelope to Keith.

He forgot about the conversation with the count. The message was from Mrs. Beresford. She'd found a promising lead—nothing more specific—and wanted his permission to spend a good chunk of the money he'd given her for the research expenses. Of course he'd let her.

He bowed to the count. "Thank you for your time, my lord." He turned to the butler. "May I have a horse ready? I need to go to the village."

twenty

VIOLANTE HADN'T RIDDEN in years, but the moment she jumped on the saddle, her training came back to her. Keith scowled as they went at a well-paced canter up the hideous road to the village. It was better to ride a horse than take the carriage.

"What's this mysterious message you must send with all urgency?" she asked.

She'd caught a glimpse of the message he'd received earlier after he'd told her he needed to go to town. She'd insisted on going with him, and he'd relented. Although she'd done more than take a glimpse at the message. While he'd changed into his riding habit, she'd read it out of curiosity. But she hadn't understood it. Something about some money and expense claims.

"I can't tell you," he said without looking at her.

"Nonsense." She trotted closer to him. "Who's Mrs. Beresford?" She couldn't completely remove the annoyance from her voice.

He whipped his head towards her. "How do you know that name?"

"I read the message, and I apologise but...is she your mistress?

You can tell me." She closed her hands around the reins. "I knew you hid a mistress from me. A widow, I guess."

He showed a charming, lopsided smile that made her tingle. How silly of her. He shouldn't smile in that fashion. That wasn't the reaction she expected. "Are you jealous?"

"Well, you're my husband."

"Husband of inconvenience."

"Indeed."

"So you *are* jealous." Too much amusement rang in his voice.

"I simply don't like being lied to, as does everyone. You were quite convincing when you proclaimed yourself to be celibate. What if the count learns you have a mistress? You're being unfaithful to me. Your reputation will be ruined." Yes, she was jealous.

"I was convincing because I told the truth." He wasn't amused now.

"Then who is this woman?"

"Vi—"

"No, really." She pointed a finger at him. "We're here under false pretences. We're partners in crime, and we must be honest with each other. I need to know what you're doing and what secret you're hiding. We've already made a faux pas with the count. I'd like to avoid another one."

He stared at her with awe. How odd. "Mrs. Beresford has nothing to do with the count. I swear it."

"Who is she?" If Keith's secret was so innocent, why didn't he want to tell her? She didn't have faith in people's compassion. If the count discovered she and Keith lied to him, and that Keith had a secret mistress, he would kick them out.

He sighed. "I didn't want to tell you until I was sure, but I hired a couple of private detectives, Mr. and Mrs. Beresford, to search for your mother."

"What?" The air was punched out of her lungs. She nearly slipped off the saddle.

"I didn't want to give you false hope before they investigated."

"Why would you search for her?" She pulled the reins to stop the horse. She wanted to focus on him.

"Because it matters to you." His eyebrows knit together. "The fact you didn't have the opportunity to talk to your mother before she disappeared hurt you deeply, and if there's something I can do to alleviate your pain, I'll do it."

She drew in another breath, but it seemed her lungs didn't work properly as she realised something utterly astonishing; something she should have understood earlier—he loved her. He truly did. He hadn't told her that, but it was clear now. She hadn't asked him to find her mother. Dash it, she hadn't even thought about asking him. But he did it before she knew it was what she needed. He anticipated her needs. If that wasn't love, she wouldn't know what it was.

"Violante." He reached out and touched her cheek. "I'm sorry. I should have told you first. But I had no idea if Mr. and Mrs. Beresford would find anything. I didn't want to cause you more pain."

His love overwhelmed her. In a good way, but still, she couldn't deny the storm of emotions in her chest. After having fended for herself for years, after having been lonely and not taken care of, he gave her everything she needed and more. A tear slid down her cheek.

He caught it before it wet her chest. Concern furrowed his brow. "I'll ask them to stop the search if that's what you want. Don't worry. Besides, I don't know what they found. Mrs. Beresford merely asked permission to spend some of the expense the money I gave her. That's all."

She threw herself at him, which wasn't the most brilliant thing she'd ever done. Her horse got startled by the sudden move, the jump was awkward, and she hurt herself in the process, hitting her knee against the pommel of the saddle. Not to mention she risked falling on her face on the dirt road.

Keith caught her by the waist as she bent forwards between the two horses, but her horse decided he'd had enough of these crazy humans and trotted a few yards away. Served them right.

Violante's stomach dipped as saddle and horse disappeared from underneath her bottom.

"Bloody hell." Keith kept holding her, stopping her from falling and keeping her safe. As usual. He climbed down of his horse and put her down on the ground. "Are you all right?"

A bit sore, especially her ego. "Thank you." She wrapped her arms around his neck and hugged him tightly. "Thank you, Keith."

He hugged her back. "Anything for you."

If she had any doubts about his love for her, they were good and gone.

"But you have to consider Mr. and Mrs. Beresford might not have found anything." He put his hands on her shoulders. "Their search could bring nothing."

"I don't care. It's what you did that matters."

The lines on his forehead vanished as he smiled. "Let's hope what they found is important, and that—"

She cut him off with a kiss. A savage kiss. She'd never kissed anyone so aggressively. But he matched her wild passion, kissing her deeply. His tongue thrust inside her mouth and danced with hers. She returned the favour, exploring his mouth. Their teeth clashed. Their lips pressed hard against each other, and she was wheezing, but the desire igniting her blood didn't want to settle.

They broke the kiss together, panting. More than a kiss, it'd been a fight.

He stroked her cheek. "You're the most important thing in my life. No, let me express myself better. *Be with me always—take any form—drive me mad! I cannot live without my life. I cannot live without my soul.*"

Wuthering Heights. No, she wouldn't cry. Crying would ruin this moment.

She cupped his face. "Thank you for your kindness and care." She couldn't express her feelings better, but she'd find a way to.

"Let's go." He helped her to her horse, his smile radiant.

They rode the rest of the cursed road at a good pace, smiling at each other as if they were on Windy Ridge again. At the post office, she couldn't remain still. Now that she knew what his wire was for, she couldn't wait for Mr. and Mrs. Beresford's reply. She hadn't realised how important seeing her mother again was until now. She owed that to Keith. She owed him many things.

"When are they going to answer?" she asked once they left the post office.

"It might take a day or two."

She clung to his arm like a vine. "Imagine if they find her. I wonder—"

Her happiness died a swift death at the sight of a familiar, bald, and broad man walking down the cobbled street. His large figure was at odds with the fairy-tale-like beauty of the narrow road. What was George the Blade doing in this godforsaken town?

"What is it?" Keith asked.

She ushered him to a dark corner. "Over there."

He followed her gaze and grunted. "Is he the thug who attacked us in that alleyway?"

"George the Blade," she whispered. George entered a public house and disappeared from view. "What is he doing here?"

Keith led her towards the horses. "I think a more pertinent question is, is he looking for you?"

Violante trembled by the time she and Keith arrived at the manor. She was so shocked she hadn't spoken during the ride.

Too many strong emotions had overwhelmed her and tested her heart that day. Seeing George in the village reminded her of where she had come from and where she might end up if she wasn't careful. The flowers for the celebration had arrived, judging by the pretty, colourful floral decorations all around the yard. A cascade of geraniums and orchids stood out. Tulips adorned the front door, but they couldn't brighten her mood.

"You took only a ring from George the Blade, right?" Keith helped her off her horse in the manor's front yard.

"Yes. I don't have it anymore." She removed her gloves, walking towards the front door. "I can't believe he chased me here for the darn ring. There must be another reason. Or maybe he doesn't know I'm here."

Goodness, with George here, she risked more than the wrath of an outraged count for having lied. She risked prison or worse.

"Do you think his presence here is a mere coincidence?" He clicked his tongue. "I doubt it. If he wants money, we'll give it to him."

"I don't want you to pay him." She put a hand on his arm. "It's not fair. You shouldn't be involved."

He narrowed his gaze at her. "Just this once, let me deal with the situation. If he wants money, I'll pay him, and that will be the end of it."

She stepped into the entry hall, handing her coat to a passing servant.

Other servants were around, including Fletcher and Murray, so she waited for them to leave before talking again. "What if he doesn't want money but something else?" she whispered.

"Like what?"

"To kill me?"

Keith lowered his eyebrows in a deadly expression. "I'd like to see him try."

"I wouldn't." She let out a nervous chuckle.

"Lord and Lady Ashford." Lady Diana came towards them. "What do you think of the flowers?"

"Beautiful," Violante said.

"My cook is baking the braided bread. If you stand near this hallway and breathe in, you'll catch a whiff." Lady Diana inhaled deeply. "Isn't the smell delicious?"

"Yes." Goodness. Violante was being rude.

The countess's smile dropped, likely because Violante didn't show much enthusiasm. "Anyway. Mr. Wellington arrived half an hour ago. He's having tea with my husband in the sitting room."

Oh, dear. Violante tottered on her feet. Now Paul? . What next? Had all the planets aligned against her?

"Are you all right?" Lady Diana touched Violante's elbow.

"Yes." She massaged her forehead. "The ride tired me a little."

Keith coiled an arm around her waist.

"A cup of tea then," Lady Diana said. "Isn't that what the English drink whenever something happens?"

Violante would need gallons of tea after today. If the count learnt she was a former thief from George, he'd call the police, and she'd rather not have another brush with the coppers. She neared the sitting room on unsteady legs at Keith's arm. The reaction was silly of her, but after all that had happened, she was too shaken for more surprises.

Lady Diana brushed past her and spread her arms, showing off her tight gown that enhanced her curves. "Here we are."

The chatter paused as Violante and Keith entered the sitting room. Paul turned around to face them.

Seeing Paul after all those years sent a shock of stillness through Violante. He was more handsome than she remembered, but his blue eyes held their old wariness and nervous glint. The last time she'd seen him, he'd been stuffing his pockets with her father's money and the family's jewels. Anger burned the back of her throat as if the robbery had happened a moment ago. She thought about Keith and his love for her to help her calm down. His love was more important than anything else. She could face anything as long as he stood by her side. Her control was a way to repay him for everything he'd done for her.

Paul had smiled at the countess but became serious when he saw Violante.

"Ashford!" Paul's cheerful expression returned briefly and he shook Keith's hand. "Good to see you. I didn't know you were married." A strained note intruded into his words.

"It happened recently. Paul, this is Lady Ashford, my wife." Keith raised his eyebrows. His voice dropped an octave.

Paul gave him the slightest nod. "Lady Ashford." He kissed her shaky hand. "It's a pleasure to meet you."

She swallowed past the lump in her throat. She could only manage, "Thank you."

Sir Nigel studied them from a corner of the room. She'd never met him when she lived at Sharpe Manor, but he might know Paul. But even if he did, it didn't matter. Paul's past wasn't a secret. At least not all of it.

Paul stepped back from her and started to chat with the count about travelling from New York City, ignoring her, which she appreciated. She had to take a few deep breaths to stop the tremor from going through her. A part of her was eager to confront Paul. Another part didn't wish to talk to him at all.

Keith touched her hand briefly. "Are you all right?"

"I'm fine."

She jolted when the butler announced the dinner would be served in an hour. Violante had barely time to go upstairs and change. This time, she asked for Mrs. Collins's help to speed things up.

Mrs. Collins tugged Violante's dress up her body with a brusque gesture as Violante stood behind the screen.

"Careful," she said. "The fabric might rip."

"Well, you're rich enough to buy another one." Mrs. Collins made short work of buttoning the dress. "Unless the money is fake as everything else."

Violante didn't care about being addressed as Lady Ashford or about the curtsies, but Mrs. Collins crossed the line. "You should mind your tone."

"Or what? You're forcing me to lie."

"You accepted Lord Ashford's money for that."

Mrs. Collins finished buttoning the dress, scoffing. Then she left without a curtsy.

Violante partly understood Mrs. Collins. She'd been asked to lie to an Italian count. Money or not, if the ruse was exposed, she'd be in trouble. Although she could leave whenever she wanted. Keith didn't force her to stay.

He entered the bedroom, wearing a freshly pressed suit. "Is everything all right? I met Mrs. Collins in the hallway, and she looked furious."

"Nothing you need to be concerned with. Instead, did you notice Sir Nigel?" she asked. "He had a strange expression."

He straightened his cravat. "He met Paul years ago at Hampstead, so he might dislike the idea of dining with two former servants. But I agree. Something is going on. The way he stared at you and Paul worries me." His expression softened as he looked at her. "You are lovely as usual."

"You look dashing, too." She rose from the vanity and tugged at the decorative sash around her shoulders.

"Please don't." He moved the sash aside to stroke her naked shoulder, leaving a trail of fire on her skin. "I prefer when you undress yourself."

Her cheeks warmed. "Actually, so do I, when you're around."

"I like that." He kissed the crook of her neck, and she sighed shamelessly.

His lips had cast a spell on her because whenever he kissed her, she wilted and wished for more.

The dinner gong rang out, reminding them they didn't have much time. He held the door open for her.

In the corridor, he leant closer to whisper in her ear, "When we are alone—"

Whatever he meant to say was cut off by Sir Nigel who brushed past them down the stairs. He bumped into her, hitting her back with his elbow, and didn't apologise.

"Ouch." She nearly lost her balance and gripped the bannister not to fall.

"Excuse yourself!" Keith snapped at Sir Nigel, steadying her.

"Is 'bugger off' all right?" Sir Nigel strode towards the dining room.

"Ass," Keith hissed.

"Leave him. Don't fall for his baiting tricks." She hooked her arm through his. "Focus on the count."

twenty-one

VIOLANTE COULDN'T REMAIN still during the dinner, despite the fact the cook had done an excellent job. The braided bread was fragrant and perfectly crunchy. The broad bean stew was spicy and not too salty.

Every time a servant entered the room, she champed at the bit to ask if a wire for Keith had arrived. Paul didn't look at her once, chatting politely with the count and making a point of ignoring her. His accent sounded different. No longer British but had a certain lilt when he dropped his 'r's. Instead, Sir Nigel shot her glares for whatever reason, and the countess was uncharacteristically silent, focused on her meal. She smiled only when the cherry tart with cream was served.

"A toast," the countess said without enthusiasm. "To my husband Giuseppe for this lovely Italian dinner and because today is his name day. A simple dinner to remind us we're all humble human beings. Happy Saint Giuseppe's day."

Everyone raised their glasses, but the guests had to be preoccupied because the toast lacked gaiety. What a pity. Violante had looked forward to celebrating Saint Joseph's Day, but she wasn't in the mood for a party. The fact it was also Father's Day added a hint of sadness to the evening. Her papa would have loved this dinner. He would have laughed and hugged her. Keith was right. She should keep those precious memories away from the darkness.

When the men retired to the smoking room, Keith paused to give her a heated glance, which lifted her spirits. She smiled at him, following Lady Diana to the drawing room.

"You seem quiet, Diana," she asked, sitting down on the sofa.

"A little tired." Small saffron roses with red dots, like the one Keith had given her, adorned Lady Diana's hair.

"Are those roses from the maze? I haven't seen them in other parts of the garden. Their colour is so peculiar. They're surely a special type. I've seen that Sir Nigel had one in his jacket as well." She must have said something wrong because Lady Diana's hand froze with the cup of tea halfway up.

"Yes, I took a stroll in the maze today." The countess sounded defensive. Another fax pas on Violante's part. She must have hit a nerve. Although, the countess owned the grounds and the maze. It was perfectly normal she strolled in it.

Violante hurried to say, "I didn't mean to pry. Keith and I got lost in the maze, and we spotted those beautiful roses by the fountain."

"Yes." Lady Diana put her cup down. "I love them. They're an Italian variety. Venetian Roses, they're called. Did my husband and yours find an agreement?"

Fine. The countess wanted to change the subject.

"Not yet. The count seems interested in supporting Sir Nigel's project." Disappointment crept into her tone.

The countess brightened. "Sir Nigel offered my husband a hefty share of the hotel's profit."

What? It was Violante's turn to remain frozen.

"A quite generous share, I have to say." Lady Diana patted her curls. "The deal will require us to travel to London more often than usual, but it's a small sacrifice. You can't blame my husband for wanting to be part of what promises to be a great enterprise compared to your husband's charity. The hotel is going to make us a fortune."

"But my husband is making an honest effort at improving people's lives while Sir Nigel means to kick people out of their houses to build a luxurious hotel," she said. "Which one of the two projects is more important?"

"There will always be people in need. We can't take care of every poor in the world. We wouldn't make any money, otherwise." The countess laughed.

Yes, there were too many people in need. But men like Keith and the count could help one person at a time. Violante's papa had been a businessman as well, but she'd seen both side of society—the rich one and the poor one. But as someone who had lived on the street, the countess's laugh hurt. Deeply. Poverty was no laughing matter.

She stood up, fighting the urge to talk back, or worse, to burst into tears. "If you'll excuse me. I'm afraid I need to retire. I feel a bit sick all of a sudden."

The countess nodded. "Have a nice cup of tea."

"Good night." She bunched a fistful of her skirts and left of the room.

The count didn't want to do business with bachelors because he valued honesty and commitment, but a charity was disgraceful because it didn't produce money. Now she understood Keith's frustration and doubts.

Mrs. Collins came out of a door. She sighed when she saw Violante and muttered something under her breath.

"My lady," Mrs. Collins said in a tired tone, starting to follow her, but Violante didn't wish to talk to her.

"I'm all right, Collins. Thank you. You may retire."

Mrs. Collins released a breath. If she'd had enough of pretending Violante was a real lady, that made two of them. "Good night."

Violante went up the stairs when Paul's voice reached her ears from the count's study.

He was standing in the doorway. "Goodnight, my lord. Thank you for the meeting."

"Thank you, Wellington. I'm glad we found an agreement on that shipping. I'm sorry our time was cut short, but I must attend to my correspondence."

"I have another project I'd like to discuss with you tomorrow," Pauls said.

"Of course, goodnight." The count closed the door to his study.

She waited for Paul in a dark corner. "Paul," she said quietly when he walked past her.

He came to a quick stop in the middle of the hallway. "Violante," he whispered, gazing around as if they were two conspirators.

She stepped out of the shadows, a little worried by the hostile expression on his face. "We need to talk."

"Not here, for Pete's sake. Someone might see us." He pivoted and marched towards the other side of the hallway.

"Wait." She grabbed his arm and tugged at it until he turned towards her. "I want what you owe me." Short and not so sweet. Straight to the point.

He opened his mouth but closed it as the count opened the door and stepped into the hallway.

The count approached them gingerly and narrowed his gaze over her hand on Paul's arm. "Lady Ashford. Is everything all right?"

"All is well, thank you, my lord." She withdrew her hand. "I was saying goodnight to Mr. Wellington on my way to find my maid when I stumbled and he steadied me."

"I heard voices," the count said.

"I was retiring to my room." Paul offered a shallow bow, already walking away.

"So was I. Goodnight, Mr. Wellington, my lord."

"Goodnight." The count kept frowning.

She hurried to her bedroom and shut the door behind her.

Keith was already there, fastening his nightshirt. "Is something the matter?" he asked before she said anything.

She removed her shoes, being careful because she didn't want to ruin a pair of fine silk slippers. "I couldn't talk with Paul. The count interrupted us."

He sat on the bed. The nightshirt left naked a triangle of golden skin on his chest, and she couldn't stop herself from noticing it.

He followed her with his gaze as she discarded her gloves and removed her earrings.

"I promised you I wouldn't interfere, but I asked him about the money he stole," Keith told her.

She plonked down onto the bed. Her beautiful skirt frothed around her. "Did he answer you?"

"Nigel interrupted us. If Paul refuses to talk to you, I can engage Mr. and Mrs. Beresford's help again and trace your mother's pendant. I mean, the money is gone, but the pendant might still be found. At least you'll have it back."

"You would do that for me?"

He shrugged, and his nightshirt opened on the front, revealing more of his smooth, broad chest. "Of course, I would."

The sadness of the evening evaporated. She put her hand over his. "Thank you. You keep helping me, and I keep being horrible to you."

"Not true." He brushed his knuckles against her cheek with a feather touch.

A flutter started in her stomach, and the instinct to lean against his hand was too hard to resist. He cupped her cheek and caressed its curve with the rough pad of his thumb.

"I wish you only joy. You know that, don't you?" he said, lowering his voice.

She pressed her cheek to his palm. "I do." She had no doubt. In fact, she felt guilty for that infamous day when she'd told him to leave. She wondered if she'd ever stop feeling guilty.

He brushed a curl of hair from her face, his gaze lighting with awe. He didn't need to say anything because his love warmed her chest. But, if she was going to be honest, the tingle in her body demanded more than a simple, warm touch. Much more.

She turned around. "Would you unbutton me, please?"

His sharp intake of air sent another shiver down her back. He trailed his fingers from her cheek to her neck and down to her back. He repeated the caress until a sigh escaped her. Goodness, his touch was heaven and hell rolled up together. Heaven because it felt blissful, and hell because it made her want to do wicked things.

He swept her hair aside, and she closed her eyes for a moment. The room was so quiet only the crackling of the fire in the stove and the loud pounding of her heart filled it. He undid the first buttons slowly as if savouring each moment. As the gown sagged down her body in a swish of silk, he paused to run a finger over her spine. He stopped where her corset started before resuming unbuttoning her. Between her chemise and corset, not much of her skin was exposed, but his heated touch seemed everywhere, reaching parts of her she'd thought dead. He stroked her shoulders, pushing the muslin sleeves of her gown down her arms. Cool air hit her skin when he didn't touch her. When the last button was undone, her bodice gathered to her waist.

"Done. I've done my part," he said in a husky voice.

Oh, she understood what he meant. It was her choice now. She could keep playing this game of longing and touching, or she could hide behind the screen and pretend nothing had happened. She touched the front of her corset, pondering what she had to lose. Not much. Whatever virtue she might have had, according to society, was long gone amidst sleeping under a bridge with other people and stealing a wallet. But that wasn't the only argument in favour of yielding to Keith's passion. She wanted it, too. She wanted him. She wanted everything.

He waited, silent and still behind her. She had the feeling she could sit there forever, and he wouldn't prompt her. He would wait for her. But she didn't want to wait.

With trembling fingers, she undid the first hooks of her corset. The hesitation from a moment ago was gone. The more hooks she unfastened, the more determined she became and the faster she went. He stroked the back of her neck lightly. His warmth reached her skin as the corset dropped to her hips. He pulled it away and tossed it somewhere, leaving her in the flimsy chemise. Her breathing quickened as he lowered the satin straps holding the chemise up and kissed her shoulder. It was a light, almost shy kiss, but it set a fire in her veins. The stubble on his chin scratched her skin in the most delicious fashion. She wondered how it'd feel on her breasts or between her thighs. She couldn't stop a moan.

He moved closer until his chest touched her back. His lips trailed a scorching path along the curve of her neck. He put a hand on her waist, and the heat of his skin reached her through the single layer of fabric separating them. A combination of anticipation and eagerness tormented her as he slipped a hand under her chemise. No barrier now. It was skin against skin. Heat against heat.

He drew small circles on her belly with his thumb while his warm breath feathered her neck. A sweet tension coiled in her stomach and exploded when he inched his hand up. Her nipples tightened painfully, chafed by the chemise. She and Keith both groaned when he cupped her breast and fondled it.

Heavens. The feeling of his thumb stroking her nipple ignited a throb between her thighs. He tweaked and pinched her nipple gently until it hardened and puckered. She arched her back, pushing her breast deeper into his palm. He kept scattering butterfly kisses on her neck and shoulders. She sagged in his arms and wasn't ashamed of that. After all those years of deprivation and hunger, his touch chased away all the horrible memories and triggered another type of hunger.

He slid his other hand under her chemise, tearing a gasp out of her when he cupped her other breast. The calluses on the pads of his fingers only added pleasure to his strokes. He untied her chemise and gave it a quick yank, baring herself to him. The sharp breath he sucked in thrust his chest further towards her back. He watched her from above her shoulder, caressing her breasts with devotion. The longing overwhelmed her. She was one breath away from begging him to do more, anything to stop the ache in her core.

He showed no mercy, tugging, pinching, and rubbing her nipples until she moaned shamelessly, moving her hips back and forth on the bedcover. The ache between her legs was an inferno spreading throughout her body. She had to squeeze her thighs together to ease the throb. But it was no good. Between his soft lips on her neck and his fingers tormenting her nipples, she burned from the inside out.

"I can help with the ache," he whispered, biting the curve of her jaw. Goodness, he knew.

"Please."

He pushed her legs apart with one hand, the other still fondling her breast. She'd seen many a couple having a tumble. There was no privacy among the people who lived on the streets. Sometimes she'd come close to having a tumble herself, but she'd always changed her mind. The fear of catching a disease or being with child had always stopped her. Now she wanted whatever Keith had to offer because she trusted him with her life and vulnerability. She closed her fists when he ran his finger over the slit of her drawers. She had to watch, see what he was doing. As his big fingers brushed her tender flesh, he hissed a breath.

"You're so wet." He pinched her nipple harder, sending a shot of pleasure to her aching nub.

Yes, wetness pooled between her legs, driving her mad with need.

He explored her folds and sank a finger inside her. Her inner muscles reacted, squeezing around the welcome intruder. The ache was no better though. She was going mad with it as it kept growing and burning, and the more it burned, the wetter she became.

"Please." She widened her legs, desperate for more.

He rubbed her nub with his thumb while sliding his finger in and out of her. She wanted to scream. His touch felt so good. It looked so arousing. The more she looked, the more energy built within her. Where would that energy go? How couldn't she burst with it?

She was on the cusp of something monumental. He kept a steady pace, rubbing her and pinching her nipple until the release shuddered through her with shocking power. She cried out, bunching the quilt with her clenching fingers. How could she have imagined something like that? He didn't stop but let her enjoy every ounce of pleasure.

Finally, she understood the reason for the screams, groans, and shouts. She sagged against him, wheezing, as if she had run for miles. She wanted to do it all over again, but at the same time, a sweet exhaustion took over her.

He slowly removed his fingers before holding her. He didn't say anything, just held her and kissed her neck. She had no idea a release could be that good and devastating at the same time. She closed her eyes, panting, happy to be in his arms. He whispered something she didn't catch. She understood only, "You're safe with me."

She couldn't agree more.

twenty-two

KEITH COULDN'T STOP smiling as he woke up with Violante lying next to him.

Last night, she'd fallen asleep in his arms and hadn't woken up when he'd tucked her under the covers. Surely, the tiredness was a good sign, wasn't it?

One hand rested next to her pretty, pouty mouth, and her long eyelashes fanned over her cheeks. Her chest rose and fell slowly. One might say she was ruined now that he'd touched her, but he disagreed. It was he who was ruined. Utterly, completely ruined forever. Because now that he'd touched her and heard her moan, he didn't want to let her go. Ever. She bewitched him, and he was more than happy to be enthralled by her.

He held her closer, inhaling her sweet scent. His shaft twitched, eager for some action since last night, but he shushed it. It wasn't the time. She wasn't experienced. He could tell by the way she'd behaved and by her tightness. She was whole and easily hurt. If she came to him again, he would welcome her, but they would go at her pace.

She fluttered her eyes open, and a flush coloured her cheeks the moment she stared at him. But there was no need to blush, no room for shame.

"Good morning." He sounded husky to his own ears. "Did you sleep well?"

The blush intensified so much even her lips reddened. "I..." She inched the cover up, hiding her face.

He kissed her forehead. "Why are you embarrassed?"

"Because I fell asleep. Because of what happened."

"Do you regret it?" He already eased his hold on her.

"No, no." She put her hand on his cheek. "You were so kind to me, but I didn't think of you. I mean, you didn't enjoy yourself."

"Don't worry about me." He kissed her inner wrist. "I'm happy you liked it."

"So I did," she whispered, caressing his chest. Her lips parted, but she didn't say anything.

"Tell me." Hell, that blush would be the death of him.

She inched his nightshirt aside, and he let her do it. Whatever she had in mind, he'd follow. She explored his chest and abdomen with a focus that made him smile.

"So many muscles." She rubbed his nipple, and his body tensed in a moment. "I like touching you."

Bugger him. He cleared his throat. "I like touching you, too."

"But it's my turn now." She followed the path of her fingers down to his waist.

He found he couldn't breathe properly as she pushed up his nightshirt. She gasped at the sight of him fully erect.

"Er..." He scrubbed the back of his neck, not sure if she was shocked or pleased.

"I felt it last night touching my back."

"Did you—bloody hell!" He suppressed another curse as she closed her curious fingers around him.

Her small hand didn't cover him completely, but she applied the right amount of pressure to his aching flesh. It didn't matter that her movements were tentative. He shivered with pleasure.

She stuck out her tongue as she watched her hand wrap around him. She rubbed the blunt tip with her thumb, and he couldn't keep his hips still.

"It's so thick," she said. "How can it fit?"

"With a little practice," he said among quick pants.

"It hurts, doesn't it?" She worked her hand up and down, exploring and killing him.

"At first it does, but if the partner is careful, the pain is nothing but a sting." Talking was difficult.

"I know you'll be careful." She gave him a delicate squeeze that didn't distract him from what she said. Did she just say she wanted him to take her properly? Because he looked forward to being with her.

The shock confused him for a moment. He stopped her when she sped up, rubbing the tip, and his release threatened to burst faster than he could say *tumble*. He reclined his head, a deep growl leaving him.

"Why did you stop me?" Her hand was still clenched around him.

"Too much."

"It's not a bad thing, is it?" She kissed his neck, and another shot of pleasure rushed through him.

He clenched his fists in a futile attempt to slow down the wave of pleasure about to swallow him. No point. She stroked him again, and he spent in her hand. The release was so intense that it was almost painful. His bollocks hurt with its power, and his brain threatened to burst out of his skull. She stroked him again until he sagged on the pillow, exhausted and full of energy at the same time.

"Did you like it?" She caressed his bollocks lightly.

He jolted. "Bugger me."

She laughed. "I gather you did."

He kissed her lips quickly before leaving the bed. "Let me."

He took a clean cloth and the basin filled with soapy water. He washed her hands while she watched him. She did that a lot.

He cleared his throat. "It was wonderful."

She wrapped her arms around his neck and squeezed the daylights out of him, causing him to spill some water. "I'm so glad. I want to give you the same pleasure you give me. It's the least I can do after everything you did for me."

His smile dropped. He disentangled from her embrace. "What do you mean?"

"You gave me a job, new clothes, and you're looking for my mother. You even gave me so much pleasure. I had to return the favour." Concern tightened her features. "I've seen couples making love. I know men always expect something from the lady. They demand the lady perform as well, or they get angry."

What? The back of his mouth burned with disappointment. "I don't know what type of men you met, but I'm not like that. You don't have to return any favours. I don't want you to touch me because you think I expect that." He must have done something horrible to let her think he demanded to be pleasured by her just because he'd touched her. He put the dirty cloth in a basin. "Did you touch me because you thought you had to? I don't want you to feel forced to do anything to return a favour." He felt sick to his stomach. That she hadn't wanted any of that and had done it only not to anger him made him want to throw up.

"But..." She searched his face with her big eyes.

He walked to the screen and removed his nightshirt. Did she want him at all?

"Keith." She stepped around the screen, invading his space. She glanced at his naked body, her gaze heating. "Either you doubt yourself profoundly or you don't know me." Rising on her toes, she cupped his face and forced him to stare at her. "I didn't mean it in that way. I don't feel forced to do anything. The thought has never crossed my mind, and do you know why?"

He swallowed hard. "Why?"

"Because I know you." She trailed a hand down his neck to his chest, pausing right over his heart. "I know you would never, ever force me. I trust you with my heart and body."

"I don't expect anything, nothing from you." His voice hardened because he hated that she might have thought, even for one second, that he took advantage of her.

"I know. I spoke in a clumsy way. I simply meant that I'm yours if you'll have me, and I'm giving myself to you gladly. Not because I feel forced to do so, but because I want it, and I want you as well. I want to touch—"

He crashed his mouth over hers, overwhelmed with relief. She stretched up on her tiptoes, and he supported her with an arm around her waist. The kiss was once again a savage one, even by his standards, but she matched his passion, battling for control. He groaned when she bit his lips. The more savage she was, the more he burned. He wanted her unrestrained, free, and confident. Goosebumps pebbled his skin as she kissed his neck and chest. She grazed his nipple, and another growl left him.

"I love you." The words came out with yet another growl, and he had no intentions of taking them back. They were true.

She paused kissing him and raised her gaze to his face. "I feel it. I felt it before you said it. That's why I trust you." She caressed his jaw.

"I've loved you for years." He leant against her palm. "Not knowing where you were drove me mad with worry. I met other women, but no one could ever come close to my heart as you did."

Tears glistened in her eyes, but he was having none of that. No tears. Not now. This was a happy moment. He'd finally unburdened himself. She would make whatever she wished with his love.

"Don't cry." He kissed her cheeks. "Don't cry."

They held each other. He gladly took her weight as she sagged against him.

"I love you, too, Keith. I really do." She gave him a wet kiss on his lips.

His pulse raced, and a daft smile stretched his lips. She loved him. Could the world be more perfect?

"Do you know what that means?" She wiped her eyes.

"That we're going to be happy forever?" He caressed her lovely face.

She shook her head. "That I expect a lot of tumbles, kisses, and touches."

He barked out a laugh. He wasn't going to complain.

twenty-three

FOCUSING ON WORKING was a chore for Keith after the happy time he'd spent with Violante. He hadn't kissed her since that morning, but the sweet pressure of her body against him as they'd hugged each other was impressed into his mind and soul. Her words were carved into his memories. Her scent teased his senses. He was aware her presence distracted him from other activities. In fact, the deal with the count had taken second place compared to the urge to be with her.

Sitting in front of the count with Paul, Keith forced himself to stop thinking of her, which somehow made him feel guilty.

"Do you approve of Wellington's idea, Ashford?" the count asked from his stuffed chair.

Paul raised his eyebrows, waiting for Keith's answer.

"I do."

Keith hoped Paul's idea wasn't anything crazy. He was finally alone with the count and Paul without Nigel hovering around. The insufferable man had gone to the village to do something. Good riddance. It was his opportunity to try to secure the future of his project and have an honest conversation with the count.

Paul gave him a sceptical glance. "As I said, I'm setting up a gymnasium and youth centre in New York City as well." He showed a map of New York City to the count. "My idea is to favour cultural exchanges between the United States and Britain. The youth from New York City will travel to London and spend a few months there, and those from the London centre will do the same, if Ashford agrees."

Keith was impressed. "I say. That's a splendid idea." He hadn't imagined Paul might care so much.

Paul flashed a boyish smile that reminded Keith of their happy time in Sharpe Manor before the disaster.

"If you're involved, my lord," Paul said, "we'll add Rome to the list of possible destinations, and of course, I'd like to know if you decide to make a deal with Keith."

Despite his delightful distraction, Keith's chest warmed at the thought of having his project realised. "Imagine what travelling and seeing new places would do to these children."

The count's stubborn frown didn't want to ease. "Travelling is expensive, especially to and from the United States. And then there are the fees for the accommodation for these children. How do you plan to cover these costs?"

"I'll certainly find a way to fund the operation for my charges." Paul turned towards Keith.

"I'll do the same. I like the idea," Keith said. "Also, we can raise more money through charity events."

Paul nodded. "You're welcome to donate if you want to be part of this venture, my lord. It's a noble cause. One that has proven results."

"Such as?" the count asked.

Paul didn't seem bothered by the count's lack of enthusiasm. "Reduced criminality rates in the quarters of New York City where youth centres are operating to start with. These children receive a good education, which translates into better jobs. Thirty per cent of my youngsters aspire to go to a university. It's an impressive figure."

"University paid by the charitable trust, I suppose," the count said.

"Yes, my lord." Again, Paul seemingly failed to catch the sarcasm in the count's voice. "A noble pursuit, as I said."

"Were there any accidents in these youth centres?" The count stapled his fingers on the desk. "Ashford? What about your centre?"

There. Keith shifted his position. He couldn't lie. "Yes, my lord. Thievery is unfortunately common. There have been stabbings and fights, too."

"Mr. Wellington?" The count turned towards Paul.

"A few incidents. They happen only when new children arrive," Paul hurried to say. "Once they understand criminal behaviour won't be tolerated, they change their attitude rather quickly. Besides, what do we expect? We take these children out of desperate situations of crime and violence. Incidents are bound to happen."

"Really?" The count leant back in his chair, stroking his short beard. "Sir Nigel plans to employ only people from the rookery to improve their situations. An honest job will do wonders for those unfortunate people."

"After he forcibly takes their homes," Keith said. "It sounds like blackmail to me."

"An exclusive hotel in that area of St. Giles will never work." Paul jabbed a finger on the desk. "It'll only cause unrest."

"But many people will find a good job," the count said. "Isn't that a better form of help?"

"The education of children is the future," Keith said. "That's how we help them. That's how we build a better society."

The count remained silent for a long moment. When he spoke, he faced Paul. "Wellington, would you mind if I have a word with Ashford in private?"

Paul scraped his chair back. "Not at all." He exchanged a glance with Keith before leaving the room.

The moment the door was shut, the count edged closer to Keith. "Do you trust Mr. Wellington?"

"I do." The real answer was more complicated than that, but he didn't want to explain to the count all the intricacies of his relationship with Paul. Besides, he trusted Paul with the management of the centre.

"Hmm." The count drummed his fingers on the polished desk. "You don't have any qualms about involving him in a project as expensive and delicate as yours, do you? Trusting him with the lives of young people?"

Keith was confused. "None, my lord." Was the count searching for faults? First, he'd complained about the incidents that might happen. Now, Paul wasn't trustworthy. What was the count's point?

The count pushed aside the documents Paul had shown him. "Ashford, I like your enthusiasm and practicality."

"Thank you. But?"

"Please indulge me." The count exhaled. "I'd like you to have an honest conversation with your friend and discuss the project and his commitment to it in depth. Then we'll talk again."

"I will. Although I like Paul's idea."

"Talk to him. I'm talking to you not as a probable investor but as a friend."

"I will talk to him." Keith gathered the documents in the folder, puzzled about the conversation.

Paul would be involved, yes, and Keith trusted him with the project. Why was the count doubtful? Anyway, he would do as told and talk with Paul.

He paused along the hallway to watch out of the window. Violante promenaded in the manicured garden. Her colourful parasol gleamed in the sunlight as she twirled it. The weight on his chest lifted. Just watching her smile in the sunshine made him feel better. From his elevated position, he also had a good view of the blasted maze. It wasn't complicated at all once he studied its pattern from above. And to think it'd taken him a long time to find the exit.

Another parasol seemingly floated along one of the aisles between the hedgerows. It had to belong to Lady Diana. She seemed to pace back and forth on one spot though. Surely, she couldn't be lost. She should know the maze better than her house.

Nigel hurried inside the maze. He was supposed to be in the village.

Keith checked his watch. No, Nigel couldn't have gone to the village and returned here in fifteen minutes. Besides, he'd said he'd return in the late afternoon. Keith lost sight of him, and even the parasol vanished.

"Keith." Paul hurried towards him, breaking Keith's musing. "How did it go?"

"I'm not sure." He glanced one last time at the maze. Even Violante was nowhere to be seen. "Follow me." He led Paul to his bedroom and shut the door. He dropped the folders on the escritoire. "First, I find your idea of our cooperation brilliant. But the count is worried about your commitment to the project. Did you say anything to him that might have caused these doubts?"

"No. I barely talked to the man." Paul scoffed. "I'm fully committed. I already have a few American investors ready to help me. All facts and figures are recorded in my documents. I showed everything to him. I don't know what more I could do."

Keith shoved his hands in his pockets. "I don't think the count is going to sell to me or even be part of our project. He brings up one problem after another. He prefers Nigel's idea."

"He wants to make a profit. That's understandable. Although I'm disappointed. He claims to have strong principles, after all, and there's no need to evict anyone."

Keith rubbed the spot between his eyebrows. "Maybe we should leave it and find something else."

"And let Sir Nigel kick out honest people from their houses to build his hotel? He'll cause a riot, and riots attract the Fenians' attention."

"Good point."

"I need to think of another strategy. Maybe I can show more data to the count," Paul said.

Keith caught another glimpse of Violante in the garden, and his heart gave a kick. There she was. "There's something else I need to tell you."

Paul nodded. "Your new wife."

No, Keith wouldn't correct Paul and confess his marriage to Violante was fake. "Please give Violante what she wants."

"If she wants to be compensated, then yes. But her mother's pendant is gone. I can't help her, and to be honest, I'm not eager to."

"Why? These years have been harsh for her."

"They have been harsh on everyone. She isn't the only one who suffered."

"Why are you so unfair to her?"

Paul turned serious. "She didn't believe me when I told her about the Fenians. Her precious papa couldn't possibly be at fault."

"She was in shock," Keith said. "What was she supposed to do? And you were robbing her father's safe."

Paul pressed two fingers to his temples. "I panicked, all right? I was worried the police would arrest my mother and me. We had nothing. No money, no home, and no job. If we'd stayed, between the police accusing us of anarchism and the people hating us for having worked for Mr. Sharpe, we'd be starving in some rookery."

"That's exactly what happened to Violante." Keith arched his brow. "Have some compassion, mate."

Paul exhaled. "Fine."

"Thank you."

"You're welcome." Paul paused before leaving. "Talk to the count again if you can, please."

Keith exited the bedroom and headed towards the garden. He needed Violante now. When he arrived at the garden, she wasn't on the path where he'd spotted her earlier. He peered at the entrance of the maze, and there she was, twirling her parasol and gazing around.

He strode towards her, already feeling his chest lighter. She turned around and laughed upon seeing him, but the closer he came, the more she stepped back.

He paused. She paused.

A game. He was all for it. He ran towards her. She giggled and darted along the aisle. The gravel crunched under his shoes as he chased her in full pursuit. Her fluttery pink skirt gave her away, and he spotted her when she rounded a corner. The fluffy flounces of her petticoats created a hide-and-seek game with her lovely legs he fully appreciated. He sped up, glad he'd trained every day for the past years. Because he didn't want to lose this game.

She let out a squeal when he nearly caught her. He coiled an arm around her waist and pulled her closer, somehow avoiding the parasol.

"You ran from me," he said, breathing her scent.

"I thought you would enjoy the challenge." She closed the parasol and kissed him.

All the tension of the day disappeared. He lost himself in the sweetness of her demanding lips. Her breasts pressed against his chest as she deepened the kiss, darting her little tongue out. She was growing bolder, and he loved it. He thrust his tongue inside her velvety mouth and forgot about the world and its problems.

"I missed you," she whispered.

"So did I."

He took her hand and led her to the spectacular orangery rising from a corner. The large windows showed glimpses of orange and lemon trees, but the thick brick walls made the structure look like a cottage. Bougainville, palm trees, and other

Mediterranean plants competed for space among pools of water and marble benches. The scent of orange blossom filled the air.

"It's stunning," Violante said, admiring the luscious plants.

He led her to the end of the orangery where a storeroom would provide more privacy.

He kissed her again once he locked the door and they were out of sight. Not the most romantic of places, even though the storeroom was cosy and pretty, but he wasn't in a romantic mood now. He unfastened her dress with impatient fingers. So many damn layers. The hooks of the corset opposed some resistance, but he conquered them until only her chemise covered her beautiful breasts.

"You're quite eager—" The rest of her sentence turned into a moan when he pulled down the neckline of her chemise and closed his mouth around her nipple.

He tongued her nipples until they were two hard peaks and she writhed against his mouth. She whispered something he was too busy to understand. The skirts proved to be equally uncooperative when he shoved them away to reach her core. Hellfire. She was wet and dripping. Ready for him. But he'd rather cut his own bollocks than take her in a garden shed like an animal in heat. He ignored the throb in his shaft and sank two fingers inside her. Hot velvet. She was very tight. Sucking her nipple deeper into his mouth, he added a third finger and stretched her more. She gripped his shoulders almost painfully, squeezing her thighs together.

"Please," she begged, watching him.

He rubbed her with his thumb and kept tonguing her breast until her inner muscles milked his fingers and she moaned in pleasure. Her release transformed her face, reddening her lips and making her eyes shine with violet sparks. She was a goddess, and he was her devout worshipper.

"You're so beautiful." He kissed her, rubbing her.

She was so responsive that he wasn't surprised when she grew wet again. He worked slowly and drew lazy circles while sucking her nipple.

"Heaven, Keith." She breathed faster.

Her gaze never left his mouth on her breast. He rolled her nipple between his lips while stroking her more deeply. She bit into his shoulder, muffling her next scream of ecstasy. Spasms of her inner muscles gripped his fingers as she found her release. There was no greater pleasure than making her scream.

She sagged against him, her lips reddened. "Goodness."

He kissed the top of her head. "All for you, and no, I don't want you to return the favour."

She smiled. "You're wonderful."

Another moan came, but it wasn't from Violante. He stopped kissing her. A feminine moan came, followed by a masculine grunt. He quickly buttoned Violante up, reminding himself that she was officially his wife, so her honour was intact; but another man wouldn't see her like that, half-naked and glowing after the release.

"Who is it?" she whispered, finishing buttoning her dress.

"Let's give them privacy, whoever they are. They have my sympathy." He surely wouldn't find it interesting to see the count and the countess being intimate.

He opened the door a crack and froze. Hidden between two bushy trees were the countess and Nigel. They'd progressed well beyond what Keith had done to Violante. Lady Diana's legs were wrapped around Nigel's waist as he pounded inside her relentlessly.

Keith and Violante couldn't walk out of the storeroom without being seen. Besides, the front door of the orangery had to be locked. Great. They were stuck in their hiding place. He withdrew into the shadows, hiding Violante, but a slice of the two lovers remained visible through the slit between two wooden boards.

The tumble would be over soon anyway. Lady Diana and

Nigel couldn't go on at that frenzied rhythm for much longer. It wasn't humanly possible.

Nigel pounded with too much energy. Surely, he would soon be exhausted...any moment now. A matter of minutes. No. The two lovers changed positions and started all over again.

"Is it normal?" Violante asked, her lips close to his ear. "I mean, they're very energetic."

Keith muttered a curse under his breath. Nigel and the countess changed positions again. He took her from behind, practically holding her up with the sheer strength of his arms. That warranted some respect.

Violante tugged at his sleeve. "Can we do the same thing?" she whispered.

He nearly choked, forcing down his laugh. He nodded. "Any time."

When Nigel finally pulled away from Lady Diana, Keith sighed in relief. The two lovers whispered to each other and exchanged a few heated kisses before they adjusted their clothes and walked away.

Keith exhaled. "Bugger me," he said once the lovers were out of earshot.

"So much for the count and his high standards. His wife is unfaithful to him literally under his nose, and he doesn't even notice." Violante clicked her tongue. "Now I understand why the countess is eager to support Sir Nigel's project."

"Is she?" He checked the aisle was clear before coming out of the storeroom. Holding her hand, he walked along the aisle.

"She told me that once the hotel is open, she'd need to spend more time in London since she and her husband would be Sir Nigel's partners. Obviously, she's happy she's going to meet her lover more often. Also, now I get why she sounded annoyed when I noticed the roses in her hair. They came from the maze, and Sir Nigel had one too. I bet they got the roses the last time they were together here."

"Sooner or later, the count will find out about their tryst. Maybe they wish to get caught. I don't envy the poor sod." He pulled the front door, but it didn't budge. "Damn. They locked it."

Violante sidestepped him. "Watch me work." She took a couple of hairpins from her chignon and slid them into the lock. "Not to brag, but I'm quite good at this." Two twists, and the door opened. "Voila!"

"You're amazing." He smacked a noisy kiss on her cheek before hurrying out of the orangery.

Violante stopped walking. "If the count learns about his wife's tryst now, he'll never sign the deal with Sir Nigel." She wiggled her eyebrows.

"Yes, but..." He massaged his temple. "It's a vile move."

"The count's marriage will be destroyed." She kicked a stone. "But she and Sir Nigel are betraying the count. He should be told."

"We don't know what will happen." He laced his fingers through hers. "The countess and Nigel might end their affair soon anyway. Many of these trysts don't last. I want the count to accept my deal for the right reasons, not because he wants revenge on Nigel. That would be a very poor way to start a strong, promising partnership."

A solemn expression tightened her face. "You're a decent man, Keith, and I love you."

His chest heaved with a rush of happiness. He'd never tire of hearing those words from her. As she laughed, he lifted her by the waist and twirled her around. No matter what happened, he wanted her in his life.

twenty-four

THE ATMOSPHERE AT dinner wasn't the most cheerful. Not that Keith cared. He'd stored enough personal happiness in his heart to last for a whole year. After the last meeting with the count and Keith's conversation with Paul, the count barely talked, Paul sulked, and Lady Diana did her level best to avoid glancing at Nigel, who didn't engage in conversations with anyone. But Keith was happy to steal touches with Violante under the table.

After dinner, Violante retired to their bedroom, followed by a forlorn Mrs. Collins while he had to endure a nightcap and a cheroot in the drawing room with the gentlemen. Nigel excused himself rather quickly while Paul and the count rehashed their conversation about charity versus social order. They would never agree, and Keith was tired of hearing them talk. He went up the stairs and tiptoed into his bedroom. He shut the door gingerly. Violante should be asleep now.

The oil lamp on the nightstand still glowed though. He undressed as quietly as he could and put his folded clothes on the chair for Murray to take care of the next day.

After putting on his nightshirt, he slid under the covers, glad the bedsheets smelled like her. There was a rustle of sheets, and Violante turned towards him.

"Did I wake you up?" he asked.

"I was waiting for you, actually." She snuggled closer, her soft, warm body touching his. "Keith..."

"Yes?" he prompted when she didn't say anything else.

She whispered something so low he didn't catch it.

"What did you say?" He took her chin. In the golden glow of the lonely lamp, her hair ignited with a riot of colours.

Her large eyes fixed on him, and her lips parted.

"What is it?" He stroked her chin with his thumb. "You can tell me anything. If something bothers you, please tell me. Is it because of what we did in the maze?" Perhaps he'd been too savage.

"No." She put a hand on his chest. "It was perfect."

"Good. What then?" A hint of worry crept into his heart.

She propped herself up on one elbow but stared at the pillow. "Will you touch me now?"

He thought she wanted to sleep. Now, that was a nice surprise.

She must have misinterpreted his silence because she waved. "Never mind. It was bold of me to ask."

He took her wrist before she turned around and collected his thoughts because he wanted to be absolutely clear. "There's nothing I want more than to touch you. I couldn't think properly today because you were the only thing I could think about."

The tip of her pink tongue darted out to run over her bottom lip. "Can we light a few more lamps?"

"You want more light?" That was a first.

She hesitated again before speaking. "I like to see and watch."

Hellfire. A shot of sensation burned him. His shaft strained painfully, hard and ready in a moment. It was the first time he'd heard such a request, and it was more arousing than he expected. She wasn't so shy then.

He shoved the covers aside, making a mess in his haste to do her bidding. Matches. Where were the matches? He'd seen some earlier. Why hadn't he paid attention to something as important as the matches? He opened the drawer. Nothing. Where, where, where? The mantelpiece! He held the matches as if he'd found the Holy Grail. He burned his fingers when he lit two more oil lamps, three candles, and two gas lamps. Warm light spread through the bedroom.

"Good enough?"

She was bathed in the orange glow from the lamps. "Yes."

That 'yes' would make him climax where he stood. "And now what?"

She sat up, letting the cover slide down her body. "Come here," she whispered.

He obeyed her and waited for her next command. "What do you want me to do?"

She gave a little shrug. "Anything you want."

"Oh, fire of hell." He ran a hand through his hair. "You can't say things like that. You have no idea."

She pouted, and he had to restrain himself from grabbing her.

"I mean, it could be risky." Because he might be too wild for her.

"But I trust you."

What had he said earlier about never having heard anything more arousing than her request to turn on the lights? He'd been wrong. Her trust was the most arousing thing ever. "You must tell me if you don't enjoy something."

She nodded eagerly.

"No, I need to hear you."

"Yes, I promise I'll tell you if I'm not comfortable."

"Good." He kissed her cheek, and she giggled, the most beautiful sound in the world.

He didn't know where to start. Or rather, he knew what he wanted to do but didn't want to scare her, or worse, hurt her. He bunched up the skirt of her nightgown inch by inch, revealing her lovely legs. Her skin was silk under his fingers. He could spend the whole night simply tracing every curve on her legs, from her slender ankles to her velvety thighs.

She reclined on the pillow, following his moves with hungry eyes. He paused when he pulled the fabric up to her waist. The scent of her arousal damped the air. Every instinct inside him urged him to bury himself in her and pound hard until both of them cried out in pleasure. But her trust was too precious. He parted her legs to reveal her most intimate part. Her breathing sped up. He pushed her legs wider until he could nestle between them. Oh, he wanted to watch as well. Thank goodness for the light.

He'd take his fill of her, and she was a sight to behold. All glistening pink. He ran a finger over her wetness. Her hips jolted, but she kept her gaze on what he was doing. She did enjoy watching.

He rubbed her until her chest rose and fell quickly. When he was satisfied she enjoyed it, he dipped his head and kissed her. She cried out in surprise. The first lash of his tongue over her slit made her jolt again. He dug deeper, tasting her spicy flavour. She moaned and writhed against his lips, closing her fists, but she never looked away. He devoured her, and the more he lapped at her, the more his erection hardened. To relieve his ache, he rolled his hips while she whispered his name among pants. He added two fingers and growled deep in his throat at her firm inner muscles gripping him. So tight and slick.

He sucked and tongued her while stroking her deeply until quick spasms pulsated against his lips and she let out a scream. Her release triggered his. He couldn't stop it. The shot of pleasure was quick but intense. He waited for her to stop moving before slipping his fingers out and lifting his head. He wasn't ready for her devastating beauty.

Her violet eyes were two large beacons. Her cheeks and lips were reddened the same colour as her wet folds. She glowed from the inside out. He had to see the whole of her now. He yanked her nightgown down, maybe with too much energy. Her taut nipples flushed the same pink. He pinched one and sucked the other as if his life depended on it. Little moans filled his ears. She tangled her fingers through his hair as he drew her nipple into his mouth. Her legs wrapped around him, and the temptation to drive himself forth was a constant hammering in his brain. He reached out between them and stroked her again, finding her soaked and ready. Her second release caused her to shudder.

He didn't stop touching her until she sagged on the bed. Lifting his head from her breasts was harder than he anticipated, but it was worth it to stare at her satisfied beauty.

Their breaths mingled as they stared at each other, aware of the threshold they'd crossed. How could he live without her? He ought to say something, but every word he could think of sounded wrong or inadequate. He didn't know how to express his feelings at that moment. Even saying he loved her wasn't enough.

She caressed his cheek, and he discovered right then and there he starved for her touch and closeness. He hugged her as he'd done last night. If he couldn't find the words to express himself, he would let his body talk. She clung to him with desperation as if worried someone might rip her out of his embrace.

"Take me, Keith, please," she whispered in his ear. Her hips rubbed against him. "Please."

He pulled his nightshirt over his head and held her, enjoying the contact with her soft skin. But she was an impatient one. Her legs wrapped around him like a vine as she lifted her hip to meet his hard shaft.

"Please, Keith."

"I don't have a sheath."

She caressed his cheek. "I'm sure you know what to do. I trust you."

Her words were going to kill him. He propped himself up on his elbows and shifted his hips forwards. They both gasped when his tip slid an inch inside her.

"Painful?" He remained still.

"No. Keep going." She dipped her gaze down.

For some reason, her obsession with watching was the most erotic thing that had ever happened to him. He gently pushed on, closing his eyes when her slick velvet closed around him. A loud sigh came from her.

"This is so good." She arched her back, and her taut nipples were too inviting.

He tongued them both before resuming sliding inside her. Inch by inch, pausing to kiss her lovely nipples, he sheathed himself fully. Perfection. She gripped him like a tight fist. A release built up from his groin even though he wasn't moving.

When he started to thrust in and out of her, the pleasure blinded him. They found a rhythm, not too fast to hurt her but not too slow to be frustrating. She met his thrusts, and he pushed deeper. Her gaze was glued to their joined bodies.

"Please look at me," he said among hard breaths. "I need to see your eyes."

She obliged, and he got lost in the depths of her eyes. They never failed to shake him.

"Faster, please," she said.

They stared at each other as he shoved back and forth faster. Their breaths and heat mingled. He was sure their souls did, too. She didn't close her eyes or avert her gaze when the release caught her. Judging by the delicious flush creeping up her face, the release had to be spectacular. He felt it in the way her body quivered and her muscles tightened around him. He followed her, but pulled himself out and spent on her belly. Not the safest practice, but he hadn't thought about bringing a sheath.

He touched her forehead with his. "Violante."

She hugged him. "It was wonderful."

Still breathing hard, he wiped her belly and between her legs with clean cloths. He had barely time to finish before she sat up.

"Can we try that position from behind as the countess and Sir Nigel did?" she asked as if inquiring about the weather.

He laughed. "I'd love to, but I need a moment to recover."

"Really?" She flipped to her belly and rose on all fours, offering him a spectacular view of her supple behind.

He caressed the smooth globes and ran a finger down to her slit. Immediate hardness.

"Am I all right like that?" She winked. Oh, she knew.

"You're teasing me." He stroked her gently.

She moaned. "Is it working?"

He positioned himself behind her and grabbed her hips. "You'll be the judge."

He buried himself to the hilt with one single thrust. Heaven.

"This is even better." She rocked her hips, taking him deeper.

It was. Holding her hips, he moved back and forth, careful to watch her reaction. Her back arched as he sped up. The new release hit them at the same time. He managed to pull out by sheer self-discipline. A curse escaped him. He collapsed next to her and gathered her in his arms, unable to utter a word.

She snuggled against him, her skin almost feverish. "Fantastic."

"Yes." He panted.

"The only problem is that I can't see what you're doing in that position."

He burst out laughing.

twenty-five

"YOU SEEM DISTRACTED," the countess said as she and Violante took a walk through the garden the next morning with the countess's lady's maid.

Yes, Violante was very distracted. Her body tingled with the memory of what Keith had done to her and with the sensation of him inside her. Her plan had backfired. Sort of. When she'd asked him to do whatever he wanted to her, she'd meant it with her whole heart, and no, she didn't regret anything. Quite the opposite. She hadn't expected *that*. She hadn't expected him kissing and tonguing her between her thighs—that had been delightfully shocking—she hadn't expected to feel even more pleasure than the first time, and certainly, she hadn't expected the tender, all-consuming feelings burning in her chest after their tumble.

The need to touch him, be with him, and feel his warmth bordered on pain. She'd never experienced anything close to this maddening urge, and she hadn't planned to feel that way; it was scary. If she was going to be honest, last night she'd only wanted to enjoy herself. But something had changed between them. He'd kissed her with too much devotion, and she'd shared her very soul with him. His touch had been too deep and caring. His gaze had been too adoring. No, whatever had happened between them last night wasn't simply fun. Yes, she'd told him she loved him, and she meant every word. But now, her feelings were deeper than that.

She tilted her parasol to shield her eyes from a fierce ray of sunlight. "I apologise. I had a not-so-restful night." Not entirely true.

She'd slept more than well in Keith's protective arms, but the need to have more tumbles troubled her. Was she too wanton? Was her desire normal?

"Looks as if our husbands are talking about the deal?" The countess glanced at the gazebo where Keith and the count were talking about their business.

"This deal is very important for my husband. Personal, I'd dare to say. I still believe that a youth centre is more important than yet another hotel." She hadn't talked with the countess since their last conversation, but she hadn't changed her mind.

The countess lifted a shoulder, causing the white lace of her neckline to flutter. "It's always personal with men."

They strolled towards the hedge maze. What the point was of a labyrinth made of bushes, she couldn't understand.

She caught a glimpse of a man with a fluttering dark coat. "A man is over there behind that bush. It looks like he's hiding."

Sir Nigel perhaps, waiting for his lover.

The countess twirled her parasol. "The gardener. Heaven knows if this place needs constant trimming and pruning. Endless care and attention."

"Yes, I'm sure it must be an exhausting job."

The countess arched her dark eyebrows. "If you'll excuse me. I need to talk with the gardener."

"By all means."

Oh, the countess and Sir Nigel were going to use their mouths but not to talk. It was a miracle the count hadn't discovered them yet.

After the countess left in a hurry, Violante huffed. The situation was an injustice. She couldn't care less about what the countess did or didn't do in her private life. But the countess could enjoy her tryst, being unfaithful to her husband, while Keith's noble project was snubbed. Keith was more honourable than she was. Violante might have used what they'd discovered to influence the count's decision. Although they didn't have any evidence of the countess's tryst. If the count didn't believe them, they would make the bad situation worse.

She resumed walking alone when Paul came out of a path in the garden. It was her chance to talk to him again. He tensed when she walked over to him.

"Paul."

He seemed about to bolt away but exhaled and waited for her.

"Lady Ashford." His tone didn't lack kindness.

"Thank you for stopping to talk to me," she said to start the conversation well, just in case her temper ruined it.

"You're welcome." He darted his gaze around, like a thief.

"As I told you, I want back what is mine." She went straight to the point.

"I understand your wish. Truly, I do." He produced a cheque-book and a pen from the inner pocket of his jacket. He scribbled on a page and handed it to her. "Here. With interest."

She didn't take it. "What about the pendant?"

"The pendant isn't in my possession." He remained deadpan.

She expected that, but surely something could be done. A precious pendant like that must have been bought by someone with money or left at a pawnshop. There were chances to track it. "I want to trace it. Did you sell it?"

"No." He stared at the ground. "My mother forbade me from selling it. In fact, she didn't know I took your money until we were out of London. Anyway, we didn't sell the pendant."

Good. There was hope. "What did you do with it then?"

"I gave it to your mother."

Had the ground quaked? Because Violante felt as if she were falling. "What? Where? When?"

"I met her in New York City last year." He placed the cheque into her hands. "She was in terrible shape, I have to tell you."

She stared at the cheque. Her thoughts were scattered. "What else did she tell you? Why did she leave?"

He shook his head. "This is a conversation you must have with her. Besides, she didn't tell me much, just that the Fenians were after her."

She gasped. "Do you know where my mother is now? Is she alive?"

"No, I don't know where she is. I offered her my help, but she refused it. After I gave her the pendant and some money, she left." He touched his hat in a manner of greeting and went to leave.

"Paul." She took his arm. "Tell me. Please."

His expression softened. "I really don't know. It was a brief encounter. My mother was worried the Fenians might attack us after we'd talked to her. That's all I know. I swear."

She swallowed past the swell in her throat. "Thank you."

He gave her a bow before striding away. She stood in the middle of the path, holding the cheque.

"Are you lost, Lady Ashford?" The count seemingly appeared out of nowhere.

She stuffed the cheque in her pocket but not quickly enough for the count not to see it. "I don't think so."

He craned his neck towards Paul then watched her closely. "Sometimes we are lost without realising it. May I escort you to the manor? Your husband retired to his room to take care of his correspondence." He offered her his arm, and she accepted it although she wasn't sure what he implied with his tone."

After they stepped into the entry hall, he watched her as she ran up the stairs to her bedroom. His gaze followed her until she reached the landing. Odd.

Once in her bedroom, she paced, holding the cheque. Two

thousand pounds. She'd spent the past five years dreaming about that money and being angry with Paul. Now that she had the money, she didn't know what to do with it. In fact, she didn't want it. Keith was everything she needed. A laugh escaped her. Yes, Keith was everything, and not because he was rich. He could be penniless, and she'd still love him and spend the rest of her life with him. Well, now she knew what she had to do.

She left her bedroom and knocked on Paul's door. When she didn't receive an answer, she inched the door open. "Paul? It's me."

He came out of the screen, shirtless and towelling himself dry. "Is something the matter? The cheque is good. I promise."

"I'm sure it is." She put the cheque on the escritoire. "I changed my mind about the money. I don't want it."

He wrapped the towel around the back of his neck. "Give it to charity then. I don't want it either."

She was about to lecture him that he ought to take it, but he was right. The money could be used for charity. It'd be the best end to her five years of desiring it.

She took the cheque back. "For once, we agree."

He burst out laughing. "Truce?" He stretched out his arm.

She shook his hand. "Truce."

"I am truly sorry for how we parted."

"So am I."

"By the way, congratulations. Keith is a good man. He'll make you happy."

"He will." She exited the room to bump into the count again. Was he following her?

"Lady Ashford." He peeked inside the bedroom where Paul was still shirtless, and his features tightened. "You didn't stay in your bedroom."

"Er...no, I didn't." Obviously. Good gracious. She strode past him to go to her bedroom.

He went after her. The cheek of him. "What were you doing in Mr. Wellington's bedroom?" He sounded like a jealous husband.

"I don't think it concerns you," she said, confused by the whole situation.

The way his face contorted in shock, surprise, or anger puzzled her. Why did he care about what she did?

"I demand to know why you weren't in your room." His tone was firm.

She was taken aback. "I beg your pardon. I don't have to inform you of my movements. Not even my husband demands to know what I did or didn't do. I don't believe I owe you an explanation."

"Your husband might be negligent, but I want to know what you were doing in Mr Wellington's room right this instant." His voice rose.

"*Lasciami in pace*," she said in Italian. *Leave me alone.* She spun and marched to her bedroom before he could say anything.

The moment she shut the door behind her, a crushing wave of regret weighed on her chest. She should have answered, made up a story. She'd been rather rude to the count, not addressing him with the Italian '*thou*.' When Keith had lost his temper, she'd scolded him, but she'd done the same thing. She hadn't helped Keith's cause in the least. Quite the opposite. Curse her stupid mouth.

She plonked down onto the bed. If the deal with the count was lost, it'd be because of her temper.

KEITH BRACED himself for bad news. The count had summoned him to his study in all urgency, thundering and shaking, and judging by his scowl, he didn't have good news to share. He had no idea what had happened or where Violante was. Keith had seen her talking to Paul, and he'd left them some privacy.

"Is something the matter?" Keith asked, closing the door to the count's study.

"Yes," the count snapped. He shoved his chair back and sat down. "I'm afraid I can't do business with you."

Keith sucked in a deep breath. He'd suspected that much, but to hear it in such an angry tone hurt him. "Why?"

The count pointed a finger in the direction of Keith's bedroom. "Your wife is having a tryst with your associate. Wellington isn't your friend, and I don't want to risk my reputation and money in a business that might prove to be a huge moral mistake. I trust you, Ashford, although I have no respect for a man who doesn't understand his wife is being unfaithful to him. I don't trust Wellington. He might stab you in the back at any moment, and I won't get involved in this sordid affair of assignations and trysts."

Of all the reasons the count could have picked for not making the deal, that one was the wrong one. No respect for a man who didn't understand his wife was betraying him? He was one to talk.

Keith bit down the comment. "What sordid affair? I promise you that Paul and my wife are not lovers."

"Twice, I caught them alone in an intimate conversation. There was an exchange of money as well. I saw it with my own eyes. She was in his bedroom while he stood there half naked."

Keith released a breath that sounded like a hiss. "They've known each other since childhood and have personal problems they need to discuss, but they are *not* lovers."

The count shook his head. "I'm sorry, but I don't like this degrading situation. Your project is a good one, Ashford. Your company isn't."

"This is unfair."

"Your wife betrays you right under your nose with your friend. If you can't detect that, what else are you going to miss? Also, your wife behaved rather rudely to me." The count huffed with all the outrage of a wronged aristocrat. "I caught her *in flagrante delicto*, and she had the audacity to tell me that her business didn't concern me. Put a leash on her, for heaven's sake. Do your job as a husband and control her. If you can't control your wife, how can you control your company?"

"What?" Keith leant back in shock. "I won't allow you to disparage my wife in my presence. My wife isn't having any affairs, and if she was rude to you, she must have had a bloody good reason. I approve of everything she does. I'd rather cut my left bollock than put a *leash* on her."

The count lifted his chin. "Your wife is a disgraceful harlot who makes fun of you."

Keith slapped the count's cheek with the back of his hand. "I demand satisfaction."

The count's nostrils flared. His hair was dishevelled by the slap. "Very well."

"Choose your weapon."

"The sword. Sir Nigel will be my second."

"Wellington will be mine." He turned around and strode to the door but paused. "When I win, I'll expect an apology."

"When you lose, I'll demand one."

twenty-six

"KEITH, YOU CAN'T be serious." Violante had to speed up to match Keith's long strides. She and Keith crossed the yard to the field where the duel between Keith and the count would begin.

A duel. To defend her honour. How ridiculous. There hadn't been a duel in England in a century or more. She wasn't sure if the duel was the most romantic thing a man had ever done for her, or the most stupid. Likely the latter.

"I am very serious." Keith's voice sounded like steel against steel. He wielded his sword and swished it across the air. "The count is a pompous, hypocritical braggart. He insulted you and humiliated me. Someone ought to teach him a lesson."

"Please." She blocked his path and put her hands on his chest. "This is madness. You're going to get hurt."

Keith narrowed his eyes. "Trust me, I won't. I can handle myself in a fight, and we aren't fighting to death. The winner is the first one who draws blood." He swished the blade again. "And it'll be me."

"But...but..." She followed him. A duel was never a good idea.

"We should leave this cursed manor and forget about the whole affair."

"He insulted you. I can't allow it."

"Why don't you tell the count about his wife's affair?"

"Because I won't lower to that level. I am a true gentleman." He sidestepped her and resumed his march towards Paul waiting for him in the field.

Oh, bother. She stopped at the edge of the field, her heartbeat quickening. The count and Sir Nigel stood on the other side. Mrs. Collins and Murray were present as well, along with the entire household. Paul talked with Keith in hushed tones, shaking his head. If he tried to change Keith's mind, she doubted he'd have any luck. A few more words were exchanged among the four of them, but between her anxiety and the distance, she couldn't hear anything. Keith stepped into the middle of the field. The count copied him as the two attendants, Sir Nigel and Paul, walked towards the edge.

"Bloody ridiculous," Paul said, standing next to her.

"I agree." She wrung her hands. "Is Keith good with a sword?"

"Haven't the foggiest, but the count chose the weapon. He must be knowledgeable."

"Can Keith get seriously hurt?"

Paul lifted a shoulder. "Let's say that when two angry men, whose brains have gone on a holiday, brandish very sharp blades to hurt each other, things can become really serious."

Oh, goodness. Violante shifted her weight from one foot to another. What could she do?

The count and Keith bowed to each other. That was likely their last polite act before the bloodshed. The blades caught the sunlight as they flourished them. She winced when the two swords collided with a clicking metallic noise. She didn't understand anything about sword fighting, but the count and Keith seemed well matched. At least Keith hadn't died immediately.

Keith hammered his sword against the count's defence with so much strength the count's feet left deep marks on the ground as he defended himself. A shout rose from Keith as the count flourished his wrist and slashed Keith's arm, ripping the sleeve of his shirt.

"Keith." Violante gripped Paul's arm. "Make them stop."

"I tried," Paul said.

She might faint. "Is there any blood?"

Paul craned his neck. "I don't think so. Otherwise, they would stop."

The duel would go on then.

"Stop!" The countess rushed past Violante in a flutter of green fabric and loose hair. "Giuseppe, stop this instant." She bravely threw herself between the two duellists, oblivious to the blades slashing around. Quite impressive.

"What is the meaning of this?" the countess demanded in an authoritarian voice Violante hadn't heard from her.

Keith took a step back from her, his eyes wild. "Your husband accused my wife"—he beat a fist to his chest at the word 'wife'— "of being unfaithful to me with Paul. He called her a harlot."

"Blimey." Paul whistled. "I didn't know that."

She huffed. "As if I'd ever choose you to be my lover and be unfaithful to Keith."

"What is that supposed to mean?" Paul asked.

She ignored him.

The count paced, trying to sidestep his wife. "He and his wife aren't trustworthy. I don't want to have anything to do with their lot. He's an idiot for not realising his wife is an adulteress."

"Stop saying that," Keith roared.

The count tried to lunge, but Lady Diana grabbed his arm and blocked him again. Honestly, the woman was brave. Violante had to give her that.

"You stupid fool." Lady Diana put her hands on her husband's chest. "I am having an affair, too."

Even though Violante was aware of the lady's tryst, she couldn't help but gasp in surprise at the sudden confession. Sir

Nigel turned the colour of turnips. Paul cursed, and the count remained petrified. Murmurs spread through the servants.

The countess brushed back her hair from her face. "I've been meaning to tell you for a while."

"With whom?" the count asked in a shaking voice.

"Who cares?" Keith said. "Let's fight."

Lady Diana straightened, ignoring Keith. "It doesn't matter."

"With whom?" the count asked again.

They switched to Italian in a rapid exchange Violante could barely follow. Her Italian was a tad rusty, and their accent was strong.

"What are they saying?" Paul asked.

"I think he insists on knowing who her lover is. She accuses him of having neglected her and of being a hypocrite. I agree with her about the last one."

Keith threw a hand up as wife and husband argued with loud tones and hand gestures, talking over each other. Sir Nigel cradled his chin, eyeing the main gate as if pondering making a dash for it.

Then the word "Nigel" came out loud and clear from the countess. After that, silence dropped heavily. The count turned towards the man in question and screamed an Italian obscenity at Sir Nigel who didn't need any translation.

He legged it, unashamedly so. Violante couldn't blame him. The count looked completely unhinged with his swinging sword and red face, chasing Sir Nigel while shouting bloody murder. The countess went after them. Keith followed. The situation would be laughable if not for the count's absolute seriousness.

Paul clicked his tongue. "You know, in Italy, crimes of passion aren't prosecuted. If the count kills Sir Nigel, he won't be imprisoned."

"In Italy maybe, but the count is on British soil, and his denizen status won't save him."

"You're probably right. I guess I have to help Keith and stop the madness." He rushed after the quartet.

She followed at a slower pace, not sure she had the same courage as the countess. The count's blade seemed like a living thing with a mind of its own, and Violante didn't trust the count while he was in that deranged state.

By the time she arrived at the other side of the field, Paul and Keith had tackled the count and blocked him. The swords lay on the ground. Sir Nigel shivered and was deadly pale, but not a trace of blood strained his tailored suit.

"Calm down," Keith said.

"You can't kill Sir Nigel," Paul said.

The count shrugged himself free of Keith and Paul. His hair, wild and dishevelled, added a touch of savagery to his figure. "Lady Ashford," he barked. "Come here."

Violante stiffened, not having expected to be summoned. "What do you want?" Surely, manners didn't matter now.

"Did you have an affair with Wellington?" the count asked.

" No." She tilted her chin up. "If you really want to know the truth, Paul stole from my father some money and my mother's pendant, and I wanted to be compensated until I changed my mind. The cheque you saw contained repayment of the sum Paul had stolen."

The count's face kept reddening. "Is it true, Wellington?"

Paul muttered a curse, shooting her a glare. "It's true. It's a long story but true. And Violante would be the last woman I would ever have an affair with."

"Excuse me?" Keith said.

"Oh, shush, darling." Violante waved a hand.

"Traitors and thieves." The count surveyed the small group of astonished people like a ship captain who was facing mutiny. His gaze stopped on Sir Nigel. "You worm. Forget our deal. Ashford is going to get it."

Sir Nigel's face regained colour.

The count pointed a finger at him. "Ashford was brave enough to challenge me to a duel to protect his wife's honour. You didn't have the courage to face me or to protect Diana's honour. You ran away when your name came out. You have no honour or respect. I can't do business with you."

Violante shuffled her feet and exchanged a glance with Keith. The news was so stunning she couldn't celebrate. Besides, the way the count had decided had nothing to do with his approval of Keith's idea.

"I can't believe you agreed to make a deal with these criminals," Sir Nigel said, shaking with anger.

"Criminals?" The count scoffed. "Don't throw accusations around. You aren't in the position to."

"Not accusations, but facts." Sir Nigel waved at someone at the gate, and a tall man stepped inside.

Violante's stomach lurched. Keith tensed. It was George the Blade.

"Who's this man?" the count asked. "What's happening?"

"Violante isn't Keith's wife," Sir Nigel said in a smug tone. "Their servants told me. There was never any marriage."

"Don't drag us into this chaos," Mrs. Collins said.

"We have nothing to do with anyone here," Murray said.

Keith hissed. The count rubbed his forehead. Violante exhaled. Paul looked confused. The countess stared at Violante.

"But there's more. The fake marriage is but the beginning." Sir Nigel beckoned George closer. "This is George, an associate of mine—"

"Associate?" Violante recovered from the shock. "He's a mobster. My lord, George is the head of the rookery's mob."

"I'm confused." The count drooped his shoulders.

George removed his flat hat and pointed a meaty finger at her. "That woman is Fleet-foot Vi, a thief and a fraud. She got her nickname because she's the fastest thief in the rookery. She stole my wife's ring, and I can claim she isn't married to that man. She comes from the gutter. She's nothing but a thief. She and her fake husband are deceiving you."

"Is that true?" the count asked no one in particular.

Violante took a tentative step towards the count. "The situation is complicated, but if you give me the chance to explain it to you, everything will be clear."

"Is it true that you and Lord Ashford aren't married?" the count asked.

"Well, yes," Violante said at the same time as Keith said, "It's as if we were though."

"They live in sin, so they do, my lord," Mrs. Collins said.

"We had to call this woman my lady," Murray added.

Everyone started talking together. Paul asked Violante and Keith why they'd deceived everyone. Violante begged the count to listen. George threatened to kill her.

"Enough!" The count raised his voice, shaking a fist in the air. "I don't want to hear anything. I've had enough. No more deals with anyone. You can all go to hell and rot." He crossed the field with long, angry strides.

Somehow, Violante believed they all deserved his scorn.

"You are not leaving." Lady Diana stopped her husband, and surprisingly, he didn't protest. "We must get to the bottom of this story."

He huffed as if he didn't care one way or another.

"Nigel," the countess said, "how do you know George? Is he a criminal?"

Sir Nigel showed a fleeting smile. "Darling—"

"How dare you call my wife darling?" In a surprisingly quick recovery, the count snatched his sword from the ground and aimed it at Sir Nigel.

Violante exhaled. What a drama.

"Answer the question." With quick footwork and astonishing precision, the count forced Sir Nigel against the wall surrounding the estate. "Is your associate, George, a criminal?"

One thing had to be said about Sir Nigel. While he might be clever, he didn't shine for his courage. Faced with a sharp blade, he sweated and paled. "Lord Bassini-Verdelli, you're losing the focus of the conversation. It's Keith and Violante—"

The count pressed the tip of the blade against Sir Nigel's throat. A single drop of blood trickled down Sir Nigel's neck.

"Oh no." Violante covered her eyes for a moment.

"Yes, yes." Sir Nigel held up his hands. "George is a mobster. I called him here to discredit Violante."

"Idiot," George hissed.

"What kind of business do you do with him?" the count pressed on.

"Don't say a word, you bloody coward." George slid a hand inside his jacket.

"Money lending." Sir Nigel stared at the blade at his neck. "Usury."

The countess gasped. "Shame on you."

George unsheathed a gun and pointed it at the count. "Drop that sword, and I—"

The rest of his demands was cut off by Keith. He tackled George to the ground and wrestled with him. Violante cried out in surprise. The countess shouted as well. Chaos ensued again. Sir Nigel took advantage of it to flee. He must have beaten a world record because he dashed to the front gate faster than Violante could blink.

A loud smack rose as Keith hit George's head hard. Then the thug remained still on the ground with his arms spread wide as if about to hug someone.

"Are you hurt?" Violante ran to Keith and helped him up. A cut in his arm bled.

"Just a scratch." He stashed the gun in his trousers. "Nigel escaped."

"Good riddance," the countess said as the count said, "I'll send for the police." They both strode towards the manor, still arguing about their marital problems.

"And you two"—Keith pointed at Mrs. Collins and Murray—"are sacked. Pack up your things and leave."

They had the audacity to grumble before striding towards the manor.

"Let's make sure George doesn't go anywhere." Paul used his leather belt to tie George's wrists. "What a mess. It was like watching one of those plays full of melodrama."

Violante hugged Keith and kissed him. "But with a happy ending."

twenty-seven

KEITH WINCED AS Violante cleaned the wound on his arm with carbolic acid. The liquid smelled bitter and stung worse, but the cut wasn't deep. He wasn't sure how he'd injured himself, but in the bloody chaos that had ensued after the duel, he'd understood very little of what had been going on. His only solace was that George had been taken away by the police, and the count had withdrawn his accusations against Violante and offered her an apology. Ha! Who was the fool now?

He suppressed a shout as Violante applied more disinfectant to the wound. "You were right. I made a mistake. I shouldn't have challenged the count."

"Actually, I think it's better this way." She put a bandage around his arm. She was so close he could see the tips of her eyelashes overlapping. "The count knows about his wife's betrayal and that Sir Nigel can't be trusted. The truth is out. Sir Nigel's plan backfired horribly for him, but it benefitted us."

"The count knows we aren't married." He caressed her cheek.

"Yes, well, we've always known the risks of our ruse, and in a way, I think we deserve the count's wrath although I'm responsible for that. You were right about not wanting to deceive him. We lied to him for our own gain. Also, I'm sorry for the countess. I could have never imagined that Sir Nigel was a shark. She hasn't stopped crying since the incident."

"But we don't have to lie anymore." He took her chin and stared into her magnificent violet eyes.

"I'm looking forward to leaving this place and starting afresh. But I'm sorry for your project."

He'd think about his failure later, but at that moment, he was eager to discuss something else. "Will you marry me? For real? No more lies and ruses. Just you and me. No marriage of inconvenience, only a long, happy life."

She laughed and threw her arms around him. "Oh, goodness, yes. We could go away right now and buy a special license."

He kissed her lips, sharing her laughter. "Absolutely not. No shortcuts. I want a full wedding with the flowers, guests, food, and wine. I want to do things properly now."

She sat on his lap. "Then we're engaged to be married, and I'll soon be Mrs. Keith Ryan."

"Lady Violante Ryan, Viscountess Ashford." He kissed her again, deeply this time, pouring all his passion into the kiss.

She scattered kisses on his neck, and the absurd tension of the day lifted from his chest just like that. "We should pack. The count is going to throw us out if we stay here." She caressed his hair. "Are you disappointed about the deal?"

He held her closer, taking the opportunity to slide a hand under her skirts and stroke her lovely legs. "Yes and no. As you said, I deserve the count's scorn. I shouldn't have lied to him. I missed the opportunity to help many children and those people who might lose their homes. That bothers me the most. But he's proven to be a fool, and I'm still upset about the way he treated you."

"I don't care about the count or his moral standards. Besides, he's suffering ten times over about his disastrous marriage. He's hurt. I'd rather leave as soon as possible."

"Your wish is my command."

As they finished getting ready and packing their belongings, Keith couldn't keep his hands off her. He slipped his hands under her skirts or shirt whenever she was distracted. Yes, leaving was the best idea, so he would be alone with her.

"Keith, stop it." She laughed, swatting his hand away from her firm breast.

"Hey, I nearly died today to defend you." He put his hand on her breast and fondled it.

"The decision to challenge the count was all yours." Yet, she didn't remove his hand.

"I think I deserve a proper tumble after today." He pinched her nipple through the shirt, and she laughed.

The knock on the door tore a curse out of him. He reluctantly let Violante's enticing breast go. "Come in."

Paul inched the door open. "I'm sorry to interrupt." He was wearing his travelling coat and hat. "I'm leaving, and I wanted to apologise to Violante." He removed his hat. "Thank you for forgiving me."

She frowned. "Who said I forgive you?" Her tone was light though.

Paul grinned. "I'll make amends by helping Keith with his project as much as I can."

"Fair enough. You're forgiven."

They carried the bags downstairs. The house was eerily quiet. Not a sound came from the garden either.

"Where's everyone?" Violante whispered.

"Why are you whispering?" Paul asked.

She ignored him. "We should say our goodbyes to the count."

"Not bloody likely." Keith dropped his bag in the hallway. "He behaved beastly to you."

"Let's be civil. Come on." Violante took his hand, and together with Paul, they searched the house until they found the count in a small, quiet parlour.

He was sitting on the sofa with a glass of whiskey in his hand.

Dark circles bruised his eyes. Grass stains dotted his white shirt, and mud caked his boots. He looked ten years older.

"We're leaving," Keith said, already moving towards the door. "Goodbye."

"Keith." Violante held him back. "We're sorry to part like this."

"No, we aren't," Keith added.

"Shush." Violante waved a hand. "Because, despite everything, we respect you."

"No, we don't," Keith said.

She shot him a scorching glare. "Keith."

"My lord," Paul said when the count didn't acknowledge them. "We're leaving unless you need help from us."

Keith coiled an arm around Violante's waist.

The count dipped his gaze to Keith's arm around Violante. "You can stop the pretence."

Keith pulled Violante closer. "My marriage with this extraordinary lady might be a sham, but my love for her isn't. We're going to get married. In fact, we're engaged to be married." He couldn't stop a smile. "This trip here has been a curse and a blessing for us. I lost a deal and the opportunity to do good for the youth of Seven Dials because I lied, but I gained the love of my life."

"Well said." Paul nodded. "Can we go now?"

"I love you too, Keith." She smiled at him, and for a moment, they were alone, holding each other and staring into each other's eyes.

"Well." Keith itched to throw back in the count's face the speech about a man who couldn't detect his wife's infidelity, but Violante wouldn't approve. So he simply said, "I hope you find peace." He glanced at Violante for her approval. She gave him a slight bow of her head.

"Leave, leave." The count waved them away. "That's how I'll find peace."

The butler rushed into the room without knocking. "I'm sorry to trouble you, my lord, but there are a few people who wish to speak with Lord and Lady Ashford urgently." He dabbed his glistening forehead with a handkerchief. "They're quite insistent."

The count polished off his glass with one tilt of his head. "What is it now? Another fraud? Bank robbery? Murder? I'm almost curious."

The butler didn't have time to answer. Hurried footsteps echoed from the corridor.

Keith hitched a breath as Mr. and Mrs. Beresford strode inside. Their travelling cloaks were dirty with mud, and their faces were ashen. Surely, the damn trip down the steep road was the cause of their distress.

"Who the hell are you?" the count asked.

"Mr. and Mrs. Beresford, private detectives," the two private detectives said together.

"Goodness." Violante clamped a hand on her mouth. "What happened?"

"Private detectives?" The count refilled his glass.

Keith almost pitied him.

"Lord Ashford." Mrs. Beresford curtsied to everyone. "We found her."

"Found who?" the count said as Violante gripped Keith's arm painfully. "I don't understand what's going on."

"Please do come in, madam." Mr. Beresford stuck his head into the corridor. "Everything is all right."

"No, it's not!" The count thumped a fist against the armrest. "I'm far from all right, and you're upsetting me."

"Oh, shut up," Keith said. "Not everything is about you."

That shocked the count into a frozen silence.

A woman who looked exactly like Violante stepped into the room with uncertain steps. Aside from a few grey strands of hair and wrinkles around her blue eyes, she was identical.

"Violante," she said in a broken voice, shivering from head to toe.

A swell of emotion tightened in Keith's throat.

"Mother."

For a moment, no one moved or spoke. Violante and her mother stared at each other.

Keith touched Violante's hand encouragingly. The moment wasn't the quiet reunion he'd dreamt of for her, but her mother was there, alive and well. She hugged her mother fiercely. They both cried, and even Keith couldn't remain composed. They talked and cried together, laughing and sobbing.

The count sighed, rubbing his forehead. "What is this?"

"One of the best moments of my life," Keith said, happy and proud to have given such a gift to the woman he loved.

STILL IN THE blasted count's manor, Violante was sitting on the bed next to her mother. She couldn't believe her mother was really in front of her. Even though she hadn't seen her in years, she would recognise her immediately. Staring at her was like seeing her reflection in the mirror. Violante had taken her violet eyes after her father, but her features were all from her mother's.

"I didn't mean to leave you." Violante's mother wiped her tears, holding her daughter. "It was your father. I hated what he was doing with the Fenians and begged him to stop. Then one night..."

Violante squeezed her hand. "Take your time."

"One night, the Fenians took me away from Sharpe Manor. They forced me to write a goodbye message. Then I was tied, blindfolded, and drugged. When I woke up, I was on a farm on a remote island. I didn't know where."

At that point, nothing about Papa should hurt Violante, but the fact he'd ordered the Fenians to kidnap Mama caused her chest to tighten with pain and anger. She guessed the positive note was that Papa hadn't killed Mama.

"It took me years to escape," Mama said. "I arrived in New York City where I met Paul one year ago." She showed her the heart-shaped pendant. "He told me what had happened to your father, and after that, I return to England and did my best to search for you. I was so happy when Mr. and Mrs. Beresford found me."

"I'm so sorry, Mama. After you vanished, I thought you left with a lover. Papa..." Talking about Papa wasn't easy, not even when she talked with her mother. Violante couldn't go on. "He hurt me so deeply."

Mama patted her shoulder. "I'm to blame too."

"No, you understood who he was."

"No, darling." Mama stiffened. "For a while, I shared his ideas. The way he was treated by everyone after he returned from the war made me angry. The government didn't help him. We had to build our life back only with our work and sacrifices. I shared his resentment. When he joined the Fenians, I thought he was doing the right thing."

Violante listened in silence, but she couldn't help feeling a hint of disappointment at her mother's confession.

"At first, the Fenians didn't plan on doing anything violent. Their meetings were about organising protests, strikes, and signing petitions. But the constant rejections from the government and beatings from the police changed the mood of the group quickly. When your father started to put his military training into practice, I was concerned. Then the Fenians started to talk about bombs and revenge. Your father and I had furious fights. I tried to persuade him to leave the Fenians, but he was too convinced he was on the right path. I threatened to take you, leave him, and go to the police. You know what happened next. On the island, I was constantly watched and guarded. Not that I could go anywhere. They didn't mistreat me, but I was eager to know what was happening to you. They didn't let me read the newspapers either. I was in complete darkness until I escaped."

Violante hugged her. "You were so brave."

"We're together at last, and I'm glad you found a decent gentleman who's very much in love with you."

Violante laughed, showing her the violet ring. "We're engaged."

"About that." Mama unlatched her heart-shape pendant; its aquamarine stone shone brightly like a good omen. "This belonged to your *nonna*, Grandmother Maria. She would be happy to know you wear it."

Violante put it around her neck. The two stones, the violet gem on her ring and the aquamarine on the pendant, went well together despite being completely different, as her love for her papa and her shame for his actions were. Perhaps she shouldn't try to reconcile the two parts and just accept them for what they were.

epilogue
One year later

ONLY A FEW days were left before Keith would finally marry Violante. He'd wanted a proper and traditional one-year engagement, so the long wait was his fault, really. The past weeks had been a blur of activity but hadn't flown as quickly as he would have liked. Never mind. His waiting was nearly over. He'd waited one bloody year to marry her, but it'd been his making. He wanted a proper wedding with the banns, invitations, guests, and a ridiculously fancy banquet, and he'd bloody have it.

Sitting at his desk, he sorted out all the letters and calling cards from people who requested his presence and that of his fiancée. After a year from the bizarre events in Bakewell—the rumours about a duel, the arrest of Sir Nigel Glenister, and the capture of a dangerous mobster—people still wanted to hear the story from Violante and him. Not that he minded. Besides, all the questions and invitations were an opportunity to promote his youth centre. Any publicity was good publicity. Especially after the fiasco with the count. Keith hadn't found a suitable place for a new centre in St. Giles yet, but at least the count hadn't sold the building to anyone and no one had been evicted.

"Are you busy?" Violante inched the door open and stuck her head inside.

"Never for you." He opened his arms, and she ran to sit on his lap. She fit perfectly in his embrace. He kissed her cheek, neck, and lips.

She giggled. "Wait, we need to talk."

"About what?" He kissed her neck again, right where her vein kicked.

"I'd like to invite the boys from your centre to our wedding reception."

He paused kissing her. "You're the most brilliant woman I've ever met."

She blushed. "Actually, my mother suggested it. I told her she should rest more and not spend all her time at the centre, but she enjoys it."

"I'll be forever in her debt, especially since she brought you into this world."

She cupped his cheek. "That's so nice of you."

"I don't want to be nice. I want to be wild in bed with you." He was about to lift her skirts when there was another knock on the door. He exhaled as Violante rose from his lap. More's the pity.

"Come in," he said without enthusiasm.

"My lord," the butler said, "Count Bassini-Verdelli is here to see you."

After Keith had given the sack to Murray and Mrs. Collins, he'd employed a few people from his centre. Maybe less experienced, but more trustworthy than his former servants.

"Goodness." Violante took the chair next to Keith. "I didn't expect that."

"What is he doing here?" Keith said.

"Keith." Violante gave him that pointed look that never failed to make him feel like an idiot.

"Fine. Let him in." He exchanged a glance with her who nodded.

After the disastrous trip, Keith hadn't heard a word from the count. The newspapers had followed the drama of the count and his wife's personal life, splattering their private affair on the front page. After that, the count had retired from the public eye, understandably so.

Keith stood up, wondering what would happen. "Count Bassini-Verdelli, what a surprise."

Violante curtsied. "My lord."

The count removed his hat and swallowed hard. His gaunt face matched his dull grey clothes; they were of the finest quality, but the suit didn't spark for its colours.

"Lord Ashford, Miss Sharpe, thank you for seeing me even though I didn't send a card," the count said in a low tone.

Keith stretched out an arm towards the chair in front of his desk. "Please."

The count plonked down onto the seat with a huff after Violante sat. "These past months, the whole year to be precise, have been rather difficult for me."

"I can imagine," Keith said.

The count lowered his gaze. "I just wanted to tell you that I spent that time thinking about my mistakes. I owe you an apology. Both of you."

"All water under the bridge," Violante said.

Keith had forgiven Sir Howard. He could forgive the count.

The count shook his head. "I wronged you, and I came here to make amends. See..." He drew in a breath. "My wife left me."

"I'm sorry to hear that," Keith said. Although that was expected.

The count took a few deep breaths. "Being alone had me thinking about what I had done wrong in my life, and I did wrong to you. I can see you two are really in love, and the reunion with your mother, which I witnessed, struck a chord with me. It made me understand how difficult Miss Sharpe's life had been. Lord Ashford, the building in St. Giles is yours. I don't even expect a payment." He produced a document from his bag and placed it on the desk. "Do some good with it."

Keith remained speechless for a moment. "Thank you, my lord. Very generous of you."

"Will you come to our wedding?" Violante asked.

That cheered the count up. "If you'll have me. I've been a little lonely as of late."

Even Keith softened. "Then we'll see you soon."

The count rose with a timid smile. "Be kind to each other. What you have is very rare." He bowed and left.

Violante sat back on Keith's lap when they were alone. "The perfect wedding gift and the perfect advice."

Yes, Keith's life with her was indeed perfect.

THE END

about the author

Love stories have always captured my imagination. What's better than two people falling in love with each other? I write steamy romance, usually with a paranormal twist in an historical setting. Add a touch of suspense and mystery and a pinch of darkness. I love stories with strong, sexy heroes and mischievous heroines who pull no punches.

I live in the City of Sails, New Zealand, drinking tea (coffee gives me anxiety) and devouring books.

Join my newsletter for exclusive content and the chance to receive an ARC copy of my books. Just copy and paste this link into your browser:

Barbara's Newsletter

also by barbara russell

If you love steamy paranormal romance set in Victorian London, my
Royal Occult Bureau series is for you:

<u>The Royal Occult Bureau Series</u>

Are you into shape-shifter romance? Check out my da Vinci's Beasts
series, set in WW2:

<u>da Vinci's Beasts Series</u>

For more Victorian paranormal romance with witches and sexy warriors,
see the Knights of the White Blade series:

<u>The White Order Series</u>

Love steampunk? Check out my Auckland Steampunk series:

<u>Auckland Steampunk Series</u>

Milton Keynes UK
Ingram Content Group UK Ltd.
UKHW012250110624
443988UK00005B/314